# her sister's eye

**Vivienne Cleven** was born in 1968 in Surat and grew up in western Queensland, homeland of her Aboriginal heritage. She left school at the age of thirteen to work with her father as a jillaroo: building fences, mustering cattle, and working at various jobs on stations throughout Queensland and New South Wales.

In 2000, with the manuscript *Bitin' Back*, Vivienne Cleven entered and won the David Unaipon Award, a national, annual competition for Indigenous authors who have not yet published a book. Published in 2001, *Bitin' Back* was shortlisted in the 2002 South Australian Premier's Award for Fiction.

# Vivienne Cleven

her sister's eye

University of Queensland Press

First published 2002 by University of Queensland Press
Box 6042, St Lucia, Queensland 4067 Australia

www.uqp.uq.edu.au

© Vivienne Cleven

This book is copyright. Except for private study, research,
criticism or reviews, as permitted under the Copyright Act,
no part of this book may be reproduced, stored in a retrieval system,
or transmitted in any form or by any means without prior
written permission. Enquiries should be made to the publisher.

Typeset by University of Queensland Press
Printed in Australia by McPherson's Printing Group

Distributed in the USA and Canada by
International Specialized Book Services, Inc.,
5824 N.E. Hassalo Street, Portland, Oregon 97213-3640

This project has been assisted by
the Commonwealth Government through
the Australia Council, its arts funding
and advisory body.

Sponsored by the Queensland Office
of Arts and Cultural Development.

**Cataloguing in Publication Data**
*National Library of Australia*

Cleven, Vivienne, 1968– .
  Her sister's eye.

  I. Title.

A823.4

ISBN 0 7022 3283 1

*For my grandmother, Vera,
and my mother, May*

# acknowledgments

A big thank you to the following people. Victor Duncan, for so many things I would have to write another book just to list them all! Amanda Jones, for believing in me. Finally, for my dear children Laura and Travis.

# one

# archie

Archie Corella lifts out the last shovelful of crumbling soil. As he looks down into the wide hole, he thinks about death: ashes to ashes, dust to dust, and wonders when the time comes what sort of funeral he'll have. If it were up to him he'd be happy to lay down with the maggots in a potato sack. With that thought, he stands straight, feeling the hot pain start at the side of his face. At this moment he wants to cry out, wants to bury his head in the dirt, to surrender to the agony.

It all comes down to Murilla Salte wanting him to talk and that's something he can't do. He knows that keepin ya trap shut will save a lot of trouble, and trouble will find you when you look the way he does. Which is why Sofie Salte is the only person to understand him. And that's something.

So when her sister, Murilla, came to him yesterday and started asking certain questions about the Drysdale man, *what could he say?* He couldn't tell her the whole truth; it would cause too much grief and that's something he can do without. The thing was, what the woman asked about happened a year ago and what difference would it make to her now? Maybe Sofie had talked but he doubted that.

The scar on his face pulses with a vicious, painful life of its own. He hopes Murilla doesn't drag him into something he wants no part of, but suspects his chances are slim.

He gets to his weary feet and looks into the gaping hole. Roses, he'd plant a rose-bush in there. He loves the velvety feel and smell of them, yet they'll never grow properly for him. After a while purplish-black blotches appear on the underside of the leaves and they succumb to disease. Despite careful pruning, insecticide spray and replanting of garden beds, they just wouldn't thrive. It made him feel lost and curiously guilty.

As he kneels on the edge of the crumbling soil, his thoughts wander back to Murilla. She's like the dirt: dark and strange. He bites down hard on his tongue, the very idea of her always has the power to make his face flame like wildfire. A gut feeling tells him that she's on some sort of woman business, stuff he doesn't want to mess with. His thoughts swirl and the distant reaches of memory jolt into his consciousness. He sees a huge man with strange eyes. A ghost so vivid his skin shrinks at the memory. *Donald Drysdale.*

\* \* \*

The day Archie arrived in Mundra it was torturously hot. The middle of a drought-stricken summer. Red dust edged the blistering bitumen streets. Air steamed and spiralled from concrete footpaths, as though you could put your hands into the haze and feel the weight of the heat. Dogs lazed sluggishly under gum trees, tongues lolling out of heads, saliva dripping down muzzles to form puddles of drool at their paws, flies blanketing their mangy, flea-ridden backs. Lined up like a regiment of dusty soldiers, old men sat on wooden benches in front of the shops, their weatherworn faces battered down and a dull shade of vile pink, as though they were ready to lay down and die from heat exhaustion.

Occasionally one of them would make a half-hearted comment to the other: 'Might get some rain yet. This weather'll be the death of this town.' Their desperate faces were constantly turned skyward, as if they were willing the rain to come. Hopelessness was etched on every posture and line of their forms. Archie saw their despair but didn't let it bother him. It would rain when it was ready to.

Archie ambled towards the end of the oddly familiar street. He supposed that after a while all towns had the same look to his tired eyes. Nothing seemed to change.

He took everything in cautiously, keeping his felt hat tipped slyly to the side of his face. There'd be no telling what people would do if they had a good gawk at his dial. What they'd say wouldn't matter, words were just words.

At the end of the road he stopped. The sun flogged his back and his mouth felt parched and spitless, dust clogged up his nose and he was fast becoming tired. He sat down on a bench, placing his hessian swag carefully on the ground beside him.

Tilting his hat back an inch, he took particular notice of the town's people and was wary not to look anyone directly in the eye.

He noticed there weren't any blackfellahs on the street and, when he thought about it, he hadn't seen any all day. One thing he did know was that a town without any black fellahs was dangerous. A place he wasn't supposed to be. With that thought he turned and looked in each direction just as a large, dusky-skinned woman stepped out of the nearby shop, carrying a plastic bag in one hand and pulling a dishevelled woman along with the other. The large woman's features were rock-solid. Her eyes narrowed into slits. Archie suspected she wasn't the type of person to bandy words: her don't-mess-with-me face told him that.

As she strode towards him, her powerful legs moved like the wheels of a train, the heels on her shoes click-clackingclickclacking as she motored along. Archie jumped to his feet and walked on uncertain legs towards her. She came to an abrupt halt in front of him and peered down at him like he was a dag hanging from a sheep's arse.

For a fleeting second he nearly stumbled back from her fierce gaze. But he held fast.

She would be the one to make his decision: stay in this town or leave. He cleared his throat. 'Arrh scuse me, Missus, do ya know where a man'd get work around here?'

She moved the plastic bag from one hand to the other, watching him closely.

'Around here, eh? What, you a drifter?'

He coughed dryly, his mouth a dusty hole. 'No ... I comed this way special like just for ... well ... um work.'

Her eyes crawled from his head to his dirty, callused feet. Briefly he thought he should have bought himself a pair of shoes. But shoes and him don't mix. He'd rather wear none.

Feeling safer after a moment's pause, he brought his head up and looked at the snowy-haired woman alongside her. She looked back at him, picked her nose, then wiped her finger on her shabby dress and said: 'I be Sofie Dove.' She smiled, her penetrating eyes taking him in.

'Um ... hello, I'm Archie Corella.' She grinned shyly as he took in her form. He guessed her age to be around twenty-eight. She was a tall, gangly woman, stooping forward slightly, as though her own body was too awkward to carry. Her incredible, wild, snow-white hair stuck out in all directions like skinny, webbed fingers. The cinnamon colour of her arms and legs were smeared with what appeared to be traces of dried mud.

More than anything Archie sensed that Sofie was not the full billy can of tea. He tore his eyes away from her and looked at the big woman. Her eyes softened a little.

'Well, I'm Murilla Salte, and that's me sister, Sofie. Now, maybe the Drysdales have something going. They employ everyone round these parts.'

'Yeah, where are they at?'

Murilla offered him a smile. 'The Drysdales have a property out of town, but they also have a shop and if ya go down there ya might just catch Donald today.'

'You live round here?' Necessity forced him to ask.

She bent her head to the side, trying to peer under the brim of his hat. 'Been here most of me life. Born n bred.'

Sofie watched him, a flicker of something crossed her face: fear, doubt? He couldn't be too sure. Then she jabbed the air with her pinkie finger and said: 'They rich as fruitcake. Nutty see n all. Sofie Dove know bout em.'

Murilla chided, 'That's enough out of you, Sofie.' She offered him a look then went on. 'Sofie gets a bit confused and everythin.'

His eyes slid away from Sofie. There was something

about her that rattled him. He pulled his hat further down, wondering how much she saw.

'Where can a man find this shop?'

Murilla pointed down the road: 'Keep going in that direction. Right up there at the other end of the street; you can't miss it. There's a sign hanging from the front door.'

'Right ya are. Thank ya, Missus.' He dropped his head, then walked in the direction of the shop.

Sofie's voice raced up from behind him, shrill: 'Be careful, extra too! Me mates doned telled me, Mister Archie Corella!'

Curious, he turned and watched as the two women walked towards the end of the street. He wondered what was wrong with Sofie and what she meant by her warning. He shrugged; he was always careful.

He stood on the edge of the sidewalk and looked across at the shop sign. Archie had a good feeling about the name Drysdale. Maybe there'd be a chance for him here after all. He really hoped so because he was tired, tired of all the wandering. And if things turned out all right he could get himself a house somewhere. He chuckled at that idea — luck wasn't something that came easy to Archie Corella.

His eyes travelled over the shop-front. It had the same worn look as the others lined back against the street: the glass windows smeared with greasy hand marks and paint peeling from the dust-covered walls. Standing near the door was a rusty drum housing pink-flowering geraniums, cigarette butts and paper, all jammed together.

Sighing wearily, Archie went up to the glass door and pushed it open. A tiny jingle sounded above his head. He stepped into the dark, cool interior and blinked for a second to adjust his eyes to the shadows. Somewhere in the background a radio blared and the gravelly voice of Johnny Cash belted out a tune.

*But ya ought to thank me, before I die,*
*For the gravel in ya guts, and the spit in ya eye*
*'Cause I'm the son-of-a-bitch that named you 'Sue'.*

Noticing no one around, he greedily took in the room. Nailed to the far walls were handmade wooden shelves stacked with cartons of eggs, rusted tins of peas and beetroot, and fly-shit-spattered packets of sugar and biscuits. Humped back like old men in dun-coloured jackets were hessian sacks, the once red stencilled word POTATOES now a faded pink. In the corner an old fridge clanked and hummed.

He took in the other side of the room. Hanging near the window on a coat-hanger was a white dress, the sleeves tattered and the collar frayed. Like everything else in the shop, the dress was covered from neckline to hem in a film of dust.

Archie thought how peculiar the lone frock looked. A slight, unexpected shiver ran through him. He ignored it, nothing unusual in that. His nerves attacked anywhere, anytime. He turned to the rest of the room, taking in the cobwebbed corners, the stained wooden floor and the messy counter littered with old newspapers. Archie idled close to the counter and coughed loudly to announce his presence.

A small sound came from the rear of the shop and he swung towards the noise. A side door opened and out stepped a man.

Everything about him was giant. His trouser-clad legs were wide and thick as tree trunks, his arms were granite-like, and rising from his broad shoulders was a stocky, bullish neck. He bent forward as though an invisible weight pressed on his shoulders. Sweat ran down his jowley, crimson face and soaked the top of his open-neck shirt.

But it was his strange eyes that really stood out: one was olive green, the other nut brown.

Archie stared at him and for a buckjumping minute thought his legs might tear off out of the shop. But something, fear or curiosity, kept him rooted to the spot. The sour, sweaty odour of the man crept up his nostrils, gagging him.

'How are you going? Drysdale's the name. Donald.' On hearing his voice, Archie jumped. Drysdale's whiny tone was much like a young boy's just breaking voice. He gathered himself and replied, 'Archie Corella, how ya goin?'

Drysdale smiled, all neat small teeth. 'Passing through?'

'Well, sort of. Thought a man'd look for work hereabouts.'

'What sort of work are you after, Corella?'

'Anything. I'd be willing to turn my hands to whatever's going.'

Drysdale licked his thick lips. 'Well, my mother is looking for someone to take care of the odd jobs about the place as well as her garden.'

'Sounds good. I like gardening. Matter of fact I'm a good gardener,' he lied, jamming his hands into his trouser pockets, hoping Drysdale couldn't read the guilt on his face. He had to settle down somewhere and *soon*.

Drysdale stared, his strange eyes searching for a place to look under the brim. 'Now, Corella, do you drink or smoke?'

Archie shuffled his feet nervously and another smooth lie passed his lips. 'Nope, don't drink or smoke. Never took either habit up. Bad for the health.'

'Fine, good. Now look, I'll close the shop and take you over to my mother.' Drysdale drew his lips back tightly over his teeth in something of a smile.

Archie grinned with relief. Looked like he'd be staying in Mundra after all.

\* \* \*

Drysdale slowed the ute to a stop in front of a rusting, padlocked gate.

'Behind those bushes is my mother's house,' he said, then got out and unlocked the gate. Jumping back behind the wheel, he looked across at him. 'Paranoid about people trespassing. Damn near shot a bloke last year. Poor bastard lost his way, didn't he. That's my mother for you — losing her bloody marbles, I reckon. You know what she thinks? ... Yep, that the town has it in for her because they all want her precious plants! But that's my Ma for you, Corella.' Drysdale shook his head with obvious disgust.

Archie's eyes slid slyly towards Drysdale. He was beginning to see that Drysdale liked to talk. It made him uneasy. A man with a loose mouth was dangerous, that's one sure thing he did know.

Drysdale turned to him. 'If you do what she tells you, then everything will be fine. Sometimes she ... Well, never mind that, just watch your mouth, do your work and stay out of her way.' Drysdale swung the ute into a gravelled driveway and stopped in front of the house. He motioned him to get out. 'Well, Corella, this is it.'

Archie looked across at the run-down Queenslander.

It crouched forward out of the undergrowth as though it was exhausted from weathering too many storms. Moss-green shutters hung carelessly from large fly-screened windows. Embracing the house like a protective arm was a white rust-speckled, wrought-iron verandah. The iron was fashioned like a delicate lace petticoat. The rotting, worm-bored steps had two planks missing from the bottom and the once cream-coloured walls were skinned and blistered, the timber exposed. Up near the roof, the gutters hung precariously, water dripping steadily from their rusty mouths. And the door looked down from this sad vista, glaring back at him.

The house seemed to buckle and sweat underneath the sweltering sun. Archie could almost hear the wood expanding, as though the house was a living thing, crying its protest.

The lawn was spotted with dead patches of tufty grass and flattened with random crops of pigweed. The flower-beds held several spare rose bushes, the mildewed leaves bowed down by armies of aphids. The jacaranda trees cast mottled shadows on the house and clearing.

Towards the corner of the house, hanging from the lower branches of a tea-tree were three small aviaries, housing budgerigars, pigeons and a cockatoo. The cockatoo, excited by company, let out a noisy squawk: 'My heart's desire, my heart's desire,' as its wings beat a futile protest against the wire mesh. The words sounded eerily human.

Drysdale scowled at the cages. 'My mother's birds. Dad bought them for her. Claimed they'd keep her company.'

Archie didn't make any reply to that. Best to keep his mouth clamped. He watched Drysdale closely, but not too closely.

'Bloody pests, don't you think?' Drysdale questioned as though expecting a certain answer.

Understanding what was needed of him, Archie responded, 'Yeah, boss, if ya say so.' He shuffled his feet on the gravel, not liking the way the man's eyes drilled into him.

'Don't say a lot, do you, Corella?'

'Nope, boss, don't reckon I do.' Archie stared at his bare feet, wondering with a sick feeling if Drysdale was gonna take the piss out of him. He was used to that.

Drysdale went on, 'That's the trouble with this town, too many people talking out of turn. I like a quiet man. Someone who knows well enough to keep his trap trapped, understand?'

Archie answered, 'Yep, sure do,' understanding.

Drysdale rested a large hand heavily on his shoulder. 'The thing is this: Mundra being such a small town, and small towns being what they are, people love to talk. Especially when it comes to my family. And I expect you not to carry any sort of gossip. Get it?'

'I get it,' he mumbled, not getting it, wishing Drysdale would get his sweaty hands off him.

Drysdale contemplated Archie. 'Now, fellah, when I take you upstairs, don't look ...' He hesitated for a brief moment, then shrugged. 'Don't worry about it.'

Archie looked up into Drysdale's face. He knew what was going on. Drysdale didn't want his mother to see what a freak he was. He was used to that. Most people looked past, over and around him, never directly at him. That is, until now. Drysdale looked him right in the face, not once did he blink, or flinch. No one had done that before. Most times he scared people, made them angry, some turned their backs on him and others called him names: fucken freak, weirdo, scarface. He'd known about people and their ways and knew that fear was something that gets out of control if you didn't take certain steps to fix it. And that was one thing he couldn't do — fix his own nameless fears. They were always there, lurking like a rabid dog, snarling in the back of his thoughts, ready to pounce when the going got tough. But some day he would find what he was searching for and when that happened he would be at peace, would stop the wandering.

At times, when he trudged into some town, he could have sworn that he had arrived home — wherever that was. No amount of thinking or searching seemed to dig that information up. He was for the most part an empty cup. Nothing seemed to really exist. It was as though he had no former life, which made no right sense because he *felt* something, even if it just flittered through his gauzy mind like wisps of smoke.

'You got that, Corella?'

Jolted back from his thoughts, Archie responded, 'Yes, boss.' As he studied Drysdale, a clear understanding told him what the man was. A shyer. Shied himself away, like a snake when he feels the vibration of a man's footsteps approaching — hiding away, curling up in a hollow log, all the while watching with cunning eyes, ready to strike.

Once more, Drysdale's voice cut short his thoughts. 'Are you deaf, Corella?'

'Eh? Oh sorry, boss, what was that ya said?'

'As I was saying, you're to call my mother Missus Drysdale at all times.' Drysdale motioned him up the steps.

'No worries, boss,' he returned, hoping the old woman wasn't as bad as her son made her out to be. He suspected the odds weren't too good.

As Drysdale led him into a dark, musty hall, he snatched quick glances through the doorways and into the rooms. The smell of pine o cleen and furniture polish clogged the air.

The floor squeaked as Drysdale's boots trod the spotless black and white tiles. Archie wondered if his filthy feet would leave any dirt tracks, sort of hoped they did.

Drysdale came to a stop in front of a tall wooden door, then turned and faced him. 'Remember what I said. If she asks where you're from, tell her you've been in town for a month. You don't have to tell her *everything*.' He nodded at the door. 'And remember your manners, Corella.'

'Righto, Mister Drysdale,' he answered, pushing the heavy door open and stepping into the room with dread coursing through his body. She'd hate him for sure.

He walked further into the room, then stopped dead in his tracks. At first, although it didn't make any sense, he thought the woman was shouting at him. His heart knocked wildly as he took a step back into the dark corner of the room.

The woman's piercing voice broke through the still air. 'You ... you ...!' she screeched at the other corner.

It was then he realised there was someone else in the room.

Gathering himself together, he went forward slowly. From the corner of his eye he spotted her standing by a side table, pouring water into a glass tumbler. Her face, set hard and expressionless: Murilla Salte. She brought her head up and looked across at him with a weak smile, then handed the glass to someone sitting in the recliner.

The shrill voice barked, 'How many times must I tell

you to wipe the bloody condensation off the glass? You know how much I hate to have wet hands, Murilla!'

Murilla grimaced, the side of her face twitched. 'Um ... There's a man here to see ya,' she uttered, her tone low and respectful.

'Well, don't just stand there, tell him to come on in.'

Murilla motioned him to step forward and smiled kindly as though she knew how nervous he felt. Archie hesitated for a second; the woman's voice had rattled him. Finally he walked towards the chair, particularly careful to keep his face to the darkest side of the room.

The old Drysdale woman lounged back in the recliner, a glass of water in her hand. As his wobbly legs neared, she brought her steel-grey head up and looked straight at him. A high white dress collar framed her sallow face and shadows lay in the hollows of her sharp cheekbones. Her non-existent eyebrows, pencilled in jet-black, arched when she saw him. Her shrewd eyes were inky and impenetrable.

Archie stood before her, arms linked behind his back and a small half-hearted smile on his face. He knew she'd see how dirty he was. A hobo, that's what she'd see. White women hate dirty blackfellahs. He wondered how much she'd hate him. There was always some measure to hate. Big or small.

She rasped, 'Speak up, man.'

He coughed nervously, fidgeting with the side of his hat. 'The job, Missus. I'm here for the garden job. Your son told me to see you bout it.'

She tapped the side of the recliner with her hand. 'Ah, the job. Well, what can you do?'

He watched nervously as she moved forward to switch

on the tableside lamp. He croaked, 'Anything. I can put me hands to anythin.'

'Can't see you properly. Where're your manners, man?' She levelled a bony finger at his hat.

For some reason he really thought that she wasn't going to notice the hat. His insides churned as he turned to Murilla, looking for an escape, but she just directed her attention to the wall clock. No help there.

The Drysdale woman shook her head fiercely, brows knitted into a tight, red knot. 'Off it comes. No man has ever entered this room with a hat *on*! Not even Reginald, my late husband.'

Archie held the brim so tightly that his sweat-slicked hands ached. 'Oh, yeah, the hat. Sorry, Missus Drysdale,' he mumbled. He knew that he had two choices: take off the hat and be shit on or leave the hat and lose the job. Hat or job? He chose the hat.

She jabbed a scrawny finger towards the side of his damaged face, eyes transfixed on him. 'Whatever happened to you?'

He gave his usual answer, 'Accident, Missus.' His voice came out sounding croaky and confused. The truth was something he could not tell her because he didn't even know it himself. There was no memory to prompt why he came to be so scarred. A hard lump grew in his throat.

Caroline shrugged, took a sip of water, then, incredibly, swung her chair around to grab a gilt frame photograph on the side table and hurl it across the room, straight into a wall mirror. The sound of splintering glass echoed in his ears.

'You ... you ...!' Her scream shattered the stillness.

Archie gaped in disbelief. It was then he regretted his decision to stay. A sneaky glance at Caroline Drysdale told him that it was not gonna be an easy ride. The first woman boss in memory. And already it didn't seem too good.

Caroline's voice came out harsh and cold. She snapped frostily, 'Leave me alone. Just leave me be. Murilla, take Mister Corella out to his room.'

Murilla didn't budge; instead, she put her hands on her hips, a suspicious, annoyed look on her face.

'Caroline, you didn't take ya tablets today, did you?' Murilla smiled, but it didn't reach her flinty eyes. A chilly silence wrapped around the room. Then Caroline slowly rose from the chair. Her knees cracked and her breathing came out loud and laboured as she stood to full height.

'Why ... why must people bother me?'

Archie took several big steps back towards the door. What the hell was he to do?

His greasy hands fumbled with the door knob. He wanted out. Just as he turned the handle, the door flew open and in stepped Drysdale.

Archie veered away from Drysdale, then scanned the room. Murilla leaned above Caroline, arms crossed, face set into a rigid frown. Caroline crumpled back into the chair under the weight of Murilla's glare, staring at the shattered mirror, her mouth twitching.

Drysdale moved swiftly, his large bulk quivering.

'Murilla, what's going on?' His huge paws curled in on themselves.

Murilla didn't answer; instead, she walked towards the broken glass and started to pick it up with her bare hands.

'This is none of your bloody business! Out, out you go, Donald!' Caroline's wild hand gestures motioned her son to the door.

Drysdale threw Murilla a lethal glance and left the

room, his red face shiny with humiliation. 'Old bitch,' he muttered from the corner of his skewed mouth.

In a low, apologetic voice, Caroline said, 'That'll do, Murilla. I don't want you to cut yourself.'

Murilla shook her head with a weary motion. 'No, I don't want you to walk on it. Cut ya bloody feet off.'

Caroline sighed, her hands shaking slightly as she muttered, 'Okay, you can take Mister Corella out to his room, please Murilla.'

Murilla stood, threw Caroline an exasperated look and then motioned Archie to follow. When they were halfway down the corridor she turned and said, 'Don't take much notice of her. She's always like that. Old age and bad memories is what it is.'

He shrugged. 'Well, a man feels sorry for anyone having to put up with that. She's a funny one, eh?'

This time Archie had a good look at her. He reckoned she couldn't be any more than thirty years old. Her jet-black hair was scraped back off her wide forehead into a thick, long plait. Her dusky skin was marred only by a smattering of freckles on her arms. She was a large, statuesque woman and as she strode along, her head was held high and proud.

'Yeah, but that's the way Caroline is. I suppose ya met Donald, eh?'

Archie watched the way her thick lips moved. 'The son, yeah.'

She stopped in her tracks and gave him a strange look. 'Hmm, what ya think?'

He shrugged: 'Um ... he's right, ain't he?' Didn't want to start shittin on the boss. Not to someone he didn't know.

A tiny smile played at the corner of her mouth. 'Yeah

well, not the one to be saying much are ya, Corella. What, you shy or somethin?'

'Nope, reckon I'm not. I keep to meself is all.' He wondered if she ever kept her mouth shut. Stupid questions he had no time for. Ain't like he had much to say at any rate.

Murilla's eyes bored into his, as though she was looking for something that might be in there. 'Ya mightn't stay too long, eh?'

'A man's hoping to stay for as long as he can.'

Her laughter came out loud and empty as she threw her hands into the air. 'Huh, that's what they all say.'

He hated the certainty in her voice. 'I ain't all of em, am I?'

'I been here for ... let's see ... yeah, for years and I never saw one to stay a full month. Only last week the other fellah flew the coop. Can't say I ...' She stopped mid-sentence, a thoughtful expression on her face. 'Oh well, people have funny ways, I guess.' She shrugged.

'Dunno what other people like, but I'm stayin and that's all there is to it.'

He looked around, wondering what part of the house they were in, too many dark rooms to know what direction they had taken. Suddenly, from a corner room, Drysdale stepped out, hitching his trousers up around his chunky hips as he strode towards them.

Drysdale looked at him fleetingly then turned his attention to Murilla. He flung her a question. 'My mother, is she all right?'

Murilla turned her head in the other direction. 'Yeah, just fine n dandy.'

'Well, Murilla, you just be careful with my mother. If I ever catch you doing anything you shouldn't, then I'll get rid of you myself. My mother won't have a say in that, I can tell you.' Drysdale offered her a greasy smile, running his tongue across his lips.

'Whatever you say,' she responded distractedly.

'What, are *you* being insolent with *me*, Murilla!' Drysdale hit back in an incredulous tone, glaring at her.

She grinned, her hands opening and closing as she scrutinised his face. 'Nah, just tellin you the way things are.'

Drysdale blushed a weak shade of pink. 'Don't forget who's the boss around here. You'll do well to remember, Salte!' he spat out.

She smirked, putting a hand to her forehead, a mock salute. 'Yes, sir, yes boss.'

'Anyway, I don't pay you to stand around all day! Go do some dusting or something! And wipe that smartarse look off your face!'

She shrugged. 'Well, I can't do that. Caroline told me to take this man to his room.'

Drysdale offered a lopsided grin. 'Run along, I'll take him across. Oh, and I'd like to have a quiet word with you later.'

'If you say so.' Murilla turned and strode back down the hall, with Drysdale glowering after her.

'Obviously my mother was pleased with you, Corella. You'd better make sure it stays that way, right? Now, I want you to give this yard a good tidy up for her.' Drysdale directed him out the back door.

'Now Corella, here's something else for you to know: you must keep away from the house at all times. Ma might mistake you for someone else and start firing shots. Oh, don't look so worried, she hasn't hit anyone yet,' he laughed. 'But she's unpredictable. Right, this way we go.'

Drysdale led him to a pokey, decrepit building with fly-screen windows, a dark green overhang shading the steps and a pair of petrol drums painted off-white standing near the doorway.

Drysdale nodded at the drums. 'For the rubbish Corella. There's to be no women here. My mother hates most of the ladies in this town, so there's no need to be upsetting her. And I would appreciate it if there's no drinking or smoking here. Any number of those things will see you fired. The girls have the same rules. You'll be paid weekly. Most meals are from the kitchen, but you must eat them here. There's a shower in your room, and a radio. Finally, you must never go into that shed over there. If you are anywhere near it or accidentally go inside then it'd be best for you to leave immediately. It's my work place. My very own space, *understand*?' Drysdale heaved a large breath then pushed open the door.

'Yeah, I understand.' Archie felt a wild laugh bubbling up in the back of his throat. Boot camp, he'd come to bloody boot camp!'

'Make yourself at home, Corella. You take note of all those things and there won't be any problems. I expect you to start on the yard immediately. She hasn't been out of the house for years, but lately she thinks she'd like to take a walk. And for God's love, Corella, tidy those bloody rose bushes! She'll be most likely to blame me for the way they are.' Drysdale scratched his fleshy chin, took a last look at the tired furniture then left.

Feeling the day's walk catching up with him, Archie threw his swag to the floor and lay down on the hard bed. He pulled out a packet of Log Cabin tobacco from his breast pocket, rolled a smoke and lit up, thinking about the day's turn of events. Drysdale worried him. It was nothing he did or said so much, but he hated the man, really hated him, like the way he hated the sight of snakes. But, he supposed that when winter arrived, a warm room was better than freezing his black arse off in a dry creek bed somewhere or in a small, cold cell. He'd put up with the Drysdales, make do for a while.

Later on that night, hands aching and cracked from pulling out the rose bushes, he carried his feed of mashed potatoes and pork chops back to his room. He was so caught up in his thoughts that he almost missed seeing the shadowy outline near Drysdale's workshed. A dreadful, sour taste rose in his mouth. He wondered why Drysdale would be spying on him. Lowering his head to the ground, he continued walking. When he reached his room, he rushed inside and dropped to his haunches under the windowsill. Slowly, he raised himself and peered into the night.

In a dim sliver of light that fell from a window of the house, he caught a glimpse of the person. It was a woman. He looked harder. His first thoughts were that somehow she had gotten lost, had walked into the Drysdale yard by mistake. Then he remembered that Murilla was probably still up at the house.

White hair plastered to her skull and wet dress clinging to her angular frame, stood Sofie Dove. She appeared to have something in her hand. He craned his neck for a better view and as she raised her arm up above her head he caught sight of what she was holding.

Archie gasped.

Swaying from one foot to the other, Sofie was wavering like a ghost, her mouth moving wordlessly as she watched the shed door with odd concentration. Wriggling and jumping about in her hands was a yellowbelly fish.

It was then Archie realised the place he had come to was a place with its own shying. Suddenly the night air chilled his bones.

* * *

Now as he looks down upon the parched ground, Archie decides that he'll chance it. The roses will go in. But somewhere, as an echo in the back of his mind, Murilla carps at his thoughts. He wonders if, after all this time, she has finally cracked or found out the truth and is planning revenge against him or Caroline Drysdale.

He throws his head back and looks up into the blazing midday sun. A few ragged clouds move across the sky and gather like a slate cloak as they float in from the west. A timid breeze scurries past and he picks up the scent of rain across the dry flats, a storm coming. His ears begin to roar and the pain returns to his face. The rose thorns dig into his soft palms. Blood weeps down his hand, as the clouds blanket the sun.

Again she steals into his thoughts. She'll kill him. Murilla Salte will put him in a coffin before God does.

*That much he knows.*

## two

## murilla and caroline drysdale

The year 1981 was the worst time in the history of Mundra. That year the freakish weather was the coldest anyone in the district ever experienced. It wasn't only the farmers that went down with the killing frosts; it was the town people too. And on the odd days the farmers happened to come into town for food, the women would complain bitterly to each other. Some of the weaker ones simply just walked away, never to be seen again.

Cold seeped into the very bones and froze fingers to a stiff numbness so that you'd swear they'd snap off. The gales blew in over the dusty flats with such force that by morning everything — garden hoses, bicycles and whatever else was laying about — was soon frozen to a rock-solid lump of ice.

All over town black and grey ribbons floated and curled through the frosty air as chimneys belched smoke. House windows cracked and spaces under doorways were blocked with old towels or rolled up newspapers to keep out the biting wind. Down by the river, old Margaret Hanrahan was found sprawled across a block of wood, her fingers still twisted around the axe handle as she stared out of glassy, frost-rimmed eyes.

It was a fierce dog-vicious bitch of a winter. And the worst time of Murilla Salte's life. To start with she had no money, the house was falling apart and two months before, her mother died, leaving her the sole carer of her sister, Sofie. For three torturous months Sofie and Murilla tried to rebuild parts of the mouldering house. The toilet was always blocked, the stairs were steadily coming apart and the walls were rife with rising damp. It saddened Murilla and Sofie to see their mother's beloved house falling apart before their eyes.

It was the neglected house that spurred Murilla on. She decided to do something she swore she never would. She went to see Caroline Drysdale to ask for a job.

The first time Murilla met her, Caroline said that she had nothing going.

'It would be a lot of hard yakka and it's not only me you'd be working for, it's them in there, too.' Caroline nodded towards the dining room. Murilla understood 'them' to mean Caroline's husband, Reginald, and their son, Donald. She didn't have the time to be fussy, she knew she'd have to do something before the Council started on about the house. A few days later, for some unknown reason, Caroline called Murilla up, telling her that in fact she did now have a job. She gave no explanation for her sudden change of mind.

Every day at six in the morning Murilla would walk down the dirt road, the wind smacking her face to a frozen slab, her sandshoe-clad feet crunching over the frosty ground. By the time she arrived at the front gate she would be a shivering lump and her dress (which she was told to wear) would be stiffened ruler-straight as ice particles clung to the thin cotton.

Most mornings when Murilla first arrived at the house she would make a beeline straight to the kitchen to thaw herself out. Occasionally Doris, the kitchen hand, would sneak her a hot cup of tea or coffee, then start on with the 'I-told-you-so' speech before work began.

Floors would be polished to shining perfection. Murilla's knees would bleed as she crawtailed around the dining room, pulling a bucket of wax with one foot and clutching a filthy rag in her hand. She would buff until the floor gleamed like a mirror, and it wouldn't be finished until she could see her own face looking up from the floorboards. But wash days would nearly drive Murilla out the gate, would nearly make her throw the job in.

The Drysdale house sits on top of a small hill and when the breeze comes in from the flats it tears full force across the paddocks, knocks small trees over and whips around the yard like a hurricane. Nothing and nobody would get about in weather like that.

Murilla would stand at the wash house door for five minutes or so, waiting for the wind to die down before she went into it. Lugging a basket full of heavy, wet clothes, pegs jammed into her mouth, she would go to the line with a low gut feeling that the weather was gonna kill her, like it did Margaret Hanrahan. For a hellish hour Murilla would bend and peg, and by the time she was done her hands would be numbed blue-grey.

And all the while, up by the window, a pair of eyes would be watching. That was wash day. But there'd be other days Murilla would come to dread.

\* \* \*

Murilla lets the thoughts go and looks across at Missus Drysdale.

Caroline hunches forward on the recliner, eyes riveted to the beige carpet. A deep frown lines her brow, as though something is puzzling her. She exhales a long, exaggerated breath while idly tapping the side of the recliner. Giving the carpet another contemptuous glance, Caroline turns with calculated slowness and levels her eyes at Murilla.

'Murilla, what's on this carpet?' she shouts, jabbing a gnarled finger at the carpet.

'Nothing! Ain't a damned thing! Don't ya dare tell me it's not clean!' Murilla shakes her head with mounting fury.

'You, Salte, are a bloody liar! I can see the *dirt* on it!' Saliva dribbles down her chin and her black eyes spit.

'Come on now, don't be making yaself all sick about it. It's only a floor — *a clean floor.*' Murilla walks further into the room.

Murilla, just get moving and clean this appalling mess up!' Caroline clicks her fingers, eyes feverish with anger.

Murilla's shoulders bunch back and the bottom of her stomach knots. Small beads of sweat appear on her upper lip. She glares back at Caroline. 'Caroline, ya just don't give a person a break, do ya? I'll clean the floor after I've finished everything else. Ya life doesn't *depend* on it, does it?' She catches a drop of sweat on the tip of her tongue. *How many times have I cleaned the friggin carpet this week: twice? thrice? No a million times! Every day! Scrubbed, vacuumed, mopped. Never enough. Like she hates the floor...*

'How come you're late today? And where is Donald?' Caroline asks, peering around the shadowy interior.

'I ain't late and Donald ... Oh, I dunno where he is.'

Murilla grits her teeth. *Is she ever gonna believe that he's dead? That he carked a year ago? Arh, people tell her but she just won't swolla it. That's her mind playin tricks on her.*

'That's what you tell me,' Caroline barks. 'And is the gardener putting those rose bushes in that I ordered from Mister Freeman's?'

'I told you that the gardener left a long time ago! There's no gardener here anymore. Anyway, how'd ya remember *him*, of *all* people?' Murilla watches Caroline's face clearly. *Cunning as a shithouse rat.*

'That's a lie! That's all I get from you, lies, lies and more lies! What, you're chasing away the gardener now!' Caroline laughs loud.

'Right, that's it! I've had enough of you! I don't tell lies, and the gardener took off years ago!' Murilla casts her a suspicious look.

Caroline ignores her. Her eyes travel around the room and come to rest on a gilt-framed black and white photograph on the side table. For a brief second her pinched lips quiver slightly. She reaches out and lifts the picture up in her unsteady hands. 'Bastard!' she whispers, then puts it back on the table.

As though nothing has happened Caroline settles back into the recliner, then says, 'The Doctor never comes. I don't understand it, Murilla. Do they all hate me that much? Well, that's all right because I hate them too! And did Reginald get my birds yet? He knows I love my birds.' She stares down at her stockinged feet.

'The birds are fine,' Murilla lies. She pauses for a second and waits for the furious outburst. None comes. She goes on. 'The Doctor doesn't hate ya, and he's already been for the week. No, nobody hates ya. It's all in that head a yours.' Murilla puts her hands on her hips.

Suddenly, Caroline bursts, 'It's Archie Corella!'

Murilla stares at her. 'What?'

'The gardener! Archie Corella was his name. Never forget a name do I, Salte. Oh yes, and how could I ever forget that face of his.' She fiddles with the collar on her dress, a faraway look on her face. 'Archie, yes, that definitely was his name. Strange bird, wasn't he?'

Murilla shakes herself, then looks across at her. 'Huh?'

'Queer bird that Corella. A parrot's name.'

'Oh, yeah, he sure was.' Murilla shrugs. *Seems her memory isn't that far gone after all.* 'Anyhow, how could ya remember him after all this time?' It dawns on her that Caroline has never talked about him before. Why now? Murilla studies her face for any signs of mischief. There're none.

'What? Who ...? Oh, yes, the carpet.' Swiftly Caroline changes the subject, eyes dimmed and watery as she looks across at the window.

Murilla turns and walks over to the windows, drawing aside the heavy velvet curtains. 'Ya heard me. Corella. Archie Corella, why are ya talking bout him now?'

'Get out and get away from me! I know what you're doing, poisoning me. That's right, feeding me all those pills!' Caroline's voice ricochets around the room.

'Stop that right now! Don't be upsettin bout nothing. I've looked after ya for many bloody years! Then ya gotta have stupid thoughts like that! No, it's gotta stop. That's why no one else will work for ya. They all know what ya like. Mean as a bloody snake!'

Caroline's bottom lip protrudes and she peeks up at Murilla from beneath her grey fringe. 'Clean that mess off the carpet. Please.'

'Okay. But it's already been cleaned to nothing. Look at it, yeah, worn out. Bald patches all over the place.'

Murilla goes to the cupboard and hauls out a bucket and rag. She squats and begins to scrub away the invisible stains.

Suddenly, Caroline perks up. 'Murilla, please get up from there and leave that damned floor alone! It's like you have an obsession with that carpet! Work, work, that's all you do! Come on, dear, I want to go to bed now.' Caroline stands up slowly, a broad smile on her withered face.

'Okay then. Here, let me help you.' Murilla twines her arms into Caroline's and leads her down the hall. Caroline falters along, measuring her steps with care. The smell of her assaults Murilla's nose: rose water and dried piss cling to her like moss to a rock.

Suddenly Caroline stops in her tracks, a thoughtful expression on her face. 'Murilla, who are my visitors this evening?'

'Wweelll ... Mrs Jane Smith. Um ... the Doctor, Sofie and me.' Murilla gives her the time-honoured answer.

'Good,' Caroline mutters, then pulls forward towards the bedroom.

'Okay, now take off that frock, and I'll find a nightgown for you.' Murilla rummages through the drawers.

'Here we go.' She hands Caroline the gown.

'Don't stare, Salte, it's rude! Look the other way!' She pulls the gown across her chest.

'Sorry,' Murilla mumbles.

'Suppose you think that I'm an ugly old woman! Well, do you?' Caroline's voice shakes.

'As usual, no. I don't think any of that. Wake up to yourself, you're not a little kid are ya?' Murilla turns back around.

Caroline moves under the bed covers. 'When you see

that gardener tell him to plant those roses near the gate. I can't keep telling you what to do. Take the initiative, Salte! And Donald and Reg are about as good as a wet week!' She laughs hollowly and holds out her hands. 'My pills?'

'Here, take two.'

Before she shoves the pills into her mouth she asks, 'Salte, will you bring Sofie over to see me?'

'Yeah, but ya gotta be on good behaviour, right?'

'Humph, rubbish. I'm always well-mannered.' She lies back against the pillows.

'Oh, and give your mother my regards.' Caroline smiles, and pulls the covers up under her chin.

'My mother's dead,' Murilla whispers, tiptoeing out of the room.

\* \* \*

Murilla unlocks the gate and steps onto the dirt road, throwing a glance back at the house nestled in the bushes. At the end of the road the sun fades slowly into the creeping darkness. The hot night is filled with the clamouring of crickets and frogs. Out past the bush, Murilla hears the dull slapping of water against the muddy bank as it flows toward the weir.

Goosebumps prickle her arms and her breath comes out slowly. She is scared of that river. It's as though it gets louder each time she passes it. Sometimes on quiet nights. She hears a strange noise and thinks old man river is calling her name. Each time she stops, cocks her head to the direction and listens. It sounds like tinny voices echoing out of the darkness. Somewhere in the scrub something hits the ground. Murilla swings around wildly, heart pumping. She struggles for air. *Mrrwhooo.*

She stops short. What is it?

*Mrrwhooo.* The river?

Sounds like it's calling her up.

There! There! Murilla can hear it more clearly now.

The night closes in. The chattering whirrwhirr of insects buzzes around her head. The noise explodes. Panicked, she stumbles to the other side of the road, tripping on tree stumps and tangled roots as she rushes forward. When she reaches the other side, her breathing returns to normal.

She hates the river, always did. If she's the kind of person to believe in ghosts then she'd say that Donald Drysdale is haunting her. Tracking her down like he did in life.

Her footsteps hasten as she nears the end of the dirt road and the bitumen comes into view. The town lights cast a faint yellow-blue glow across the tar.

Back from the road a small, white house crouches, lace curtains fluttering in open windows, garbage bins lined neatly beside the front gate and a light shining from the verandah. Murilla senses eyes watching her from a dark window and suddenly the verandah light is switched off. One day, Archie Corella, she thinks, then continues towards the last house at the end of the street.

The flickering TV light streaks out her front door. She treads up the creaky steps and stands in the doorway, looking in at the curled-up form on the couch. Tiptoeing into the room, she starts to head over to the TV when Sofie sits up, yawning.

'Hey, love.' Murilla sits down beside her.

'Why for you see Archie?' Sofie puts a ragged, bitten-to-the-quick fingernail in her mouth and watches Murilla with sulky suspicion.

'Archie ... what ... have ya been up there, Sofie?' Murilla catches her by the bony wrist.

'Um ... no. Sofie go nowhere.' Sofie blinks, a guilty look creeping over her face.

'Sofie, don't lie! Look at ya! All soaking, bloody wet! Ya been in the river again, haven't ya?'

'With me mates. I sawed the fish down there n they telled me I was gettin a better swimmer than em!' Sofie jerks back slightly.

'I told ya! Keep away from there. Bad place, Sofie Dove.' Murilla twines her arms around Sofie's shoulders.

'Hain't bad, Rilla. Me mates, they done told me things.'

'What things?'

'Oh, stuff.' Sofie fidgets.

'Yeah, Dove, like what?' Sofie's eyes spin around the room, sliding away from Murilla. Lying eyes.

'That a man was there. The big man of the scary house.'

Murilla's skin crawls, a faint shiver prickles the back of her neck. 'What man, what scary house?'

'Mister Drysdale.' Sofie smiles.

'Sofie, he's dead. Donald Drysdale died years ago. Drowned in the river.' *Sofie can't help it. Get things messed up in her skull. Way she were birthed.*

Sofie goes on, 'He done tell me mates he love em.'

'He told the fish he loves them?' Murilla watches her closely. She wriggles uncomfortably under her gaze.

'Yeeeppee, that's the story of it. Reckoned he was gonna be gettin em stuff. Worms n that ta eat. Ya reckon he will?' Sofie smiles almost knowingly.

'And, Missus Dove, when did all this happen?' Murilla pretends not to take any interest, and stares at the peeling paint on the loungeroom door. Sofie hates people staring at her.

'Um … When the sun jumped outta the sky. I swummed away. A fish ya see. Yellabelly. A bubba one. No one can rightly catch a fishy when it swim too fast. I swummed up the river too! Weeds holdin Sofie back …!' She stops and puts her hand over her mouth.

'Sofie, Sofie, what is it?' Murilla reaches out for her. *Maybe something's happened. Can never be too sure with Sofie.*

'Cos I be a river girl n em friends helped me too. I get right cold. So, I say, Sofie Dove, getcha arse home cos Rilla be sad n mad atcha. Swim home. Home I swimmed. No more friends, see. I be gooder now. Archie a true time mate.' She stops and gives Murilla a vague smile.

'A story? Is this one of ya make up stories? No, Sofie, don't look away from me. Tell Rilla trues. Have ya been over to Archie n he told ya things?'

'Um, we mates.' Sofie wrings her hands.

'Archie's been telling ya stories, is that right?'

'Archie be tellin me everything. But ya go there pestin him! He don't like pesters, Rilla!' She flings Murilla's hands away, then jumps to her feet to look down at her.

'Hmmm, right then.' Murilla lets it slide. 'But I only got one thing to say and you know what that is. If I ever catch ya on that friggin riverbank I'm gonna get Nana Vida over here to keep an eye on ya while I'm at work!' Murilla threatens, one finger pointing to the door.

'No! No! She's not me sister's eye! You be me eyes, Rilla!' Sofie flings an arm into the air, a wild look spreading across her soft face.

'Righto, love. That's all Rilla ask for. That river is a dangerous place to be, for anyone.'

'Rilly, you're me eye ain'tcha?' Sofie moans, hugging herself.

'I'm ya eye, Dove. Always was n always will be.' Murilla pulls her close and cuddles her.

'Archie don't like anyone pesting him, Rilla,' she whispers in her sister's ear.

'Yeah, Dove, whatever you say.' Murilla mumbles.
*First thing tomorrow, Archie Corella.*

\* \* \*

'The Doctor wants to see you. He's downstairs in the dining room.' Caroline nods to the doorway.

'Yeah, what for?'

'How the hell do I know!' she splutters indignantly.

'I didn't think he was coming until next week. He certainly didn't tell me about this change of plan!' Murilla folds her arms; a seed of doubt crosses her mind. 'Unless, of course, you told him to come.'

'Well, I'm not his boss, now am I?' Caroline's bottom lip drops and she pouts like a sulky child.

'I'll go down and check. And I think ya need to get out of that chair and take a small walk around. That thing can make ya lazy. A bit of exercise never harmed anyone.' Murilla leaves the room, knowing that she's wasting her breath trying to get Caroline to do anything.

She enters the dining room and looks around. 'Doctor? Doctor Sheffield, are you here?' There's no sound.

Jesus Christ! She lied! She storms to herself. She pelts upstairs, huffing and puffing. She flings the door open, 'You bloody liar, Caroline!'

'What's the matter, Salte? The good doctor not in?' Caroline laughs, slapping the bedpost with glee.

'Why? Why do you always do this to me?' Murilla seethes. 'Is this some sort of mad game with you?' Murilla moves closer.

'You're the one talking about exercise all the time. I

figured a little bit of leg work wouldn't do you any harm.' Caroline grins.

Murilla threatens, 'Well, you know what I'm going to do? Yep, I'm gonna phone the doctor and tell him about your childish ways. Then I'm going to get him to write down the days when he's due here.' She smiles: *take that*.

'You just do what you have to.' Caroline picks at the bedclothes. 'Anyway, Murilla, I don't see what you're all upset about. It was only a joke. Har, har, see I'm laughing.' Caroline curls back her crusty lips.

'Have ya taken all your medicine today?' Murilla goes to the cabinet, yanks it open and rummages through the assortment of pills, finally settling on a small bottle. When she turns around, for a horrible moment she thinks Caroline's having a heart attack. Caroline's face tints shocking pink.

Murilla rushes forward. 'Caroline, are you alright?' Then she stops with a sinking feeling as she sees the mortified look on Caroline's face. The familiar sour odour of piss invades the closed room.

Caroline looks at the far wall, ignoring the piss that seeps into the bedclothes. She bends her neck and folds her hands demurely in her lap.

'Yes, I'm fine. And don't look at me like that!' she snaps, twining her legs tighter together.

Murilla reaches out for her. 'Come on, into the bathroom.'

'Get away, leave me alone!' Caroline spits defensively, gripping the bedpost.

'Might be a good idea to go into the bathroom, Caroline.' Murilla looks away. She turns around when she hears Caroline get up from the bed.

Caroline, her gown crumpled and soggy, holds her

head high with a proud tilt and begins, 'Can Sofie come visit?'

Murilla scans her face. 'What do ya want with Sofie, Caroline?'

'Company. It seems no one else bothers about an old lady.'

'Now come on, none of that talk today.' Murilla guides her into the bathroom and shuts the door.

Feeling like a bag of bones, Murilla drops onto a chair. She casts a glance towards the bed and wonders how long she can keep this up, knowing Caroline is becoming worse by the day.

The bathroom door swings open. Caroline floats into the room in a gauzy, brilliant pink gown that swishes as she moves past. Rose water chokes the air. Murilla stares up into a made-up face: bright green eyeshadow creases her lids and a thick blood-red crooked slash of lipstick smears her mouth. Perched elegantly on top of her wiry hair is a black cloche hat with a white feather poking from the side which jiggles up and down as she moves.

Caroline swings slowly towards Murilla. 'You like?'

Murilla plays the game. 'Oh, sure do! Now where are ya going so fancied?'

'My husband and I are off to the races. After that we'll dance the night away. And of course we'll be attending a private function at Mrs Henry's first. She'll have her usual banquet, seafood and chardonnay.' Caroline slides with effort to the side table and picks up a tumbler of water. She takes a delicate sip. 'Perfect! A chardonnay I see!'

'Um, yeah I had to order it special like.'

'What do we have here? Oh, lobster! How perfect,

Maureen!' She runs a hand across the table and pretends to pick something up.

'I wouldn't serve anything less, Caroline.' Murilla sweeps an arm across the phantom buffet table.

'Well, Maureen, I've been thinking that perhaps I'll have a little do of my own. Maybe I can ask that lovely young girl from town — Murilla, that's her name — to make me some pâté and petits fours. Naturally, you'll be invited.'

'Thank you, Caroline. It all sounds so flash!' Murilla throws her arms open enthusiastically.

Caroline salutes her with the tumbler. 'Who else do you think deserves an invite?'

'The Doctor and his lovely wife, Sofie Salte, and, um ... Joyce Hall and ...' Murilla stops, looks at her reddening face and takes a deep breath, knowing what's coming. Knowing what Caroline wants her to say. 'And Polly Goodman.' There, she said it.

'No! Oh no! Not that woman! That dirty ... that foul ...! Murilla, help me! Murilla!' Caroline screams, then crumples to the floor in a pink heap. 'Do it, Murilla,' she whispers into the folds of the gown.

'Right, that's it!' Murilla swings to the empty corner. 'Missus Goodman, you are a friggin cow! Caroline Drysdale hates ya guts! Ya keep away from this house and from her! Otherwise I'll ... I'll do something I shouldn't. Get ya arse out of here ya bitch! There's to be no party here n ya tell that to ya high bitin mates too!' she screams into the corner.

Caroline gets to her wobbly feet, her face bleached white as she clambers into the recliner. Her frail body trembles. 'Is she better than me? Prettier?'

'No, she's not! Never were, never will be!' Murilla bends down and looks into her watery eyes.

'She hates Murilla,' she whispers. 'You know that, don't you?'

'I know she hates Murilla. Murilla hates her, too.' She folds Caroline's bony knuckled hands into hers.

'She took him away from me. I was nothing. The bird in the gilded cage! Huh, that's a fine laugh! Gilded cage!' Caroline laughs bitterly.

'Yeah, funny.'

'She was caught, you know. Oh yes, Murilla caught the bitch at it. But Polly ...'

'Polly what?'

'She tried to ... it was both of them. Donald and Reginald. They hated me, Salte. Tried to drive me out when I discovered that ...' She stops and moments later her chin falls to her chest.

Murilla lays the crocheted rug across Caroline's pink gown. She walks over to the window and looks out. The skeletal trees bend in death, their gnarled branches reaching skyward like the grasping talons of a witch.

Everything that was once alive and green died a long time ago.

Nothing will grow in the yard now. The dirt seems to have some sort of sickness. It's as though when Reginald Drysdale died he took something away. *Took part of life with him into death.*

# three

# unwanted truth

Archie Corella looks down into Murilla's thunderous face.

'Ya know, Corella. I know ya know! I was there before you were. Something happened and I wanna know what! I got eyes, man, n I see things. Who was the girl, Archie?' Murilla needles, her face glazed with sweat.

'Murilla, I swear to God,' he lies. 'I don't know watcha talking about, woman!' *She will hound me forever unless I tell her everything. Until then she'll never rest. That's the kind of person she is. But if I tell her, she might do something stupid. Get me, get the old woman.* It was a long time ago but he'd never forget it. The look on her face was murderous; her flinty eyes could have scraped flesh from him. It was something small that triggered it off, the wrong rose bush planted in the wrong flowerbed.

Archie has a dreadful feeling that if she ever finds out what he thinks he knows, then there'll be no place on earth for him to hide.

Fear keeps him rooted to the spot. A mad desire whips through his mind: *maybe he could give her a hint. Let her work it out from there. Nah, she wouldn't fall for that.*

Murilla's large frame advances up the steps. 'I think

ya do, Corella. I know what Donald Drysdale was and you know what he was. Spit it out, man!'

'Um ... Yeah, but ...' He lays down the garden fork and watches with dread as she steps onto the verandah.

'What ya scared of, Archie?' Murilla's voice lowers to a cracked whisper.

'No, no it's not that. I, well, I don't know anything! Murilla, a man don't know what the hell you talkin about!' Archie shakes his head. *Just go away, woman. Go away.*

Her eyes narrow dangerously. 'The shed. It happened in the shed.'

A frown creases his face. 'Donald's work shed?' *The work shed, this is where it all comes down to.*

'Don't play Jacky with me, Corella! The shed! Now, I know ya used to spy out of that little window, from the quarters. Ya saw something! One last time, the girl — was it my Sofie?' Murilla yells, near delirious.

'No! No! I don't know ...!' He takes a trembly step back.

Archie breaks from her gaze and looks out at the unfinished garden. He'd have to put some horseshit into the ground soon, fertilise it all. That's the problem with gardens and such — have to be digging, fertilising and weeding, have to keep ...

Murilla shouts, 'If I ever find out that ya lied to me, Archie Corella, I'll bury you in one a those holes over there!' She points past the steps.

He looks around, then moves closer to her. 'The ... the ... the old woman,' he whispers in a fractured voice.

'Corella, ya tellin me Caroline knows something?' She scowls.

'She ... she knew ... but then one day ...' Archie swallows the lump in his throat.

'Yeah what, come on out with it!'

Then it dawns on him. Someone has talked. 'How? How did you find out?'

'I got ears, fellah. Now, get on. I haven't got all friggin day to be standing here yakkin.'

'The old woman found stuff in the shed. If memory serve me correct it were the day you was down town ...'

'Stuff?'

Archie stutters, 'Umm, yeah ... cclloo ... ggirrll ... little ddrreeess ... girls ...'. His ears ring and his heart pounds furiously. He doesn't want no part of this.

'Caroline found them?'

'Shh ... ssshhheee ... sheeee ...'

Suddenly Murilla is upon him, shaking him by the shoulders. 'Corella! Archie, are ya right, man?'

He can hear her but he can't see anything.

Darkness closes in. He feels himself drop into it.

'Archie, Archie.' Her voice floats above him.

He opens his eyes. Murilla stands over him. He wonders where the hell he is. He gets up on one elbow and looks around. It's his bedroom.

'You fainted, fellah. Want some strong black tea?' she offers, voice edged with worry.

'Tea would be good.' He fainted, that wasn't anything new. Too much pressure and he'd go down like a sack of shit. He looks up at the ceiling. If he told her what he did know and what he thinks he knows, then that'd mean talking to Sofie. No way he could risk that.

A few minutes later Murilla comes back into the room.

'Here, it's hot. Might clear ya head.' She hands him the mug.

'Murilla, I can't tell you much. Just because I worked

there doesn't mean I saw *everything*. Have you talked to Doris?'

Archie looks down at the teacup. Maybe she'd annoy Doris about it and forget about him. He doesn't like his chances. One thing he knows about Murilla Salte is that she is like a dog with a bone. Won't let go. And if he's right, she never will until she finds what she's looking for.

'All right, Archie, I have ya word on that. But ...' she stops. Look, I'm not a hard person but I got my sister to look after.' She eyes him suspiciously. 'Ya care about her, don't ya, Archie?'

'Please don't let this change things. She's all I got!' he croaks.

'Now, don't get all upsettin, Archie. If I thought anything funny was going on then I wouldn't let Sofie hang around here, now would I?' She shakes her head, walks over to the far wall and drags a chair across to the side of the bed. She sits down, then reaches over and pulls the grubby white sheet over his legs.

'How's the old woman?' He watches her closely.

'Still a handful, if that's what ya mean,' Murilla grunts.

'Her health been good?' He sips his tea.

'Nah, she fallin to pieces,' she shrugs, eyes roaming the room.

'What, she's that *sick*?' A suspicion crosses his mind. He doesn't like the way her eyes avoid his.

'Ya know what it's like. Startin to see things now. Threatened to kill herself the other day — all shit, mind ya. The only thing wrong with her is that mad head of hers. Yep, always reckonin every day she gonna die — been sayin that for years.'

'How do you put up with her?' Archie wonders how

the two of them stayed together this long and who hurt who the most.

'I pay her no mind. I been looking after the oldest kid in the world for years.' Murilla laughs, but it doesn't come from her hard eyes.

'She'd get on anyone's bloody nerves. I tell you this, I'm glad a man don't work there anymore! Arrhhh, suppose I shouldn't be too hard on her. She done all right by me, I guess.' He puts the cup down beside the bed.

'Sometimes I could just ...!' Murilla stops abruptly, her mouth twists to one side. 'Oh never mind. Look, Archie, if Sofie comes over later will ya make sure to keep her away from that riverbank, huh. Seem you the only one she'll really listen to.' She stands. 'Are ya right here?'

'Yep, good as gold.' He smiles feebly. *It's not as though I don't like her, sure I do, just that I don't trust the woman.* He watches her large shoulders as she passes through the doorway. Then, lying back onto the pillows, he wonders when everything started to go wrong. He goes back to the summer of last year.

\* \* \*

He'd been working for the Drysdales for three months when the boy disappeared. It had happened the same day as the hospital held the street parade. He was told that the parade was an annual thing, raising money for sick kids and their families to go to the bigger and better-equipped hospitals in the city. And every year without fail the whole town chipped in and supported the event.

Being such a special day the Drysdales had given him time off, telling him to start work the next morning. Having nothing better to do he decided to walk over to Mary Street, maybe have a beer or two, and give the hospital a small donation.

Dressed up like a real gentleman, he strolled down the sidewalk taking everything and everyone in. The school band was there, leading the march: drums were bashed with fierce effort, cymbals clanged and flutes struggled to be heard above the racket.

Dotting the pavement like a carnival sideshow were old women wearing hair-nets, shouting and pulling people up to buy a six-pack of lamingtons or some homemade tomato chutney. 'Three dollars a dozen! Merle Drewson's best lamingtons since winning last year's cooking competition!' they bawled in high tones.

'Here, over here, the ladies of the Red Rose Committee have the best pickles and home-baked bread in the entire district! Buy three, get one free!' shouted a well-dressed, horse-faced woman, casting him a sly glance as he went by.

Towards the end of the closed-off street was a merry-go-round, the red, white and blue painted horses bobbing above the crowd. Archie stopped and looked across. He thought it was her. Dressed in a bright red frock and a pair of clunky brown sandals was Sofie. She cooeed and laughed, one hand gripping a pink cone of fairy floss.

Every time the music started up she sang along with it, her voice drowning out everyone else's.

*That sweet summer we had my love, my love*
*Then you had to go away*
*Tears of sorrow that I have shed for my love, my love, my love*

Archie watched her with a smile, how she loved that song.

He turned his attention to the other side of the road. Standing with one hand on her wide hip and the other jammed into her skirt pocket was Murilla. And with mouth flapping, Doris stood beside her. He offered them a smile and raised his hand in greeting.

Archie searched for the bar, then spotted a line-up of farmers and town blokes hanging around a wooden stand. Feeling hot and dry he ambled over, painfully conscious of his hat, the tan shirt and second-hand polyester trousers he wore. Oh well, he had to look halfway decent. Weren't like he could afford new stuff anyway.

Archie paid for a tin of beer and downed it in two gulps, then lit up a cigarette and watched as the parade moved sluggishly down the sizzling road.

Suddenly a loud scream split the air. His arms banded with goosebumps as he looked through the crowd and spotted a wild-eyed woman staggering drunkenly and shouting at people, 'My son's gone! He's missing!' She pulled on shirtsleeves with fierce desperation as she fought her way forward until she stood in front of the bar. 'My son Kenny's gone! Help me, please someone, help me!' she implored, fat tears rolling down her freckled child-like face.

Some men turned and faced her; others laughed into their hands. After a second, a man wearing a stetson hat and red cowboy shirt said: 'On em drugs are you, Miranda? Don't tell me that Kenny's lost *again*!'

The girl stumbled back, reeling as though hit midsection. She placed a hand across her heart and her eyes roamed from one man to the other. Some men had the decency to look shame-faced; others just mumbled that she was a good-for-nothing druggie, that she wasn't good enough to look after a mongrel dog.

Finally a sympathetic voice piped up, 'Go see Dave Warner.'

Miranda's face flushed a deep pink and she looked at

the line of men with such hate-twisted features that for a strange moment everyone froze. 'Bastards! Fucking bastards,' she choked out in a small, cracked tone.

From the side of the bar, a man with grey hair and sunburnt features stepped forward. 'Okay, Miranda, how long has he been gone for?'

'Orh, Dave ... well, he was at the merry-go-round for a bit. I just turned my back to say hello to Doris and when I turned around he was gone,' she sobbed.

'Did you go and tell Arty to broadcast it across the speakers?'

'Yeah, but no one's seen him. *It was only for a minute that I turned my back!*'

'Right then, you blokes get your arses moving! We've got a kid to find,' the copper barked at the line of gawking men.

Tipping his hat to the side, he watched as a few stragglers followed the copper. Archie wondered if he should help, but it weren't likely he'd be able to find the kid. Nope, he was flat out finding his hair comb in the morning, let alone a kid.

But they wouldn't find the boy. There was never any hope with such thick scrub. The thing was, the Stewart River flanked the entire town and very few people, even those that lived in the district and spent their lives fishing and swimming there, would ever really know it like the back of their hands. Except for one person.

But none of them knew that.

Throughout the entire night, men and dogs combed the riverbank. Flashlights lit up the night like glowing insects. Voices demanded that Kenny appear. By this time, the boy's mother was heavily sedated and having a spell in hospital.

Soon the rumours started. Miranda killed her son. The boy drowned. The river flushed him out onto Top Paddock, old man Cleaver's property — *and he likes young boys*. But none of these things were true.

Days later they brought in the divers. Some people just shook their heads with despair and repeated, 'A small boy like that doesn't have a chance in hell, not on the river.' All hope for Kenny had been surrendered. The town went into mourning. Afterall, it was something that could happen to *anyone*.

Archie would always think of how she begged, see the look on her face as some of the men laughed, and part of him would remain guilty. He should have stopped them. Any decent man would have.

But as things turned out it was on the fifth day that something happened.

Archie was on the riverbank digging up sand for the flowerbeds when he spotted a yellow shape flittering on the horizon above the bushes. First he thought it was a wild dog. People were always dumping unwanted pets on the riverbank.

But then Archie noticed how tall and swift the shape was. Curious, he walked further up the bank and focused hard.

There: a flash! Something was definitely moving like it had fire up its arse.

He put the shovel down and, careful not to be seen, crept along. The branches and dead leaves crunched under his heavy tread as he stepped into the scrub. Again the thing flickered, jumped and moved in all directions. Then it came to a stop.

As he straightened up, the figure turned around and looked him directly in the eye as though knowing he was there all the time. A guilty flush crept up his neck and he felt stupid, as though someone had caught him doing something he shouldn't.

'Archie Corella.' She smiled, fingering the hem of her yellow dress.

Archie scratched his neck and slowed to a lazy walk. 'Hello, Sofie.'

'Ya spy me?' She frowned, the edge of her mouth quivering.

'No, no ... Well ... um, I thought I'd come this way for a walk.' Archie dropped his eyes feeling as though she could read the lie in them. Suddenly within a terrifying instant a dark shape appeared and curled around Sofie's leg. It was a brown snake.

Archie stuttered, 'ddoo ... ddoonn ... doonn ...' His hands trembled and his heart galloped. *Oh no, not this again!* Snakes scared him more than anything else in life. Archie's eyes remained on the twisting brown vision as it uncoiled then slid slowly across her bare foot.

He was struck dumb. He moved his head an inch and looked into her eyes. She stared back at him, not a flicker of fear in her.

He waited for what felt like hours but the snake refused to budge. It had settled on a good, warm spot. Knees creaking and ears pounding like gunshots, he moved ever so slightly. Knowing that if he scared it the snake would respond by lashing out.

Then something happened. It was unexplainable that day, as it would be later. Archie would never be able to tell anyone that what moved him was the look in Sofie's eyes: trust. It felt as though when he moved he flew through the air, even though he was airborne for only a fraction of a second. When he looked down, the snake was writhing in his hands, spots of blood seeping from its cruel mouth. He had broken its neck without even realising it.

When he looked up, Sofie was off again tearing through the scrub, hands fighting tree branches that threatened to smack and claw her in the face.

He threw the snake onto the ground and raced after her. 'Stop! Sofie, don't run away! Stop!' he screamed hoarsely. Then, to his amazement, she stopped.

Casting rapid, furtive looks to each side, Sofie parted the thick shrubs and stepped into them. Shaken by the confrontation with the snake, Archie thought what he heard next was something he'd imagined. Yet it was *there*, loud and clear. The voice of a child.

He parted the bushes and stepped into the clearing. There she was, sitting on a log and holding a young boy in her arms. He looked at her and grappled to find some reasonable answer. The boy had dark brown hair, piercing blue eyes and a freckled nose. He knew without doubt it was the lost boy, Kenny Austin.

Archie opened his mouth to say something but words and thoughts refused to come together. He scrutinised the kid and apart from being filthy there seemed nothing wrong with him. Finally, he managed to open his mouth, 'Sofie, that's Kenny, ain't it?' He walked towards them on the log.

'Yepee, reckon that's right,' she answered, ruffling the boy's hair.

'You found him ...?' He didn't believe that for a second. The kid looked too well kept.

'Sofie done found this here bubby in that bush, see.' She tugged at her ears.

'When'd you find him?' He had a terrible feeling that

something else had happened, that Sofie didn't find the kid at all, she stole him.

'Ummm, can't say, Archie Corella. Sofie loses stuff every day.' She pulled a piece of buttered bread from her pocket and shoved it into the boy's grubby hand.

'Sofie, ya tooked that bubby didn't ya?'

'Nah! Nah! Don't be dobbin, Corella!' Sofie yelled, tears gathering in her eyes.

'Oh ... oh ... yoo ... yoouu ...' He stopped, took a deep breath, then steadied himself against the trunk of a gum tree. 'Trouble, oh God, there'll be shit every which way.'

'Is my bubby!' She wrapped her arms tightly around the boy, a look of fierce determination on her face.

'He's gotta go back, Sofie.'

'Nope! Getcha arse outta here! Thought ya was me true time friend!' she sobbed.

He looked at the two of them on the log. Common sense told him that it amounted to kidnapping and that meant all sorts of grief.

'I'm ya mate, Sofie, but he's gotta go back.'

'Why for? He's mine, ain't he. Sofie find him. Finders keepers, losers weepers!' she garbled, panic-stricken.

'Sofie, there'll be trouble. What about his mother? She's sad ya know.' He tried to be soothing, but his head throbbed.

'Sofie sad!' she responded, pulling at greasy strands of her hair with anger.

'The police have been looking for him. Now look, we'll have to take him in. I'll tell everyone that you found him and was too scared to tell anyone, okay?'

'No bubby for me?' Sofie crossed her arms.

'No. He ain't ya bubby. He belongs to that Miranda girl. Ya don't wanna see her cry, do ya? Now say after me, I found the baby and was scared to tell anyone because I might be in trouble. I looked after the baby and gave him tucker.'

'I found the bubba n was scared up cos Sofie be in trouble. I gave bubba tucker too. But Sofie ain't hard hearts. Can she have nother bubba?' Sofie looked at him with anxious eyes.

'Oooh ... I suppose so. Just remember what I told ya to say.' He bit his lip. For an entire hour he made her repeat the words.

'Good! Joy for the moon, joy for the spoon!' Sofie laughed wildly as the three tracked out of the bush.

An hour later they were in the police station. Dave Warner was the first person Archie looked for. They were there for hours, answering questions. Warner wasn't such a bad cop after all. When he finally got the garbled story out of Sofie, he just shook his head sympathetically. It was decided that the story would go no further than with those that sat in the room.

That was the strong will and cunning of Sofie Dove. And only one of the few things to test him. There was something else she would do later on that would bring Archie to his knees. And all the while he fought the ghosts that came for him.

\* \* \*

Archie yawns and the thoughts disappear into the back of his mind. Sighing heavily, he gets up from the bed, picks up the empty mug and goes into the kitchen.

He checks the time: three o'clock. Sofie would be on her way over.

Just as he turns to put the cup into the sink the sound of knocking reaches his ears.

'Archie Corella! Sofie Dove be here.' She shuffles her feet, casting swift glances past his shoulder.

'Hey, Sofie, come in.' He opens the door wider and lets her through.

'I see Rilly was here. Why for?' She plonks onto the kitchen chair.

'Um, she wanted some garden stuff,' Archie lies, then turns and plugs the kettle into the power point. 'Tea, coffee or Milo?'

'Sofie have Milo.'

'Murilla told me you have to stay away from that riverbank. It's dangerous down there, Sofie.'

'Poop, poop. I swimmed all the way to the weir n all. I getting a better swimmer, Archie Corella.'

'You'll get drowned is what'll happen. Sofie, please stay away from there. If you want to go swimming, just come and get me and I'll go with you.' He places the steaming drink in front of her.

'Rilly angry at Arch?' she frowns.

'Nuh, why?' He watches as Sofie fiddles with the cup.

'Stuff that happens. Bout that scary house man, the girls n all.' She chews on her lip.

Archie feels his gut turn to water. 'What things?' He looks down at the floor. She won't tell him anything if he looks at her. That's the way she is.

'Ar ... um ... stuff.' She giggles then covers her mouth.

'Man stuff?' Archie offers the bait.

'Of the scary house.' Her eyes widen.

'The Drysdale house?'

'They nutty n all, rich as fruitcake. Ya be careful, Arch, he be watchin ya every move.' Suddenly, she jumps to her feet and before he can move she's halfway out the front door.

Archie realises he's touched a raw nerve. He has a suspicion that what he witnessed a year ago could well be what he thought all along. Sofie was hiding something. He puts a hand to his forehead, cool down, cool down. He doesn't want to see any carnival lights today. Only one thing he can do, and in his books the right thing: protect her.

Archie's thoughts veer to Murilla — yep, he'd even take her on if he *really* has to.

He races out onto the verandah, 'Stop! Sofie, stop! Where ya going?' he shouts.

'Swimmin!' Sofie throws behind as she tears full gallop down the dirt road.

He watches until she disappears into the bushes. He decides to follow, to keep an eye on her at any rate.

The faint roar of the river reaches Archie's ears. At first he fails to understand what the low rumble means till something in the back of his mind jars. He pulls to an abrupt halt. Something isn't right. Then the clear light of understanding sifts into his mind. His heart trips. 'Sofie! Sofie!' he yells gutturally.

He rushes headlong into the scrub, tearing away gnarled branches that rake their scrawny fingers along his face. Archie's legs pump hard and his ankles bleed as tree limbs lash at him.

'Sofie Dove!' Archie's scream startles pigeons out of the treetops and as they take flight they seem to echo his call, *Dovedovedovedove!*

Wiry branches reach out to snag the bottom of his trouser leg and he trips face forward into a muddy ditch. A slow warmth dribbles down the side of his face and specks of blood splatter his hands.

The roar becomes louder.

He brings his head up and looks across at the thrashing, raging water. Stumbling uneasily to his feet he grabs hold of a paperbark gum. He gapes at the sight before him. Looking across at the water he knows nothing will be the same again.

The torrent spins and whirls as it bashes into the muddy banks. Small tea-trees snag underneath the greedy, sucking mouth of the water. The noise is deafening.

Swimming and bobbing her way upstream is Sofie.

He's gonna see her drown and there's nothing he can do about it. A desperate madness grips him.

He scrambles down the rock face, grabbing hold of the outcrop. She's going against the flow!

When he reaches the lowest part of the ledge, he turns around slowly. He's lost her. Somewhere high up in the ghostgum the brassy cry of a Kookaburra rings out. Archie looks down.

Sofie stands below him at the edge of the water, mud smeared on her face, and river weed clumped in her hair. In one hand she holds a cod.

'Sofie! Sofie!' Archie cries out, his voice edged with hysteria as he stumbles down the slope.

'Archie Corella!' She smiles.

'What are you doing?' Archie grabs her shoulders. *How can she do this to me. I thought she was gonna drown!*

She holds up the struggling fish in his face. 'Me mates, Arch, I swam with me mates, heeeyyy.' Then she kneels on the edge of the bank and gently releases the fish into the rushing water.

'Sofie, how'd you do that?' Archie asks in amazement. All this time he never knew. He should have but didn't.

'I'm a fish, Arch. Fish swim in water. Can't ya know that?' she glowers.

'You'll drown, that's what'll happen!' he yells.

'I can't be drownded. Arch, I can't get drownded!' She flinches away from him, her bottom lip twitching.

'It's bloody dangerous, Sofie. *You will* drown.' He shakes his head, looks at her, then at the river.

One thing he does know: Sofie is one hell of a swimmer. In that small moment a terrible, unwanted truth slides into his mind.

*His Sofie Dove has murdered a man.*

# four

# the house of mud

Sofie's dreams rise from a fragmented landscape inhabited by a chorus of bruised whispers. She tosses and turns, the bedsheets twisting around her sweat-drenched body as she treads a shifting dreamscape. Waking in the darkness she cries out and sits upright in bed, tears and sweat mingling. She walks over to the window and peers out gritty-eyed into the moonsoft night. She looks in the direction of the river and her expression deepens into a mask of fear. Through a swirl of dreamshadow, insistent thoughts come to tell the story of an unhappy girl.

*Once upon a time it were a sad day. The trees they bend over and cry from sadness — cry eye all ova the place. The river wash up all the tears.*

*There was a man, he name boo, Mister Peekaboo. He be waitin by the bushes, the river bushes.*

*Mister Peekaboo grab a hold a Sofie! Oh, bad troubles there. He turn wild as the bull, he bust a gut: Get over here!*

*Sofie, she cry up. Oh, ya must scat cat! Sofie wanna run too fast. 'Boo, getcha fucken arse way from here!'*

*The moon sick up n all, even too the stars felled outta that sky. Dark n everythin. Peekaboo twist yellagreen eyes.*

*Come on, girl, he say, laughin way down there.*

*Grabbin Sofie he has hands into that place, pink, soft place, bad man.*

*Scat Cat! Sofie's words big, heart beatin too fast. Too scaredy, she want her sister's eye, Rilly, RILLY.*

*Then he finish up, look at Sofie n smile. Off in the bush he go. Gone to the scary house.*

*Sofie hide, crybubby, then crawl to the water. Deep, the mud pulled in the water wash her all ova. Sofie clean, no more cry eye. Sofie ask many things to the river.*

What to do
*Only one thing to do*
What that is
*Cut his water off*
How to
*Bring him this way*
When
*Next time he be gettin that sad girl*
Oh see then he get red bad mad
*He ain't a true time friend*
I seee
*He gotta be doin time*
Time in the drink
*Yeeeeaaaahhhh that'll be a lesson for all bulls*
How Sofie do that
*Sshhhsssshh drop to the guts n crawl in*
Oh cold water
*Shush now member what boo said they all blame the girl cos she got that thing n she a girl n girls dirty*
Oh I crybubba
*Dontcha cry*
*Here the secret*
the bad one

*Naaahh not the bad one the good one*
*When one sleep goes come to the river*
uh-huh when the sun drop over
*Yeeaahh that time*

Mister Peekaboo comed down to the river that awful scat cat day. Not even knows, as mad as he were that it were his big time.

Sofie say: Swimmin.

Boo say: Yeah, with no clothes on.

Laugh he do. His trousers everything off. White like fish belly in the water. He swims right in the middle and a thing happened. The secret thing.

'Help me! Let me go! Let me go you, little bitch! I'll fucking kill you! You bitttchh!'

That Sofie knew that no person can help when the river say what gonna happen. That the way things be. Dancin on water won't do good a tiny bit.

Face blue like the sky hands reachin at Sofie he go bubblin under there to the fish house. That ol house a mud.

He be no more Mister Peekaboo. He be keepin company with em all — eatin weeds under the river. Ain't like Sofie hard hearts just it were the goodest thing to do.

After when the sun felled outta the sky, Sofie swummed up the river. Swim on home fishy. Weeds mud n leeches catch to her.

When the men came n pulled Peekaboo outta the water, they sayed: 'Poor bastard, wonder what he was doing down there. Never thought him one for taking bush walks, har, har.'

Then police came n asked all questions to everyone at the scary house. He ask why for Sofie was on the riverbank. Someone saw her there but no words can say a thing when people dunno bout stuff.

Walking along fast as he did the man knocked on the biggest wooden door. 'Missus Drysdale, it's Dave Warner. Open up, I need to ask you some questions about your son.'

She open the door, cranky mad, she say no words bout that Sofie.

The policeman walk out of the room n seein Sofie he bust a gut: 'Stop! Stop right there!'

Sofie stop all right. Heart jumpin she look at him. She says down inside herself, don't let the eyes give you up. Were always the eyes that tell on people. Sofie, she knowed that n wished she had her sister's eye.

He ask: Sofie, did you see Mister Drysdale fall into the river?

Sofie say: 'Ain't never saw no one fall, no sir, Dave Warner. Sofie Dove see nothin.'

'Right. If I need you again, I'll see Murilla, okay? Okay fellahs, we're all finished here now.'

When the sun finish, Sofie run back down to her friends n she ask bout em coppers. Will ya tell on Dove?

*We never say words*

Ain't like we was true friends

*He jumped into us he did*

The man did he ask bout Mister Peekaboo fallin? Murilla she be sad if she know bout such things yell unhappy words at Dove.

*Yeah, he asked all sorts of things did sofie see mister drysdale fall in the river asked at the scary house doris murilla archie the old woman they say no words Sofie she stucked that ol pink snake in her mouth cry n all let me go let me go she cry too loud mister peekaboo smack her in the gob 'stay put' he rousin to her then he lift that pretty frock up n hands crawl spider legs all ova that sofie he sayed if you tell I'll kill your mother oh no she won't say no words that a true see now whatcha gotta know is this mister peekaboo can't be killin anythin we'll fix him eat his guts out like worms n stuff sofie dove dontcha cry now crybubby be no more egg white for you*

I close me ears to ya, makin Sofie scared ya is

*Gone bubbyloo crybabbycrryybabbyyy that's right cry that old boo outcha system wash his white arsehole away up river he done with hurtin black girls white girls he snake cut off right at the top cry now gone cry him right outcha sofie*

Reeling back from the window, Sofie cries out into the solemn silence. 'I hate ya! Getoutta me, getoutta me brain!' She throws herself back onto the bed, pulling the covers up over her head, mewling and shivering in the hot night.

*\* \* \**

In the morning, Sofie wanders into the kitchen. The smell of bacon, eggs and toast fills the room.

Murilla is at the stove, egg lifter in hand. 'Hey love, ya want some toast?'

'Toast for Sofie, Rilly, yes please.'

Murilla turns back around, grabs the warm plate off the stove and passes it to her.

'Love, how would ya like to go n see Missus Drysdale today? She'd like to see you.'

'Yepee, see the old one!'

Murilla's face etches into a concerned frown. 'Now listen, whenever Caroline talks it might be a good idea just to shake ya head and pretend to know what she's saying, okay? Caroline can be ... oh, never mind.'

'She's right, Rilly. Sofie knows careful.'

Murilla pours herself a cup of tea, then resumes cautiously. 'I know, love. But don't pay too much mind to Caroline, sometimes she ...um, she gets lost in the head like ...'

'Like Sofie.'

'Yeah, sorta.'

'What she want with the Dove?' Sofie breaks the toast into tiny pieces, watching butter and honey ooze onto the table.

'What ...?'

'Why? Why she wanna see me?'

'Well love, sometimes she gets a bit lonely and likes to talk to different people. No one visits her anymore, can't say a woman can rightly blame them either, especially on her bad days.' Murilla sighs, 'None of the women in town like her but then who do those bitches like?'

Sofie drops her eyebrows. 'They bitches?' She contemplates the word *bitch*. Dog bitch? Bitch dog?

'Well, not all a them, just the ones that think they're better than anyone else.' Murilla's face darkens in a look of disgust.

'How for?'

'Wha ... Oh, Sofie, bad manners don't pick your nose, it'll cave in. Well, love, sometimes Caroline gets a bit mean with people. And sometimes people get a bit mean with her. The way of the world, Dove.'

'We go n see the old one now?'

'Righto then. Let's just clear the dishes first, love.'

\* \* \*

The Drysdale house looks desolate, shutters are drawn tightly and doors closed. A small breeze scatters leaves across the unkempt ground.

Murilla studies the fenceline, then the trees. 'Funny thing that, the birds are all gone now. Gone.'

Sofie follows her sister's gaze. 'They don't like it here, Rilly. Birds don't go where the sun don't live.'

'Guess ya right, Dove.' Murilla reaches into her shirt-pocket, pulls out a key, opens the door and steps inside.

Sofie scans the musty smelling room. *Wooden chairs cry, creeaak n grrooann. Tick tock, the tall clock yells. Down along the wall, a bubby mouse pelts long like it done got a tick on its back, clicking its smallest feet on the wood as it shies off. Dark n cool as river water the hallway opens its mouth. Way off the wireless sing a song. With those little people inside ya'd think they squash like oranges in a bag — all bunched together like that. Where Rilly go?*

Murilla walks over to the loungeroom window and draws back the dust-laden drapes. Then turns to Sofie. 'Love, I'll just go into the kitchen for a bit n get Caroline her afternoon tea. Have a look around if you like. It's been a while since you've been here, hey.'

'Yeeppee, a woman n work is never done!' Sofie laughs, that be funny.

'You got that right, Dove.' Murilla heads off into the kitchen.

In a far corner, Sofie spots the TV set. She carefully turns the knob and the screen jumps to life. Excitedly she plonks onto the lounge chair. *Oh, they be shadow people.*

On the screen a man talks to a woman: 'There was never any doubt, Victoria, I've always loved you and damn it I always will. Marry me.'

Victoria, she says, 'Love is blind, Brock. I have my family

to think of and a business to take care of. I cannot commit to a man that's jilted me once before.'

'How can I go on? You have my heart and soul. Leave with me at once!

'Brock, I think there's something you should know ...'

'One of your dark secrets.' He laughs.

'I'm pregnant. Yes, Brock, I'm having your baby!'

Sofie's heart thunders with joy. She drops to her knees and crawls closer to the picture. *Oh, such a thing! She's having a bubby! Marry him, please Victoria! Be happy like ever after n all.*

'Don't tease me, my love.'

'It's true, but I can't have this baby. I ... my career ... my business ...'

'Are you telling me that you're considering a termination?'

'Yes.'

'I can't believe this! For God's sake, it's my baby and I want us to have this child!'

'It's my body, and I think you should appreciate that. Brock, I don't want any children at this time in my life.'

'Victoria, I cannot allow you to kill my child!'

Music and a voice says, 'What will Brock do? Stay tuned for the next episode of *As the Years Go By*.'

A bitter disappointment rushes through Sofie. She glares at the screen. *Can this be true? Victoria, she gonna kill that bub ... Not gonna marry Brock?* A sharp rage grips her. *Oh, Sofie can't like that. Victoria, killer bubbbbbbbyyyykilllleeeeeeerrrrrrr! Bitch, cow, fuckerdoodery ...!*

She swings around, grabs the poker from the mantle and hurls it at the screen.

Glass splinters through the air. Sofie screams at the wrecked screen. 'I hate ya fucken guts, ya bitch n all em swear words.' *Sofie, she can't have bubs cos Rilly sayed n that Victoria bitchtoria wanna be killin em!*

Murilla tears into the room, dropping the teatowel as she stands gazing at the smashed set.

'Oh my God! Oh Jesus Christ! Sofie, what the devil have ya done?' She puts a hand to her heart.

'Ain't done things ... Nothin ... Yeah, what bout that one killen bubby! Ya should stop her now. Gorn, gorn, stop her, Rilly!' Sofie drops to her knees, sobbing.

'Orh, come on, love, stop crying. I've told ya again and again, no TV. This is what happens.' Murilla walks over to Sofie who grabs her legs tightly. 'Oh Dove, it's all pretend. There's no real people in there, just actors pretending it's real.' She bends down and strokes Sofie's head. 'The baby don't happen. There's no baby, Dove.'

Sofie pulls herself away and sits back on her heels. 'Ya lie!'

'No lie, Dove. They're like a dream, not real even though they seem to be.'

Caroline Drysdale walks into the room, casting a bewildered expression towards the smashed screen.

'Oh, Caroline, it was an accident. Sofie ...' Murilla averts her eyes.

Caroline frowns. 'Sofie?'

'They killen bubs there, old one.'

'Who, Sofie? Who's killing babies?'

'That Victoria on there,' Sofie's finger jabs the air. 'She says her careerin more portant n marriage n happy after. She don't want bubbies! Such a thing!'

Caroline places a hand on her shoulder. 'Oh, yes, I see. Well, Sofie, some women just want that in life — a career and nothing else. But I'm certain that by tomorrow Victoria will have changed her mind.'

Sofie's face lights up with hope. She grabs Caroline's hands and shakes them fiercely as though the answers will fall from her palms. 'Yeah, old one, how can ya know?'

'I know a lot of things, Sofie. I know that Brock will marry Victoria and they'll have that baby and live happily ever after.'

'True. Can that be on Sofie's head true?'

'You bet your life.' Caroline turns to Murilla, a smile edging her lips. 'Now, Murilla, if you'll clean this mess up I'll take Sofie into the kitchen for some bickies and Milo.'

'Sorry, Caroline. I didn't think she'd ... I'll pay for a new one.'

'It was old, and anyway I don't watch a lot of TV and I swear I feel like doing that to it myself at times!' Caroline takes Sofie's arm. 'Come along, child.'

In the kitchen Caroline pulls out a chair and sits down beside Sofie. 'Here, have a biscuit.'

Sofie grabs the biscuit and between bites, queries, 'Ya was young?'

'Yes, a long time ago.'

Sofie stops chewing, 'N ya have bubbies?'

'Well yes, one baby.' Caroline's face takes on a soul-yellow cast.

'I ssseee.'

'It's a funny world and things have changed since I was your age. A wife was expected to look after house and husband. Really there wasn't a great deal you could do outside the home. That's unless you joined a women's committee or the like.'

'Oh, like the rose red ladies?' Sofie snatches another biscuit.

The lines on Caroline's face deepen. 'Yes, like them.

Even then you weren't always guaranteed acceptance into *their* committee. Humph, anyway I don't care what they say — it was that Goodman woman, Sofie. She ... it was all her fault!'

'Old one ...' Sofie reaches across the table, trying to grab Caroline's hands. *She looks angered n sad all together. So sad, a sad one.*

Caroline jerks forward in her chair. 'Huh? ... Oh, sorry. Now, where was I ... Yes, committees. The Red Rose ladies have always been a bunch of cows! I don't want to be in their group anyway. And ... and that Polly Goodman!' she shrills, eyes feverish with anger.

Murilla walks into the room, hands on hips. 'Caroline, what's going on here? Sofie?' A thick silence sits in the room as she looks from one to the other.

'Rose red ladies make us mad, Rilly.'

Murilla purses her lips tightly. 'Oh no, not this today. I don't want ya to be thinking about them women. No use bein upset bout them, let it go.'

Caroline lifts her head, 'Murilla, can we do some chutney? Maybe some carrot cakes and pies?' she asks in a small, child-like tone.

The side of Murilla's face tics. 'Why? Now, why would you wanna be cooking?'

'It's my kitchen, Salte!' Caroline blurts out defensively. 'Don't you dare start on me today.'

Murilla drags out a chair and sits down in front of Caroline. 'The kitchen's shut and there'll be no mess here today. Bugger the cakes. Now, we all know you're the best cook in this town but enough is enough, Caroline, please.'

Sofie covers her ears, 'Don't shout, Rilly. Sofie help the old one.' *Rilly mad up now.*

Caroline pushes on, 'Get the cake mix together, Murilla, please. Eggs, flour, sugar, milk, oh, and some icing sugar.'

'No! No. No. I can't put up with your crappy moods today. Leave it for another time.' Murilla stands to her feet, face fixed hard.

Caroline smiles winningly. 'I want to show Sofie how to make a cake.'

'Well, I'm sure Sofie can wait until next time.'

'No!' Sofie bangs a fist on the table. 'Cake! Cake today!'

'Geez, a woman just can't win.' Murilla backs down. 'Sofie, get the milk and butter from the fridge.'

Caroline throws Sofie a mischievous wink, then looks at Murilla. 'Maybe I can enter my carrot cake into this year's cooking competition. I mean the hospital still has the annual fete, don't they?'

'Yep, that's one thing ya can count on, the hospital having the fete.'

'Old one n Sofie go.'

Murilla turns swiftly. 'Shhh, Sofie, that's enough.'

Sofie's face drops. 'Why, Rilly, I bein gooder?'

Caroline cups a hand to her ear. 'Murilla, what on earth are you whispering about?'

'Nothing. Not a thing.'

Caroline smiles smugly, arching her eyebrows at Murilla. 'Yes, Sofie, you and I will go. Get those ingredients over here, and smack a smile on your face, Murilla. You're turning into a right sour puss.'

Murilla shakes her head vigorously. 'It'll end like it always does. Let it go, Caroline!'

'Talk nonsense. I have no idea what you're on about.'

'Ya know what I'm on bout. Ya gotta stop this!'

Sofie bursts out angrily, 'Rilly, dontcha be yellin at old ones.' *Rilly all mad now. Mad Rilly.*

'Sofie, just sit there n shut up!'

'Murilla! What's the matter with you these days? It's only a cake.' Caroline stiffens.

Murilla's face twists into resignation. 'Yeah, to me it is. But you ...'

'You what? Go on and say it, Murilla.'

'Rilly, dontcha be mad. Please stop. Please stop.' Sofie rocks in her chair.

Murilla, muttering angrily, crosses the room and slams the flour down on the table. 'They don't want ya! They never did!' She says in a low, vexed tone.

'Who? Go on, Murilla, spit it out. You've come this far.'

'Ya know who I mean.' Murilla reaches across and grabs Caroline's hands. 'Please, don't do this to yourself, Caroline.'

'Who do you mean? Enlighten me.' Caroline's voice is stony.

'Cake. Pretty please with sugar n all on top, Rilly.' *Bake me a cake mister baker man.*

Murilla places a finger to her lips. 'Shh love, hang on a minute.' She turns back to Caroline. 'They are never gonna let ya in.'

'See that's where you're wrong. I heard that a new member joined only last year. I'll get in if it kills me.' Caroline tightens her lips.

'And kill ya it will. How many times do I have to go through this with ya? It'll all end in tears — yours.'

Caroline sits tight-mouthed, her hands on her lap. Murilla shrugs with forced indifference. 'Yeah Caroline, right.' She turns to Sofie. 'Bring that mixing bowl this way, love.'

Caroline whispers, 'They'll never get the better of me, Murilla.'

As though deaf, Murilla doesn't respond. She grabs Sofie's arm and steers her to the door. She looks back. 'They'll be the end of you, Caroline,' she says with conviction, then leaves the room.

Walking away from the house, Sofie looks back and spots Caroline's shadowy figure framed in the kitchen window, holding a measuring cup up to the light.

As they tread down the gravel driveway, certain questions edge Sofie's mind. 'Rilly, why ya nasty bad to the old one?'

'She's gotta learn.'

'What? She be clever.'

'To learn that sometimes ya can't always get what ya want. No matter how hard ya wish it.

'Sofie, this town holds a ... well, some people in this town don't like Missus Drysdale and even some of em hate her.'

'Sofie n old one go to the fete.'

Murilla halts and turns to face her sister. 'She won't be going, Sofie. Hasn't been out of that house for years and she ain't gonna start now. Ya shouldn't pay too much mind to her, love. Says the same thing every year. When the time comes she just looks out across the paddock, then the rest of the day she spends talkin bout getting a new frock. By that time the show's over.'

'Rilly, the rose red ones make old one scaredy.' Sofie waves to the empty window.

'Huh, I guess that's something I never really thought of. Always thought they'd be scared of her.'

That night Sofie thinks about the old woman, and the Red Rose ladies, too.
*Sofie don't like the way peoples carry on.*
*Ain't right to be so mean.*
Thoughts tell her many things.

# five
# doris and nana vida

Doris looks across the road at the place by the river. Tall, straggly gums droop over the house like scrawny old women huddled over the warmth of a fire. The front part of the house is lined with rusted copper tubs full of white chrysanthemums. A rickety fly-screen door hangs off its hinges, the mesh clogged with dust and dead flies. Calico curtains hang from the windows like neatly ironed skirts.

Doris turns her attention to the other side of the house. A flock of crows land on the clothes line. All of a sudden they swoop down on the verandah railings in a knot of black feathers.

She steps towards the house and makes her way to the door, lamingtons in hand. All at once panic grips her. Why is she doing this and what can it prove? Biting her lower lip, she casts aside the doubts and knocks loudly on the door. She hears the scuffling of feet and the door slides ajar. Nana Vida peers out.

'It's me, Doris.' She holds up the pack of lamingtons. 'Thought we'd have a cuppa, eh?'

Nana opens the door wider. 'Come on in, Doris, don't stand on ceremony.' Nana motions her into the room and they go to the kitchen. She shuffles to the stove, puts the kettle on, then pulls out a chair and sits. 'What brings ya over this way, Doris? Haven't seen you about for a bit.'

'Well ... I ... um, I need to find something out.' Doris pauses, taking in Nana's face. She wonders if she should go on. After all, Nana might not tell her much either. It seems no one wants to tell her anything.

'Find what out?'

'I went to see Treacle Simpson and Pearl Midday about history ...'

Nana interrupts. 'What history, Doris, and why?'

'Ours. I need to know about our life in Mundra. I ... I feel ...' She stops, casts a glance at Nana, then pushes on. 'I know this is gonna sound silly but I feel lost here. Like I don't belong.' She's always felt as if she doesn't belong, even though Mundra has been home to her since she was a child. There's an emptiness she can't explain and somewhere in the recesses of her mind she's always known it's to do with the town's history.

Nana taps the table and watches Doris closely. 'Aye, well, Treacle n Pearl don't talk much anyways. So don't feel bad about that, my girl. I always thought one of you would come here one day. Always thought it'd be Murilla, though. It was only a matter of time.' Nana nods her head, slowly, wearily.

Doris feels a quiver of excitement. Finally someone will tell her something. But common sense reasserts itself and she wonders why Treacle and Pearl have been suspiciously quiet. It'd be foolish of her to think that they're not hiding something. She knows they are. So it's with doubt and confusion that she looks at the old woman.

'What do you mean "only a matter of time", Nana?'

'People talk, Doris. Even if Pearl and Treacle won't,

plenty of others will. I know what ya mean about feeling lost. And when people start feeling lost, they start searching for something to fill the emptiness. So go on, my girl, and ask me what you want to know.' Momentarily surprised, Doris scans her face. She never expected this. She begins, 'So you reckon Pearl Midday was the first one here?'

Nana pauses for a moment, as though gathering her thoughts. 'Aye, that would have been 1932 or thereabouts. They turned up here in a horse and sulky. Later on they applied to the Aboriginal Protection Board to get married. The Board said that they couldn't wed because Pearl didn't know the value of money. Oh, that caused them some grief. But there weren't a thing they could do about that. At that time your grandfather was working outta town there on the Barenteen property, ringbarking, horse-breaking and what not. Eventually Pearl got sick of moving around, so they built a humpy down there across from the old rubbish dump.'

Doris frowns. 'So my mother spent all her life here in Mundra? What about Mertyl Salte, was she here at that time?'

Nana cuts a lamington into small, bite-size pieces then says, 'She did. Never left, not once. Mertyl turned up about the same time as Joe and Lillian Gee ... but ...' She stops.

'But?' Doris prompts.

'I ... Pass me the teapot, will you, love?' Nana says, a deep frown cutting across her leathery forehead.

Doris pushes the teapot across the table. 'So, Nana, who were the Gees?'

At this, Nana's face seems to collapse, her lips tremor

slightly and she gazes out of the window. 'They ... um ... well ... they lived out on the reserve.'

She closes her eyes for a moment, then opens them. In a hoarse voice, she says, 'Joe put up a tent there for the family. I can't really remember what year that was, but they were good friends with Mertyl and Roy Salte. There would have been about six or seven of us fellahs in the town at that time. Not in town, but living on the edges, you see. The way things were back then was that blacks weren't welcome in town, white fellahs didn't want that ...'

Doris notices the sudden change that has come over her. 'Nana, do you feel okay?'

'Aye, yes ... yes ... I'm good,' Nana replies swiftly, clearing her throat, then turns and reaches into the fridge to haul out a bottle of beer and a bottle of lemonade. 'An old woman's joy — shandy. Want a glass?'

'Yeah, why not?' Doris chews her bottom lip. Something's not right here.

She drums her fingers on the table. 'The Gees, Nan, what about them? I mean, didn't they leave at some stage?'

Unexpectedly, Nana responds in a sharp tone. 'There's not too much I can say. Memory, ya see. I'm getting old.' She turns and looks at a spot on the far wall.

Nana turns back. 'Just be careful, Doris, you might find something you won't like.'

'Only interested in our history with this town is all.' She meets Nana's rheumy, grey gaze.

'Doris, some things are better left where they are.'

She feels the weight of unease and wonders at Nana's swift change of attitude. 'I might find something I don't like? What are you on about?' She watches Nana fiddle nervously with the glass.

'Some things are better left alone,' Nana replies in a tight tone. 'And some people like to be *private*. I tell you, maybe it's best to let it pass. Ain't no reason to be going round upsettin fellahs.'

Annoyed, Doris responds, 'Who's gonna be upset, less they have something to hide?'

Nana purses her lips. 'No one got anything to hide. You just can't be digging into other fellahs' lives like that, ain't good manners. Your mother taught you better than that.'

'I'm not digging. Anyway, what's wrong with me finding out a bit of history? Ya can bet that Murilla'll be interested too, once I tell her.'

Nana offers a vague smile. 'Murilla Salte, haven't seen her around since Mertyl passed on. How's the girl, Sofie?'

Feeling frustrated at Nana's obvious attempt to drop the subject, Doris shrugs, then replies, 'She's all right. Haven't seen her around much, she's always with that Archie Corella whenever I do see her. Funny sort of bloke. Like it's a disease for him to talk.' She reaches over and grabs a lamington.

'What! Doris, what are you saying?' Nana croaks, her face draining of colour. She clutches the edge of the table so tightly that the skin on her knuckles turns a mottled purple.

Doris jumps to her feet and races around the table. *What? What's happening!* 'Nan, Nan! Are you alright?'

Nana wheezes, a deep cough racks her body. 'I ... I ... just lost me breath for a minute.'

She places a hand on Nana's shoulder, then offers her the shandy. 'Here, have a drink.'

Nana puts a hand to her heart, gazing up at her with

something like fear. 'You say Archie Corella? Doris, that can't be right, less his ghost be roaming around.'

Doris sits beside her. 'What do ya mean?'

Nana wrinkles her brow. 'I mean, Archie Corella died years ago. Weren't no other Archie Corella lived in this town.'

Doris looks at her closely. 'There is *now*. He used to work for Caroline Drysdale, gardening, handy-man work. Matter of fact he lives over there on Artbuckle Street.'

Unsteadily, Nana gets to her feet and walks to the window. 'The Archie Corella I knew died after an accident; horse kicked him in the head. He was ... um, he would have been twelve, thirteen, years old. Was only one mob a Corellas in this town. Don't make ...' She stops abruptly, and turns to face Doris. 'How old this fellah?'

Doris shrugs. 'Oh, I reckon he'd be fifty-odd. Terrible scar down the side of his face. A bit of a loner, I think.'

Nana grabs hold of the side wall, her hands trembling violently. 'Doris, let sleeping dogs sleep. I tell you this because there's something in this town that can hurt a lot of people — you, Murilla, everyone.'

Suddenly she feels the room is suffocating her. She walks over and touches Nana gently on the shoulder. 'Something, like what?'

'You'd think old age would give ya peace, let bad memories fade and the good ones get brighter. I'm an old woman now and I made me peace with this town. Doris, you mustn't hurt anyone by asking stupid, useless questions! Please, for the love of your mother, leave well enough alone.'

Doris steps back, flushed with guilt. 'Nan? I didn't mean to ...'

Nana searches her eyes. 'Promise me you'll drop it?'

'But … I won't hurt anyone …'

'Promise me, on your dear mother's head,' Nana whispers gravely.

'Please, Nan.'

Nana, her voice low and laced with threat, replies, 'If you keep this up, you can get out of here Doris Christines and don't ever come back!'

Doris steps back. Nana means it. Every word. She should have never bothered her. But her earlier suspicions are aroused. Someone is hiding something about the town. 'Sorry … Nana … sorry … I just want to know is all. Why do I always feel lost, tell me that?'

Nana, as though deaf, doesn't respond. Instead, she takes Doris by the elbow and steers her out the door. Doris decides to let it go today.

\* \* \*

Next day, feeling heavy hearted, Doris returns to Nana's. She finds her in the kitchen.

'Nana,' she begins as she moves into the room.

Nana turns and in a cajoling tone says, 'Doris, don't be worrying your pretty head about anything. Now look, us women'll take a cool drink out onto the verandah, eh?' Nana plonks herself into a chair. 'Here, pour me a drink, please.' She hands Doris the glass.

'Anyhow, Doris, how's the kids?'

'Good. But they ain't so little anymore.'

'An old woman doesn't get about much and sort of forgets that kids grow.' Nana laughs, smoothing down the hem of her dress.

Doris lets the conversation flow. 'Yep, Tulleh starts high school next year.'

Nana looks at her over the rim of the glass. 'You don't work for the old woman Drysdale anymore?'

'I left there a long time ago. Murilla's still there, though. Don't ask me how she puts up with Caroline. That woman would drive any sane person mad! Oh, but I suppose she was all right to me. It was the husband and that son of hers that used to give me the creeps. Oowwhh, bloody two of a kind, them.'

Nana sits forward. 'Course she were a Hughes before she met Reggy Drysdale. Her mother's name was ... oh, my mind gets messed up at times ... yes, it was Lucinda. Good people they were, Lucinda and Barry. Now *there* was a woman who would stop ya in the street and actually *talk* to ya. Weren't anything fancy about the Hughes. But things changed when their only girl married a Drysdale. In the end I'll always believe that's what killed em.'

'Because Caroline married Reg?'

Nana pauses in concentration. 'That's it. But it goes back to the time when ...' She stops as a ratty cough shakes her feeble frame. 'Now where was I? Oh yeah, that goes back to when she was first married and lost the baby girl. Um, she couldn't carry the baby, you see. Her body couldn't cope with the stress of carrying such a large child. Were after she gave birth to Donald, that was his name weren't it?'

'Donald, yep, that was him. You know, now I could be wrong on this, but I'll always reckon they hated each other's guts, his mother and him. I went there one day to cook a few meals for a party they were having. First thing I thought was that Reginald was having a go at Donald. I walked into the hallway and there he was, all red-faced, with his hands around Caroline's neck! Donald was choking her! It was Murilla who fought him off.

'The only reason, I reckon, Murilla helped Caroline was because later on Caroline might have sacked her. And at that time Murilla was having all sorts of problems.'

'Yeah, that Donald was an odd fellah all right,' Nana answers, shading one eye and peering across the road. 'Doris, who's that walking down the riverside there?' She points in the direction.

She gets to her feet for a better view and looks across. 'That's Sofie Salte.'

'Sofie Dove, eh. Now there's a girl who loves water. Course she would, being who she is.'

Doris sits back in the chair and stretches her legs. 'What d'ya mean?'

'Her father was the best swimmer in the district. That man could walk on water, I swear! This might sound crazy to you, but I think Jimmy Salte had some sorta special power. I saw him once, and never'll see that sight again in me life. One of old man Cleaver's heifers got caught in the river, were his prize pet, Daisy. Oh yeah, plenty of tears that day. Anyway, Jimmy was working on the fence-line that day, and Mertyl had asked me to drop a bit of tucker off for him, for his lunch. When I got down there old man Cleaver was sobbin his guts out, and tryin to get down the bank. Jimmy saw him and said: 'Will you look at that, Vida. People just don't have any respect for the river. It'll kill him it will.'

'In flood? The river was in flood?' Doris interrupts.

'No, not at that time. But, the cow made me nervous, thrashing about and all the while mooing like it were crying for Cleaver. Yeah, *crying* for him. Jimmy looked at Cleaver then looked at the drowning cow. He told me he was going in. I pleaded with him, started bawling, as a matter of fact. I knew the beast could drag him down — kill him, while he was trying to save it.'

'It was in the middle of the river!'

'Aye, it were. The most dangerous place for anything or anyone to be. Well, Jimmy went in and swam across. Meantime Cleaver was shouting and the heifer, knowing his voice, started to panic, yeah *panic.* Jimmy reached the cow and tried to pull it across the water. See, it had a bell collar on, so he grabbed the collar and tried to pull it forward. Daisy fought him with everything she had. Kicked like crazy and refused to move. It was an hour later when the thing happened.'

'The thing?' She bends forward.

Nana nods. 'Aye. See, all this fighting with Daisy sort of knocked the wind out of Jimmy. He turned around. I reckon he was trying to judge the distance of the riverbank and how far he could get with her. It was then she swung back around and collected him full force in the head. Cows have strong, hard heads. Cleaver saw it and yelled across at me to go in and pull Jimmy out.'

'You'd of been terrified, Nan.'

'I've never been so scared in my life. I was watching Jimmy drown right before me own eyes. The thing is, I can't swim. Then he went under. I screamed for a good, well ... seemed like hours. He was dead. I turned on Cleaver, yeah, smacked him right in the mouth, swore at that old bastard and nearly pushed him into the drink!'

Doris takes a quick breath. 'But ... No, oh no! Don't say it, Nan!'

'Minutes later, I turned and looked at the river. Standing on the bank holding the cow by the collar was Jimmy. No blood, no nothing. It was as though time stood still, as though *nothing happened*! There wasn't a mark on him!

Much later, when I thought about it, I knew how impossible it was. Jimmy Salte died that day. I knew then that the Saltes weren't normal people.'

Doris shatters the air with a nervous laugh. 'Nan, dead people don't come back!'

'No, not like that. There's things in this world you or I'll never understand. Aye, an old woman likes to think that she has an answer for everything.

'Why, I remember when I was a little girl me mother took me to this man, a special man. Blind as a bat, black as midnight skin and hair the colour of oranges. Anyhow, I were a real sick little kiddie, dunno what it were, but mum took me to him. She had me wrapped in the bark of a tree. Some magic happened that day. Beautiful man, he made me well again.'

'Laying on hands?'

Nana stands, her knees creak and a tired look crosses her face. 'Can't rightly say. But that's the type of powers he had. I reckon that were more or less the same thing Jimmy Salte had. Whatever it is, I tell you this: those Salte girls have got it in spades. And another thing, Doris, you keep your kids away from that river. It's a dangerous place.' Nana halts at the doorway. 'Remember everything I told you. One day you might need it.' She goes through the door.

Doris's thoughts churn. *Need it for what? And why?* She walks down the steps and is about to unlatch the front gate when she hears a noise.

She looks across to the other side of the street.

White hair flying out behind her, dark blue frock tucked into bloomers and a fish in one hand, Sofie runs.

She pelts towards the slope, down to the river.

Doris turns and makes her way home.

\* \* \*

Doris looks across her kitchen table at Murilla with a half-smile. 'I wasn't digging for dirt. Murilla, you can be such a pain at times.'

Murilla scowls. 'Why bother with it all. We all know where we came from. Don't need any family history to tell us *that*.'

'Someone's hiding something in this town and I want to know about it. Nana started by telling me, then she had a sudden change of heart. Said I might find something I don't like. Now what do ya think she meant by that?'

Murilla shakes a thick finger at Doris. 'Nana Vida could mean anything and I reckon you'd do well to take notice of her. Anyway, there's nothing here to find except how our mob turned up, lived down near the dump, had kids, lived their lives, and that's that. As far as I can see, Nana's right, let the past stay where it is, Doris.'

She keeps a close eye on Murilla. It seems Murilla doesn't want to talk either. 'Did you know Caroline's parents apparently died from a broken heart.'

'Caroline Drysdale?' Murilla queries.

'Only one Caroline in Mundra. Anyway, Murilla, what happened with them? The men, I mean. They hated her, didn't they?' Doris watches as Murilla purses her thick lips into a mean tight line.

'They were both bastards! And it was the best thing to happen the day he went under!' Murilla spits angrily.

'Caroline hated him too, didn't she?' She can recall many strange things that happened while she was working for the Drysdales and, for the most part, Murilla seemed to be always involved.

Murilla shrugs. 'Suppose she did, I dunno.'

'Remember that day he almost strangled her? Such a big man he were.'

'Big *demon* is what he were,' Murilla hisses.

Doris twines her hands together. She wonders if she should tell Murilla what she witnessed. Nervously, she begins, 'Murilla, something happened the day he drowned. Always thought it was strange ...' She stops mid-thought. 'Yeah, strange.'

Murilla's eyes narrow as though waiting for her to say the wrong thing. 'Like what, Doris?'

'Maybe it's nothing. I dunno ... just that it bothers me, is all.'

'Go on,' Murilla prompts.

'See, the day Donald drowned, I was in the Drysdale kitchen that morning, making up sandwiches and stuff.

'As you know, from the kitchen window ya can look down across the paddock and see the riverbank. It would have been probably a good hour beforehand when I saw Caroline walking across the paddock so fast she were near to sprinting. It was later, after Stacey Cleaver found him, that I came across Caroline in the hallway, wet from head to toe ...'

In a strained voice Murilla utters, 'No. Oh no.'

'Yes. I mean, he was her son and, well, she must have loved him. Sure he was a pain and everything, but she wouldn't do that, would she? If anyone in this town knows her, it's you.'

Murilla explodes. 'God, woman ...' Then she stops. Something crosses her face, doubt or fear.

Doris wonders if she should have said anything. She smiles with uncertainty. 'As I said, that's what I saw, Murilla.'

'Well, Doris, I saw Archie Corella there on the bank

that day. I had just finished hanging the washing on the line and happened to look across the yard and lo, Archie comes along the side bank! Wet, soaking bloody wet!'

Doris feels the back of her neck prickle. 'Murilla, maybe they done something to him.' None of it ever sounded right to her.

Murilla grabs hold of Doris's wrists. '*Doris, don't you dare say any of this to anyone!*'

Doris pulls back in pain. 'Let go! Christ Almighty! All I'm saying is that's what I saw.' She looks at Murilla with fear.

Murilla sits back in the chair and says, 'Talk can run on mighty fast legs. You'll do well to remember that, Doris. Yeah, we all know Caroline can be bloody nasty, but there's no need for any person in this town to bring her down *again*!' What's done can't be undone. Ya might hate her, as I'm sure a lot of people do, but Donald Drysdale just drowned, nothing more.' Murilla sits back in the chair, arms folded across her chest.

Doris tightens her jaw. 'No need to get like that with me, Murilla Salte!'

Murilla's face relaxes into a weary expression. 'Oh look, sorry, Doris. Just that lately I been worried about Sofie, is all. Took her over to Caroline's place, what does she do? Smashes the TV. Picks up a poker and hurls it into the screen! *Because the woman on screen is gonna have an abortion!* Doris, it gets me down to no end.' Murilla sighs and her hard eyes soften.

Doris reaches across and takes hold of her hands. 'She'll be okay, just that she's probably missing her mother. She wouldn't know what has happened to that world of hers. You've had a bad time, Murilla, and no one can blame you if you get a bit off colour every now and then.'

Murilla frowns. 'She's having nightmares. Last night I woke to her screaming bout the fish, Red Rose ladies n Corella. Maybe I should keep her away from him, huh.' She twists her hands together.

Doris shakes her head. 'No, that won't work. He's the only one friend she's got. What, you don't think he's like *that*, do ya?'

Murilla's face goes expressionless. 'No, I reckon he's pretty straight. I've asked her, she says he's not like that. Thing is, Sofie gets her stories mixed up. Sometimes I have to wonder at that mind of hers. Maybe I should take her to the doctor?'

Feeling sympathetic, Doris tries to reassure her. 'She'll get over it. Even I have nightmares. The Red Rose ladies! And what would set that off?'

'Caroline and her talk.'

'That figures. Listen, if ya want me to come over and keep an eye on her while you're at work, just let me know.'

Murilla gets to her feet. 'One last thing, Doris. If ya wanna do a family history, or town history, or whatever, why not just concentrate on ya own mob n their past.'

'Don't believe I'll worry about it anymore. Seems everyone's against it to start with.'

'Come on, don't be like that.' Murilla smiles.

'Like a secret society, this town. No one will say anything.'

Murilla pushes the chair under the table. 'That's the way things have always been. Ya don't question stuff that belongs to anyone else. Me own mother taught me that. Go digging ditches, ya bound to fall in. Right then, I'm off.'

Doris goes to the front door, opens it and watches as Murilla goes out through the gate.

She watches as Murilla ambles down to the end of the street. The sunlight flickers out through the tops of trees and casts long ragged shadows across her wide shoulders. For a minute she stops, looks up at the sky, and then continues.

Before she shuts the door, she casts a glance to the far corner of the street. Sitting on the verandah, head turned towards the disappearing figure of Murilla, sits Archie Corella, a thermos and garden spade beside him. As though knowing she's watching, he turns and gives a small wave. Doris waves back then pulls the door shut.

*Remember, Doris, ditches are deep.*

## six

# the dead birds

As Archie watches the disappearing figure of Murilla, the old blood courses through his veins — fear known and unknown.

At times, he really feels that he's a no one. For days on end he'll keep the front door shut and sit inside the dark, cool house like a cockroach, too afraid to face the light. And all the time he'll rack his mind for anything that'll tell him who and what he *really* is. He thinks that's part of getting old — memory rushing away like water soaking into the earth. Memory, that sometimes refuses to tell him anything. But, eventually, he does learn something: he has no past. History is the backbone of all life, that much he knows, and if ya don't have history, ya don't have life.

Reaching down, Archie lifts the mug off the floor and pours a cup of tea from the thermos. He sits back in the rocker and looks up at the darkening sky. A pair of magpies swoop down and land in a paperbark tree on the footpath.

Up at the end of the road a deafening bang echoes down the street: a car backfiring. At once, something tells him that he's seen this before, *as though it's happening again*, and he knows that can't be right.

How many towns has he been to and thought exactly the same thing?

At times, he really thinks he's going mad, especially when the images come to him like a flickering film, fuzzy and distorted at the edges. Then there are the smells, weak as the scent of watery perfume.

But it's the voices that drive him to despair, echoing and pleading, mocking sometimes. For some reason he always feels guilty, like he should *do something*. When he tries to think back to when this started, he gets lost. He can remember things that happened a minute ago, even a year ago, but any further than that he runs into trouble. Although, there's something about this place that kindles his memory. Maybe it's tied up with Sofie, Caroline or Donald. He just cannot remember.

\* \* \*

Archie never did like Donald, from day one he hated the man.

It wasn't anything he said that made him uneasy; no, it was another thing altogether. Like an awareness based on instinct.

Automatically, his thoughts fly to Sofie. *It was her I seen on the riverbank when Donald died. Sofie who drowned him!* Yet Archie's always had a flicker of doubt about that, mainly because Drysdale was such a huge man. If he'd seen big, strong Murilla there, he'd believe she was capable of such a thing. Murilla would have been able to do it easily, and she had put Drysdale well and truly in his place one time. Archie knows her and Drysdale had a thing going on between them, hated each other more than the Devil hates a Christian. Although, he could swear that Donald was actually scared of her, tried to keep out of her way. He'll never forget the time with the birds and the Red Rose woman. That would have been three to four days before Drysdale went down in the drink. Now that was *something*.

\* \* \*

That day Archie was out in the yard, weeding and tidying a flowerbed, when a dark blue sedan pulled up at the gate. Archie unlatched it and the car came through, stopping at the house. Out stepped a tall, horsey-faced woman. She had salt-and-pepper hair scraped back into a tight, headachy knot and lips so thin and miserly they seemed non-existent. In her stick-thin arms she held a cardboard box. She strode to the door, heels crunching on the gravel.

She pulled up before him. 'Caroline in?' she asked and turned up her nose as she saw his dirt-caked trousers and the patty of horseshit he held.

'Can't rightly say. Suppose she is. I never saw her leave.' Archie watched the way her eyes roamed the yard.

She raised a finely arched eyebrow. 'Fine mess here, isn't there?'

Archie threw the patty onto the ground. 'Needs a bit of a cleaning.'

'Well, I suppose you'll be eating this ... this here for morning tea.' Her laughter came out cold and scornful.

Archie looked at the box. 'What?'

'Carrot cake. She makes them every year, poor Caroline. She can't cook. Though I must give her huge points for trying. We Red Rose ladies have strict principles. Of course, you wouldn't know ...' She paused, moving the box to her other arm.

Archie frowned. 'Red Rose ladies?'

She gave a delicate little cough, then replied, 'Our committee.'

Archie scratched his head, then it dawned on him. 'Orh, like women's business.'

'Oh, that's exactly right! Must say, you're a very perceptive man …' She relaxed her eyebrows.

Archie offered her a warm smile. 'Archie Corella, missus.'

'Well, Mister Corella, I better go in and deliver her the usual news. I do it every darn year!' She smiled, her teeth glinting as the sun caught the front of a gold cap.

Archie watched as she moved with renewed intention in her step. She didn't knock on the door, but banged, loud and impatient, as though she just couldn't wait. It was Murilla who answered. For the first few seconds they stood there scowling at each other. Then Archie was out of earshot but he could see Murilla's face darken and her mouth moving at breakneck speed.

The Red Rose woman took an unsteady backward step, her hands open wide. 'Please listen', they seemed to say. But the more she spoke, the more Murilla advanced towards her. They came within hearing distance.

'Murilla, I'm not the only one to make these decisions,' the Red Rose woman said in an exasperated voice.

Murilla's voice took on a hard, hysterical edge. 'Why? Why? Is it because of me! Is it because of Polly Goodman!'

'Oh come now, Murilla, I have no idea what you're on about. If you and Polly had words, then that's your business, and certainly doesn't affect our decision.' She shrugged her shoulders.

'Is it too much for you to let her in?'

'Everyone goes through the same process. Caroline

Drysdale is no exception. Why, even I had to go through it all. Just that Caroline doesn't have the right qualities to be one of us.'

Murilla crossed her arms. 'Qualities? Yeah, and what would they be, *Tamara Dalmaine*!'

'Community involvement and a good honest attitude towards other members of our committee. Honestly, Murilla, I can't see why *you* would be so upset about all this. Why doesn't she just give up?'

'Maybe *I'll* put in to join. Now, I wonder what excuses you'd give me: that my house needs bulldozing, that my sister's a retard! As a matter of fact, I think I will join up.'

Archie watched with amusement as Murilla smiled venomously at the woman.

The Red Rose woman frowned. 'Now, now ... It has nothing to do with your sister or *that house*.'

'Yeah, what then? Because the Red Rose ladies are a *whites* and *bitches* only committee!'

'How dare you? The audacity! We aren't *racist*.' The woman had a look of sham horror on her heavily made-up face.

Murilla aped, 'We aren't racist,' then rolled her eyes heavenward.

Archie almost cracked up as he watched them. That Murilla sure was something.

'Tell her that we've decided to let Patricia Purnell in on this year's round.' The woman handed Murilla the box. It only took a few seconds for Murilla's face to darken to blue-grey.

'You *bastards* are all the same! That's right, ya all think ya got dibs on everything and everyone. Who do you think you are? You women make me sick. Oh yeah, keep Mundra the way you want it!' Murilla shouted, her hands curled into fists.

The woman looked at Murilla as though she had something hanging out her nose. Archie always believed that's what started it all off, that look.

Then, in a blink of the eye, Murilla had the woman by the shoulders. Instantly Archie knew what Murilla was gonna do. Throwing the shovel to one side, he rushed at them. Oh yeah, he didn't wanna test Murilla, but he had to make an effort. Secretly he would have loved to see the smart-arse Red Rose woman get her comeuppance.

'Murilla, ladies, come on now. Break it up.' Archie had to suppress a wild laugh.

The Red Rose woman shot Archie a desperate look. 'Oh, please get this creature off me!'

What could he do? He had no choice: he laughed and laughed, his eyes running as he tried to take reasonable control of himself. The women looked at Archie like he was a madman — at that minute he *was*, mad with laughter. Finally, Archie offered: 'Please let her go, Murilla.'

Murilla swung on him. 'Please piss off, Archie.'

Not wanting to get into an argument with her, Archie searched the yard for someone to help him. At that moment Drysdale walked out of the shed, a fishing rod in his hand.

Archie yelled, 'Mister Drysdale!' Then pointed at the women.

Drysdale galloped across the yard, his red face going white, and pointing a rigid finger at her, he cried, 'Murilla Salte! Murilla, you let Missus Dalmaine go!' Murilla released the woman, then turned and faced Drysdale.

'What do you think you're *doing*?' Drysdale demanded indignantly.

'Nothing,' she spat. 'That's right, nothing,' lips pulled to one side of her face.

'Who gives you *the right* to assault people on this property?' The blood vessels in Drysdale's thick neck stuck out as he shouted at her.

She sneered. 'Get outta my way, Drysdale!'

Drysdale advanced towards her. 'You're sacked! That's right, finished up here! Get off *my* property!' His large arms swung backwards and forwards in a dangerous motion.

At that terrible moment Archie could see that Drysdale was racked with violent anger. He truly thought Drysdale would have scared her. And if he could have placed a bet, it'd have been that Drysdale would squash Murilla like a bug, if not literally, then by fear alone.

So it was to Archie's total disbelief that Murilla smirked: 'Ya scare me, Drysdale, ya really do.' Then she laughed right in his face.

Drysdale reared back as though she'd hit him in the gut, his face colourless and his lips tinged a steel-blue. 'You bitch! I'll get you if it's the last thing I do!' Then, incredibly, he loped off in a huff down towards the riverbank.

Archie looked over at the Red Rose woman. She had made her way back to the car and was shaking her head as she watched Drysdale and Murilla.

Murilla spun on Archie and waved her large arms. 'What are ya lookin at, Corella?'

'Nothing, nothing,' Archie answered, then turned and made his way back to the flowerbed.

\* \* \*

It was later on that night another terrible thing happened. Archie was in his room listening to the radio when he heard strange noises. Originally, he thought that it was radio crackle and static. But when he got up from the bunk and made his way over to the window he saw what was making the noise.

The birds were going crazy, squawking and beating their tiny wings against the cages. The noise was panicky and so urgent that Archie decided to go out into the night and see what was bothering them. Grabbing hold of the night torch, Archie flicked it on and shined it into the cages. There was nothing there. No birds. Once again he wondered if his mind was playing games, if in fact he had dreamed it all up.

Weren't nothing new. He'd seen, or thought he'd seen, a white dress hanging in his closet once — five minutes later it was gone. That was the kinda tricks his mind played. He began to make his way back to his room.

There! Something moved and then a noise; no, a twitter. Archie swung around and pointed the torch at the ground. At once, he thought the thing in the dirt was a fluffy, coloured doormat. Until it writhed like a choppy sea of coloured fluff.

'My heart's desire, my heart's desire,' squawked the cockatoo, its wings beating a futile rhythm against the dirt.

The birds! They were all on the ground dying. Some fluttered weakly, others were already rigid with death. Unable to move, Archie heard, rather than saw, a movement to the left of where he stood.

Archie listened to the way the ground responded to the heavy tread and knew it was the footfalls of a large person. The dry twigs snapped smartly underneath the weight of the bulky steps. There were only two people who walked like that: Murilla and Drysdale.

Archie croaked, 'Anyone there?' He moved his wrist slightly so the torch light beamed slowly across the ground. 'Anyone there?' He tried again then swung around and faced the direction where the noise had come from. The torch beam played over the undergrowth. Ragged shadows fell from the trees and the glowing, yellow-mustard eyes of a feral cat blinked back at him. No one was there, he expected that. Archie whirled back around and faced the cage, then crouched to his knees to have a better look.

How did they die? He played the torchlight across to the seed feeder.

No, he couldn't see in that far. Archie got up and opened the wire latch and walked in, careful not to step on the birds.

There. He saw something. He picked the feeder up and scrutinised the seed. Tiny white clots of powder were mixed in with the grain.

Poison.

Someone had poisoned Caroline's beloved birds. He'd have to go on up and break the news to her. Wasn't something he wanted to do but there was no point in leaving it till tomorrow. She might look out of the window in the morning and see them there on the ground.

Responsibility weighed heavily on him. There'd be hell to pay.

Archie wandered across to the door, knocked and waited for someone to answer. Of all the people he hoped wouldn't answer, Drysdale stood towering over him.

'Yes,' Drysdale growled, pulling the door slightly so that he couldn't see in.

Archie touched the side of his face nervously. 'I need to see your mother.'

Drysdale looked at him with a flicker of suspicion. 'Why, man?'

'About the fertiliser.' That was the first thing to come to his mind.

Drysdale peered down at him, his strange eyes oddly ablaze. 'Fertiliser? Can't this wait until morning?'

'Nope, it can't. Caro ... Missus likes her garden kept and I need that fertiliser first thing tomorrow.' Archie was losing it.

Caroline Drysdale's voice broke through the air. 'Donald, who is it?'

Archie yelled past Drysdale's shoulder. 'Missus, Missus, I need to see you.'

She hobbled to the door and peered out at him. 'Archie, what's going on?' she frowned.

'Missus, all the ... the ... birds are all dee ... ddeeaa ... dead,' Archie stuttered.

She looked at Archie incredulously, one side of her face twitching. 'The birds are all dead! My birds? Corella, what are you on about?'

Archie could feel his chest tighten. 'Sssoommmee ... one ... poison.'

She stumbled backwards, one hand clutching her heart. 'Someone poisoned all my birds? Is that what you're saying?'

Archie nodded, then pointed in the direction of the cages. She blanched. Her eyes bulged from her head and her breathing came out in fractured bursts. She looked at her son, then as if in slow motion, she buckled.

Her knees cracked as she hit the floor and sprawled across the floorboards, arms flung out wide, resembling the form of the crucified Jesus Christ. Her dress had ridden up around her waist, exposing a pair of white bloomers. Archie felt a deep sense of mortification. Turning towards Drysdale, Archie saw that he was no longer there. Had left the room. Had left his mother on the floor.

Archie reached out to her hand. 'Missus Drysdale. Missus.'

Her eyes flicked open, a vague film of confusion screening them. 'Whaaa ...?'

'Ya had a faint, Missus. Here take me hand and I'll help lift you up.'

He lifted her by the elbow and steered her to a chair.

'Archie, what?'

'Fainted, ya fainted was all.' Sweat dotted his forehead.

She eased into the seat. 'The birds ... when?'

'About ten, twenty minutes ago.' Archie scratched his chin. At that moment, as he looked at the feeble old woman before him, he knew he was catching another side to her that he'd probably never see again.

She tilted her greying head to one side, as if to hide the tears that welled in her eyes. Her face was a plane of stark emotion. In her despair she looked ancient.

Once again his feelings got the better of him; he really felt for her. He wanted to say something comforting, wanted to tell her that they would have died fast and probably without pain. But he couldn't.

She brought her head up and searched his face with such concentration that he started to feel uncomfortable. He shuffled his bare feet on the floor and looked the other way. Finally, she whispered, 'Archie, can you do something for me?'

'Yeah, missus.' He noticed the way her head rocked from side to side, searching the room.

'Go over to Purcell Street and bring Murilla back, please.'

He didn't hesitate. 'Yes, right away.' So it wasn't Murilla out there. Drysdale was the one that poisoned his mother's birds.

As Archie made his way towards the door, he stopped and swung around to face her hunched form in the corner chair. 'You be right?'

'Thank you, Archie, yes. Archie, thank you for this.' She smiled. Seeing her like that made him wonder at the demons she faced. Something was rotten in the house of Drysdale, and the thought made his scalp creep.

Archie hurried out into the night and bolted over to Purcell Street.

When he got there he thumped on the front door. 'Murilla! Murilla, ya gotta come now!' Archie yelled, not caring how loud his voice sounded in the sleepy night.

Murilla came to the door, flicked the front light on and peered at him. 'Corella, what is it?'

'She sent me ...' Archie began his heart thudding.

'No, oh bloody no! What'd he do! Corella, what did he *do*?'

'The birds! Poisoned. All dead.' Archie garbled, panic driving into him as he watched her face shade into one of her blue-grey looks.

'Is she right? Where is he?' she yelled.

'At ... back there. Was right when I left her.'

'Right, let's go.' She pushed past him and galloped down the street, the dressing gown flapping round her ankles. Archie panted after her.

When they reached the padlocked gate, she didn't even

bother to unlatch it. She lifted her dressing gown and hurled herself over the fence.

As he belted after her, he noticed all the house lights were on. Someone was still there. He hoped that Drysdale was in bed, or anywhere else for that matter.

Archie trailed her into the hallway.

The old woman stumbled to her feet and hobbled forward into Murilla's arms. Tears fell freely from her anguished face as she sobbed loudly, her skinny arms clutching desperately at Murilla. Then Murilla said one word: 'Donald.'

The old woman garbled, 'Upstairs.'

Indecision froze Archie to the spot. Should he follow her? The old woman looked across at him, the tears now dried on her face.

'Thank you, Archie,' she whispered hoarsely. 'Please don't think this happens all the time.' She said it as though this were the worst thing in the world.

Archie was about to answer when he heard a racket coming from down the hallway. It was Murilla's loud voice that reached his ears. Then something hit the floor in a dull thump. Forgetting himself he raced down the hall. Someone had been hurt, he just knew it. He pulled up at the doorway and looked in.

Backed up against the wall, eyes popping from her head and blood seeping from her nose, was Murilla. Drysdale had his huge hands twisted around her throat and his knees jammed between her legs. It would have been only for a second that Drysdale turned towards the doorway and glared at him. Turned his back.

It was then Murilla screamed. Well, it was more of a deep, guttural howl that shattered the air like the shriek of a madwoman.

Terror gripped Archie.

Murilla threw one arm into the air, like to reach something above.

Archie swallowed the thick lump in his throat.

She moved an inch.

Drysdale backed towards the far wall.

She passed her hand across her nose and brought her hand up to her face and looked at it.

Archie looked back at Drysdale. The man was inching backwards towards the far corner of the room.

Then Murilla lunged at him.

Drysdale never stood a chance, not with the way she moved. Later, Archie would swear that no one or nothing could move that fast. It was like a blur, a pink streak that cut across the room. She clutched Drysdale around his neck.

'Bastard! Don't you think I don't know what ya dirty little secret is!' she shrieked, gripping his throat harder.

Drysdale struggled to break away. 'Get off! Ya black bitch!'

After a couple of quiet, eerie seconds, she loosened her grip and pushed him so violently that he fell.

Drysdale ran a hand across his throat. 'You ... you ... One of you will ...' He left the threat unfinished and pulled his torn shirt across his milky-white chest as he got to his feet.

Murilla spun around and glared across at Archie. 'Corella! What are ya doing in here?'

He didn't answer, well couldn't really.

Feeling another presence, Archie turned and saw the old woman, her eyes glimmering dangerously as she looked into the room.

'Get up, Donald!' she said in a level tone as she looked at her son.

Drysdale yelled shrilly, 'Piss off you!'

Murilla snarled, 'Remember Donald, I *know things*!' Her red-rimmed eyes drilled into Drysdale's.

As though it were just another day on the home front, Drysdale strode from the room. His face was twisted into a hate-filled grimace. Every step he took he muttered, 'I'll get the both of you.'

The old lady turned to him. Not an element of her face suggested that anything had happened, and if there was something unpleasant, well, she'd just keep calm and ignore it.

'It's all right, you can go back to your room now. Oh, and Archie, can you go across to Betty Frost tomorrow and ask about a couple of budgerigars?' She asked this in a tight, quivery voice.

'Yeah, right you are. Tomorrow, first thing on the list.' Archie watched as the old woman gathered herself together and was led by Murilla down the corridor.

Archie went back to his room.

A terrible despair seized him. The Drysdale house was riddled with secrets, a place full of shying. A place he couldn't be. Archie didn't have the heart to stay. He wasn't one of them, nor would he ever be. These people lived and breathed in a chapel of grief and hurt.

There was no sleep for him that night or any night he stayed there. He did think, though, that he'd seen the worst of it. He guessed it would all blow over and everything would be back to normal pretty soon.

How wrong he was.

It would be a week later, after he stumbled into Drysdale's work shed and found the girls' dresses, that he resigned. First time he ever walked off a job.

\* \* \*

As he looks out into the darkness, somewhere in the distance he hears the voices.
*Heeeellppp mmmmmeeeee*
*Heeeellppp mmmmmeeeee*
*Help me heeeeellllppppp mmmmeeeee*
*Please help me*

'Leave me alone. I'm an old man, go away,' Archie whispers to the still air.

His head aches as the pain creeps to the top of his skull. He ignores it as best he can. But now he knows the time has come. Some part of him welcomes release, yet he wonders how he'll get away from her anger.

He won't. He'll have to face Murilla, tell her what Drysdale did to Sofie. Whatever happens next will be out of his control.

The dead man with the strange eyes has kept his promise to Murilla: he does get her back in the end.

Leaves her with a lifetime of sorrow.

# seven

# sinner's day

'You were on the riverbank that day, weren't you?' Murilla probes Caroline.

Caroline's voice is abrupt. 'Murilla, what day? Anyway, what are you on about?'

Murilla focuses on her. 'You know very well what day. The day he drowned.'

'Donald. The day Donald drowned?'

'Yeah, that's right.' Murilla lifts the tea tray and places it on the side table.

Caroline looks towards the window, her lips tightening. 'No ...'

Murilla stirs. 'Caroline, don't lie, now tell me what happened.'

'Don't you start up today. I'm tired and can't put up with your sulky moods, Murilla.'

Agitated, Murilla puts her hands on her hips. 'There's no point in trying to hide it. You were there.'

Caroline stares down at the knitting needles with odd concentration. 'Not that day I wasn't.'

'Oh yes, you were. So was Archie Corella.' Murilla grins: *There, you can't fool me.*

Caroline blanches and the cup and saucer rattle faintly in her quaking hands. 'What?'

'Archie was there. I seen him, didn't I?' Murilla pulls a chair across and sits in front of her.

'He was?' Caroline studies the tray.

'Caroline, you were seen. Someone saw you down there. If ya got something to tell me you better do it soon. People talk ya know.'

'Why must people bother an old woman? Why can't they just let these things alone?' Caroline utters.

'They can't leave it alone if they think ya had something to do with that ... thing.'

'They can go to hell! That's right, the whole damned lot of them! I don't give a ... I don't care about any of them. They've been on my case for years! What have I ever done to deserve this kind of treatment?' Caroline shouts, her eyes watery.

'Listen, just shut up and listen for God's sake! If anyone saw you do anything, there could be trouble. I gotta know what ya were doing down there.' Murilla watches Caroline warily. *She knows something*.

'I was down there, that's true, but I didn't see anything. I came straight back here,' Caroline shrugs.

'That's a lie, a lie ya hear me! I'm tryin to help ya here but you just won't budge, will ya?'

'I was there for maybe half an hour. I went down to see if Donald was going to open the shop. When I got there I couldn't see him anywhere. I saw Stacey Cleaver on the other side of the bank. She waved, then walked back up the embankment, went back to her place, I suppose. Anyway, that was that. I came straight back here.' Caroline's eyes dart around the room.

Murilla leans back in the chair. *I'm not going to let you off so easy on this one.* 'How come ya were soaking wet?'

'Wet! I wasn't wet!' Caroline responds loudly, slapping the side of the recliner with her hand.

'They'll lock you up, is what'll happen. Take ya away to prison. How can I do anything when ya won't tell me the whole truth?' Murilla grits her teeth. *Sometimes you can be so bloody stubborn.*

Caroline refuses to meet Murilla's eyes. 'I didn't do it! No, Murilla, no.'

'Someone did it. That much I know n it weren't me. We all hated him as much as you did. Yeah, at times I felt like doing something bad, could have strangled him even, but common sense kept me head. These people aren't gonna care, they don't know what he did to ya. The thing is, no one knows anything about *them* but us.'

'I'm tired, Murilla, so tired. How could a person go so wrong in life? What happened to Caroline Hughes? I lost her when I came to this place. Lost everything, everyone. Some day soon I'll die, no one will even notice. It'll be as though I never existed. Passed through and lived an unremarkable life, because I was always an unremarkable woman. No, before you say anything, I'm not feeling sorry for myself. I've come to that point now where nothing matters.' Caroline gazes towards the window.

'I'd miss you, and don't talk nonsense.' Murilla gets up and walks across to the table and pours herself a cup of tea.

Caroline erupts into bitter laughter. 'When I first met him I thought everything was fine. Actually thought I was privileged to be the chosen one. Oh, how happy I was when he proposed. Thought I was the best and prettiest girl in Mundra …'

'You were!' Murilla interrupts.

'Oh come now, Salte, I know that's not right.' Caroline shakes her head firmly.

'Yes, Caroline, it's true.' Murilla offers a smile.

Suddenly, Caroline stops. 'I'm tired, Salte. I want to go to bed. I've had enough for today. My body isn't what it used to be.' She stands and the knitting falls to the floor. Murilla takes her arm and leads her down the hallway and into the bedroom.

'Sit there while I turn the covers back.'

Caroline falls into the chair. She begins, 'Salte, can ...'

Murilla turns. 'Yeah?'

'Nothing. Nothing.' Caroline makes her way wearily to the bed.

'Have ya taken ya tablets?'

'No. They're over there by the dresser.' Caroline points.

Murilla picks up the small bottle. 'This is a full bottle.' Her pitch rises. *The Doctor wouldn't have given her a full bottle.*

Caroline barks, 'Just give them to me!'

Murilla swings around. 'Where'd they come from?' *Snaky, bloody snaky at times. She's like that. One minute fine, next cunning and sneaky.*

'I don't know! Go away, leave me alone.' She puts the sheet up to her chin.

'I'll find out, always do. Ya can't pull the wool over my eyes, Caroline Drysdale.' Murilla points at her.

'Where's Sofie?'

'At home. Why, what now?'

'Just asking, is all. Maybe we can bake a cake sometime. Sofie likes my cakes.'

'No. No. No. Get that idea well and truly out of your head.'

'Oh, mind-reader now, are we?' Caroline pouts.

Murilla sits on the side of the bed. 'I know what ya up to and it ain't gonna work. Never did, never will.' Murilla watches her closely.

'I'll bake the cake in the morning. You can take it over for me, if you will. This will be the last time, yes, the last cake for those women to laugh at.'

Murilla looks at Caroline with suspicion. 'That's it? Ya giving up?'

'Well ...' She smiles vaguely.

'I don't believe it, after all this time ya realise ...' Murilla stops. *Is this one of her tricks?*

'I don't care for those cows anymore,' Caroline whispers fiercely. 'They're not worth spitting on.'

Caroline falls back against the pillows. 'So tired. So tired,' she mumbles, shutting her eyes.

Murilla walks over and pulls out a chair from the corner, dragging it across to the window. She turns to see if Caroline is really asleep or playing fox with her.

Caroline's hands clutch the edge of the sheets tightly. Dribble escapes from her mouth and a fine glaze of sweat spreads across her forehead. *She can't even find peace in sleep.* She moans softly, a growl catching in the back of her throat. *I wonder if they've returned, if they're back to torment her again like they did in life. Like they did to the both of us.* A chilly feeling passes over Murilla.

Murilla looks out at the barren yard. Dead leaves scuttle across the dry, cracked ground and birds dip and dart catching insects in their beaks. From the corner of the house a feral cat eases along on its scabby gut, its yellow-red eyes zooming in on a sparrow. It moves along with sneaky concentration, its huge malformed paws taking up ground as it slips in for the kill. Suddenly it strikes.

It grabs the bird in its twisted jaws and lifts the tiny body, crunching and chewing as it ambles off into the bushes.

Murilla wriggles on the chair; her legs are numb. She stands for a second and stretches, then sits down, arms on the window ledge and chin resting in her hands.

The cat comes back out from the bushes and turns its head, as if looking for another victim. Looking into the cat's sick eyes, Murilla's reminded of them. The Drysdale men.

\* \* \*

Reginald Drysdale was a lofty, pencil-thin rake of a man. When he walked he gave the impression he'd smash anything underfoot if it didn't move out of his way. You'd always hear him before you saw him.

His long, triangular face was always a light shade of red, as though anger was constantly brewing. Sitting neatly on top of his narrow, bloodless lips was a thin, perfectly even, grey-black moustache. His pitch-black hair would be oiled and parted to one side of his head, not a single strand out of place. Whenever he moved there'd be a trail of cologne — musky and sickeningly sweet. He lathered it on. His eyes were much the same as Donald's: one olive-green, the other nut brown.

Then there were his clothes — navy blue suits, real leather shoes, crisp white-collared shirts and fancy trousers.

It was on a Thursday that Murilla came across the Sinner's Day. She had just finished folding the laundry, arranging the pegs in the basket and tidying the wash house when she heard someone cry out.

At that time she thought it might have been Doris mucking around in the kitchen, joking with the Cleaver kid, Barry, who dropped the papers off for the Drysdales. Then she remembered Doris didn't work on Thursday, but Murilla had come to finish some extra work.

Murilla, carrying the laundry basket, entered the hallway and halted when she heard another cry. Maybe Donald was in his room doing something strange like he always did. Then she heard it again. Someone was *definitely* crying. A muffled noise sounding like they were in pain. Murilla walked further down the hallway and stopped in front of Caroline's bedroom door. What she heard next drove her back against the wall. The hard, cruel voice fractured the air: 'On your feet, sinner!' Then: Whack! Something was hit and hard.

Murilla couldn't move. A door at the end of the hallway opened and Donald stepped out. 'Murilla, what are you doing?' he asked in an even voice.

Murilla looked at him with big eyes, unable to open her mouth, but pointed at Caroline's bedroom door.

'Yes?'

'Your mother,' Murilla choked out.

'My mother, yes, what about her?' He ran his tongue across his fat lips.

'I ... I ... she ...'

'Anyway, what are you doing here today? No one works here Thursdays.' He paused. 'Well, since you can't answer, you can go on home now. That's it, the day's done. Come back tomorrow.'

Murilla went past him, feeling his eyes follow her until she was out of sight. She went home that day, knowing there was something wrong in that house and with those people.

The next day when she went back the house was eerily still. There was no sound except for Caroline's cockatoo screeching outside, 'My heart's desire. My heart's desire.'

She entered the lounge room but it was empty; usually, Donald or Reginald would be watching the news or something, but today no one was there.

It was when she picked up a newspaper from the chair that she heard a small scratching sound coming from the side wall.

'Anyone there? Doris, is that you?'

Cowering against the wall with a blanket wrapped around her shoulders was Caroline. 'Mhhhnnnaaarrrllll.' She tried to speak, pulling the blanket tighter to her body.

Confused, Murilla stared back at her, unable to say anything.

Caroline lurched drunkenly and Murilla grabbed her before she hit the floor. She lead Caroline to the bedroom, then eased her back onto the bed, trying to pull the blanket away from her stiff fingers. She mewled weakly in protest, shaking her head: no, no. At last the blanket fell to the floor and that was when she saw it. The photo frame had been smashed to pieces. Slivers of glass cut deeply into Caroline's hands as she clutched the frame tightly. Blood dribbled onto the fallen blanket.

The photo was of a blonde-haired baby, dressed in a pale pink gown with snow-white slippers on her tiny feet. Captioned underneath were the words *Josephine Drysdale*.

Caroline pointed at the mahogany dresser in the corner.

'You want me to go over there?' Murilla walked to the dresser. Placed on top was a writing pad and pen. 'This?' She picked up the pen and paper.

Caroline nodded.

Murilla watched as Caroline scribbled. Then she handed Murilla the paper: IT'S MY FAULT. NEW DRESS

SHOULDN'T HAVE BOUGHT IT. I SHOULD HAVE KNOWN BETTER.

'He done this to you because you *bought a new dress!*' Murilla felt her stomach knot.

*What sort of man would do this to a woman because she wanted a new outfit? What sort of lunatic?*

The bed sheet rustled and Caroline reached out to grab Murilla's hand, her lips moving wordlessly.

'I can't know what ya saying. Here, write it down.'

Murilla took back the paper: I CAN'T KEEP YOU ON HERE. GET ANOTHER JOB.

'But ... but ... Because of this?' Murilla's heart lurched.

She nodded.

'I won't say nothing, if that's what ya scared of. I need this work. The council is gonna doze me house down and I got me little sister, Sofie, to look after.' She swallowed the thick lump in her throat.

Caroline scribbled some more: YOU'RE NOT SCARED OF THEM?

'Not really, no.'

VERY UNHAPPY HOUSE THIS ONE.

'Yeah, for you it would be. Caroline, is there anything I can do?'

She shook her head.

'Is it always like this?'

'Some days,' she said in a feathery whisper.

'Ya know ya can get out of this house. I can help you.' Murilla sat on the edge of the bed.

Caroline shrank back against the pillows, her face red with shame and guilt.

'No, no shame. It ain't ya fault, Caroline.'

Yes, she indicated. It is.

Murilla adjusted the sheets over Caroline's thin legs.

'I don't see how a woman buying a frock can be blamed for what he did to ya. Anyway, how long has this been going on for? Yep, ever since ya married him, I reckon.'

A tear rolled down Caroline's cheek.

Murilla felt a sickening sense of dread. 'Look, I don't like leaving ya like this. Ain't right, is it? He might come back at ya.'

No.

'Look, I'm going down and making you some tea and toast, eh.'

She tried to smile — thank you.

Murilla knew that it was not the dress or any of the fifty-odd excuses Caroline gave her, nothing like that at all. It was because Reginald Drysdale was a madman. Sometimes she'd go to the house on her days off, using some feeble excuse to be there. Eventually Reginald found out about her unusual visits.

It was a Tuesday morning that he bailed her up in the wash house.

Her back was to the door when she heard the shuffle of feet.

'Murilla Salte.'

She swung to the door. It was him. Unease gripped her. 'Oh … um yes.' Instantly her legs felt unstable.

'I note that you have been coming over quite a lot recently. Is there any particular reason?' Reginald looked her up and down.

She choked out, 'Yeah, yeah for work.' She hoped he couldn't read the lie on her face.

'Now, dear, I don't really believe that. Maybe you have formed some sort of useless alliance with my sick wife. Perhaps she's been trying to convince you that I've been beating her, hmmm. Murilla, the poor woman does these awful things to herself. Yes, I have to go in and keep the door locked so that she doesn't hurt anyone or smash the house. I should tell you that she is a rather dreadful liar and you mustn't pay any mind to her rambling.' He smiled, his small teeth glinting. *See, I'm a gentleman, a Drysdale gentleman.* His whole body spoke that message loud and clear.

'Huh ...Oh, yeah, well I do me work and mind me own business. Ain't here to be beakin on fellahs.' Murilla offered him something of a convincing smile.

'There will be a fifty-dollar rise in your pay this week. I have noticed how clean and tidy the house is ever since you came here. Fine job, Murilla.' He smiled and looked at her in such a way that she felt the bile rise in her throat.

'Thank you.' She knew it was a bribe — ya get this bonus to keep our little secret in this house.

As he was leaving, he stopped and turned. 'Doris is to stay in the kitchen at all times. I do note she has the annoying habit of wandering out into the lounge. Please inform her not to.' He strode away, a trail of sickeningly sweet cologne lingering behind.

At the time, Murilla thought she was the only one he'd been telling lies to, trying to convince her Caroline was crazy. How stupid she'd been!

She discovered it one Saturday night during a dinner party. That evening she'd offered to help Doris in the kitchen, carrying big bowls of soup and sizzling steaks out to the table. At first, when she walked into the dining room, she didn't recognise the woman sitting at the end of the table. Hair piled up into a loose chignon, face carefully made-up and wearing a high black collar sat Caroline. She was beautiful. As soon as she saw Murilla she seemed to sigh with relief. The table was full of people, some Murilla knew and others she hadn't seen before. Seated right next to Reginald was Polly Goodman, one of the Red Rose ladies.

Polly's high wide face was caked with make-up. Her thin, large-pored nose sniffed the air like a rat nosing a drain pipe and when she laughed it hit a high false note, targeted at Caroline.

'Do you think you're up to it, Caroline?' Polly smiled, her scarlet lips stretched into a smile.

'Of course, Polly. I'm sure I could be an invaluable asset to your committee.' Caroline raised her eyebrows, seeming to mock.

Reginald picked up a fork and fiddled with it, his face deeply creased in an apparent look of concern. 'Caroline, are you certain?'

'Yes I am,' Caroline replied, playing with the collar of her gown.

'You do realise, Caroline, that you'll have to leave the house once in a while to come to the meetings.' The Goodman woman looked at Caroline like she was dead certain Caroline Drysdale wouldn't have the capacity to walk to the front gate.

'I'm up to it, Polly,' Caroline smiled, but it didn't soften her gaze.

Reginald reached over and placed a hand on Caroline's. 'Thank you, Polly. Maybe only one day at a time to start with. She's been sick and we can't allow too much too soon.'

'Oh, I see.' The Goodman woman offered a chilly smile.

'Mother's not what she used to be.' Donald's voice oozed mock sadness.

'Needs a good head doctor,' Reginald responded, tapping the table. 'No need to feel ashamed about that, Caroline. We're all friends here and I'm sure everyone understands what you are going through.'

Murilla threw Caroline a look of sympathy. She knew what they were doing. Caroline flushed and every pore showed beneath her face powder. She picked up a glass of wine, downed it in one gulp, focusing on the tablecloth.

Instead of serving any of the others seated around the table, Murilla went straight to Caroline. 'Soup?' She willed Caroline to read her eyes. *You pay no mind to them.*

'Yes, Murilla,' Caroline replied, a smile edging the corner of her mouth, as though she knew Murilla's thoughts.

'She's a cow,' Murilla whispered.

'Yes, wonderful soup. Tell Doris it looks beautiful.' A laugh sat in Caroline's eyes.

'Over here. Murilla Salte, isn't it?' The Goodman woman motioned to Murilla.

Murilla walked around the table. 'Last time I knew that was my name,' she smirked.

The Goodman woman raised her eyebrows, looked Murilla over, dismissed her, then turned on Caroline. 'So, Caroline, you have a maid now?' Her cold green eyes mocked.

'No, Polly, Murilla's not my maid. She comes over to give me a helping hand in this big house.'

'You need help *to clean*! Huh, some people are incredible!' Polly laughed hard.

Murilla walked straight past Polly and ladled soup into the bowl of the large man beside her. She walked behind the guests, fixing to ladle out the soup. In a second Reginald was out of his chair walking up to Murilla. His bony hip bumped against her, pitching her forward, the soup bowl landing upside down on the table in front of Caroline.

Pumpkin soup covered Caroline from chest to knees. She struggled to get up from the table. A small cry escaped from her lips as she tumbled back, hitting a corner table before falling to her knees. The top of her gown peeked wide open, revealing her breasts.

Donald got slowly to his feet and, with obvious reluctance, lifted his mother from the floor. 'Bloody hopeless, you are,' he whispered, his voice sharpened with disgust.

Murilla shot forward. 'Come on.' She took Caroline's arm and began to lead her from the room when she heard Reginald's voice, 'Poor girl, her mind is playing up.' The room filled with low gasps and horrified murmurs.

Murilla threw Caroline a look in an attempt to see if she too heard. 'Bastard! They're both mean bastards!' she whispered.

'You're right, Murilla,' Caroline answered in a small, choked voice. When they reached the bedroom, Murilla pulled the ruined gown over Caroline's head, ran a warm bath, then eased her into the tub.

Murilla watched Caroline with a sorrowful feeling. She could see Caroline was hurting bad, trying not to let her see the shame, holding back the tears she knew were gonna come.

Finally, Murilla said, 'It's got to stop. He done that by purpose. You know that, don't ya? They're doin somethin to you. Trying to make out you're mad.'

Caroline's bottom lip quivered.

'You ain't mad. You know that, don't ya?' Murilla handed her the washer.

She shrugged, what do I know.

'They're so bloody cruel to you. There's no right need to go on like this, Caroline. It's a hard and lonely place when ya have to go it alone. I know bout these things, Caroline, I've been there.'

Caroline moaned.

'You've got to do something, *please*!' Murilla gently shook her shoulders.

Caroline sighed hopelessly, what can I do.

Murilla went back downstairs. She stopped abruptly, there were voices at the front door.

'I'm sorry, Reg. Do suppose I never thought that she was that far gone.'

'She's much like a child. That's why the Salte woman's here, to keep an eye on her.'

'Do you think it's wise to have her come into town? What if she has a turn, Reg?'

'No. That's why you must never allow her to join the committee.'

'Yes, I'm sure I can come up with excuses to keep her from joining. Oh Reg, what can I say? A man like you shouldn't have to put up with *that*.'

Murilla stepped out from the corner. Polly Goodman was wrapped in Reginald's arms, his head bent over hers. Murilla's heart thundered. She went to make a hasty exit when she heard a loud gasp. Knowing they had seen her, she turned and faced them.

Reginald advanced towards her, 'Murilla, what are you doing here?'

Her throat tightened. 'Nothing ... I ... I ...'

'Explain yourself.'

'I ... I ...'

His eyes screwed into mean slits. 'She sent you down here?'

Murilla stepped back. Reginald's face darkened with rage. 'It would be best for all if you keep this to yourself, understand!' he whispered maliciously.

Murilla nodded.

'Okay, right we are. Clean up that mess poor Caroline made in the dining room, will you please, Murilla?' He patted her shoulder — watch your step.

As Murilla walked away she heard: 'Why, Reg, you're so patient with the hired help. Patience of a saint!' The Goodman woman laughed shrilly.

It was after this that Murilla noticed a change come over Caroline. She thought Caroline was a lot smarter than the whole lot of them — well, she was in the end. But it was Polly Goodman that set off something in Caroline that would last for years. Something that would drive her almost mad. The worst thing about it all was, by that time, the whole town knew about Caroline's apparent sickness.

Polly Goodman, being who she was, soon took it upon herself to tell everyone 'the truth' about poor Reginald and Donald living up in that house with 'a crazy woman'.

Murilla knew the real truth and for that she was as much the enemy as Caroline. Sometimes Murilla would look back and wonder why she stayed. Would have been easier just to walk away and forget about the madness with the Drysdales.

It would have been three months later that something happened. Murilla knew that one day something would give. It came as no real surprise to her when she heard that Reginald had died. But that didn't make for any peace, either for her or Caroline.

\* \* \*

Now, as Murilla looks out at the yard, she notices the cat

limping along from the direction of the river. Blood and dirt cake its mangy body. Something bigger and stronger must have attacked it.

Murilla turns to the bed as soon as she hears the sound of sheets rustling. Caroline sits back against the pillows, watching Murilla with a strange expression.

'Dreaming?' Caroline asks.

'Sort of.'

'Be careful, Murilla, dreams are dangerous.'

'They are, aren't they.' Murilla stands and goes across to her. 'Do the dreams bother you anymore, Caroline?'

'You know they do.' Caroline looks at Murilla. 'Murilla, do you believe in God?'

'Hmm, well, I suppose I do. Just that I've never given it much thought.'

'Do you think I'll ever be forgiven?'

'Yeah, he forgives, don't he?' *It's coming back to her.*

'I suppose he does. Murilla, do you ever regret coming here to this place?' she suddenly asks as though the question is the most important thing in the world.

'Sometimes. But if I wasn't here, then ...' Murilla shrugs.

'Yes, yes, that's right. Now, listen, today I'd like to go into town for a walk.'

Murilla feels uneasy. 'In town. Are you sure? Oh, hang on, what's this about?' Murilla watches Caroline closely. *Could be one of her tricks.*

'I mean it. I'd like to have a look around. That's not a *crime* is it?' Caroline scowls, her face set with determination.

Murilla doesn't like it. She knows what Caroline's moods are like. She'll probably change her mind in another hour. 'No, it's just that ya haven't been in town for years! That's what's wrong with it. Why now, Caroline?'

Caroline throws the sheets back and gets up. 'Why not? Now, that's enough of your silly questions. Are you coming in with me or do I have to go alone?'

'I'll go with you. But I tell you, Caroline, this just better not be one of your tricks or fancies.'

'No, this is no trick or fancy, Murilla. All right, get my frock, please, that new one in the cupboard.' Caroline points at the wardrobe.

Murilla's hand halts on the door handle. 'What new one?'

'The new one. The ... what colour was it?' Caroline pauses, with a look of concentration. 'Oh yes, the pale lemon dress with the tiny pearl buttons down the front.'

'No, no you don't own one like that.'

'It's there. In the wardrobe.'

'Bloody isn't.' Murilla stands back as Caroline rummages under a pile of unironed shirts.

'Uh, ha!' Caroline cries triumphantly, standing back and flourishing a parcel wrapped in newspaper. 'Here tis!' she laughs.

Murilla looks at her incredulously. 'That's the dress?'

'After all this time and it's still in good condition.' Caroline holds the frock up against herself.

'That's ...! I don't believe it!' Murilla roars with laughter.

'Cunning, damn smart, huh,' Caroline splutters as she looks at Murilla then the dress.

'Yes, Murilla, this one's for us.' She stops laughing and starts to dress.

'I thought he burnt it?' Murilla takes control of herself.

'He thought he burnt it. No, the one he burnt was an

old housedress. This is the one that ...' She stops midway through dressing and looks at the far wall.

'The one that got away,' Murilla offers.

'Yes, you could say that.'

As Murilla watches her she realises what it must have taken Caroline to do that — to keep that dress after what he did. It would seem that she got the last laugh after all. Which is why the bottom of her stomach starts to churn. Caroline's going into town for another reason. After all this time, why would she bother? It doesn't seem right.

# eight

# the moon run away

As Sofie makes her way along the embankment, something catches at the edge of her sight. Her breathing slows, she shuts her eyes tightly, opens them, then squeezes them closed again, as though they cannot be trusted, they tell terrible untruths.

A raw dread hedges her mind. On the riverbank is a writhing fish; a barbed hook juts from its gills. Its glassy eyes and bloodied scales have already attracted a swarm of flies.

With a scream, she charges down the embankment. She picks up the slippery creature and carefully removes the cruel hook. Rushing to the water's edge, she kneels and releases it back into the river's opaque depths. 'Home ya must go. Home.'

Hitching up her dress, Sofie eases her feet into the cool river. But the morning is crowded by the incessant hum of thoughts hedging her mind. *Sofie gotta fix that rose red lady.*

She peers down into the water and talks as to a friend. What bout that Polly Goodman? She a rose red bitch.

She nasty, mean. She hates the old one. What a person to do?

*Weeelll one thing ya can do fix her right up. Ya go to her place to fix her. Gee, what's wrong which ya can't ya do anythin right.*

I do stuff right I do. Ya start on me n Sofie get mixed up like a cake. Hey, ya know bout me makin a cake at the old one! Yeah n that Victoria she be killin bubs! Brock he were to marry her but oh no! She won't swolla it, nope one of em bitches think she shit don't stink.

*Everyone shit stink rilly tell ya its only a tv show n ya can't be believin things ya see brockll marrry bitchoria they'll have the bub n live happy after see.*

Things can trick people.

*Sometimes people gotta stay tricked.*

Ya near as clever as the old one.

*Heeeyyy get outta here no one smart than her*

Sofie go swimmin with ya?

*That sweet summer we had my love my love*

*Then you had to go away*

*Tear of sorrow that I've shed for ya my love my love my love*

*I'll marry ya brock I wont kill the bubby like bitchtoria no way I'll have a bubby*

*Careerin nope no careerin all I want is happy ever*

I gotta go. Business I gotta do.

*Oh yeah what*

See a woman bout a dog, hee, hee. Dog, getit.

*Good one bubbyloo now one thing don't get caught troublell find ya she got eyes they be onya*

Friggin crapdoodle. Talkin bout caught, huh, no one catch this one here.

*Ya ain't got all ya marbles that what everyone say boutcha*

I don't care what they say.

*Ya getting mad stop there now sofie mad don't make a sensible woman*

Well, stop getting on me case for sure.

*Ya go n fix polly waffle up now*

No playing ring round Rosie when I gone.

*Don't sook for nothing just hold on tight we'll keep a good spot for ya here*

*Byebyebye dove*

\* \* \*

On the Mundra streets the sticky heat is already beginning to sweep the bitumen with a heat haze. Businesses have opened early, so that the owners can close before the temperature rises. The old people sit on shopfront seats, yarning to one another, each declaring, 'This heat'll kill me, you just wait and see.'

It's on a morning like this when Sofie makes her way down the main street. Some of the early risers, Nancy McIntyre, Don Artbuckle and Freddy Wenhem all bring their heads up and watch as she goes by. Nancy frowns, 'What on earth can that girl be doing at this hour?'

The others just shrug. 'Could be anything. Anything at all with that funny one,' Freddy puts in, then turns and begins to narrate the well-worn story of the cod he landed along the Stewart River, back in the '60s.

Sofie reaches the end of the road and comes to stand in front of Polly Goodman's house. At this time of morning everything is still, except for the trill of birds. She throws a precautionary glance towards the neighbouring house.

Feeling safe, she drops and crawls along the lawn. *Sneak long like a cat on its gut lest ya be seened. See the garden!*

*Wahoo! Fucken fancy as a birthday cake. Oh look out! Comin up the street.*

Sofie jumps to her feet, smoothes down her dress and looks at the ground.

'Hello, Sofie, you're about a little early.' Nancy McIntyre says with a bewildered expression.

'Um ... hello.'

Nancy gives a delicate little cough, then asks, 'Sofie, what are you doing crawling on the dirt?'

Sofie grins widely and points to the trees, 'Just looking at the birds there. Can't let em see me, they run away, too fast.'

'Well, I'll be.' Nancy's eyebrows rise. 'Never thought you'd be the one for bird watching, Sofie. There you go. Anyway, you've a good spot here. Right then, see you later.'

Sofie watches until the woman walks across to the opposite side of the street and disappears out of sight. *Phewwee close. Now that garden. Now run fast! Run, run, run.*

She looks down at the neat bed of flowers. A moment of uncertainty overcomes her. But the steely insistence of thoughts has told her what she must do.

She hitches up her dress, pulls down her underpants and squats above the flowers. *Splish splash we having a bath, wee wee. Arh, that's good.* When she finishes she stands up, arranges herself and checks her handy-work.

A scream splinters the air: 'Hey, what are you doing there?'

Sofie swings around wildly and looks towards the house at Polly Goodman racing towards her across the lawn, her dressing gown flapping like the wings of fury.

'Sofie, Sofie Salte! What in God's name do you think

you're doing?' Mrs Goodman grabs her arm in a tight grip, bright nails dig into her flesh.

Sofie takes a small step back, a shiver of fear rushes through her. *Polly mad up.* 'Um ... pissin on ya flowers.'

Polly grips her arm harder. 'Why ... why you ...'

Tears of pain gather in Sofie's eyes. She pleads, 'Let me arm go, ya hurtin Sofie!'

'Oh no you don't! You get into that shed, madam, you'll be digging up all those plants and replacing them.'

Sofie squirms, 'Nope, nope, don't reckon I can do that.'

'I reckon you can and will. Move!' Polly releases her arm and points to the garden. 'Now!'

Tightening into a rigid stance, Sofie shakes her head. 'Not movin.'

'What on earth would possess you to do such a dreadful thing?'

Sofie points at the trampled flowers. 'This what happen when ya be mean to the old one.'

'The old one?'

'The old one in the scary house, Missus Drysdale.' Sofie wriggles under her hot glare.

As though knowing all along, Polly replies, 'That'd be right. Caroline bloody Drysdale.' Then looks at Sofie, puzzled. 'But why?'

'Cos ya mean to her.'

Polly puts her hands on her wide hips, her face set into a don't-you-dare-give-me-any-trouble look. 'Well, Sofie Salte, you've got a big job to do here. Now get that shovel. Yes, that one there in the corner.'

'No.'

'No. What do you mean no? You have just vandalised my garden and I expect you to do something about it. Now, get moving!' the Goodman woman's voice rips out.

Sofie mimicks Polly's stance. 'Fuckerdoodery!' she blurts out in helpless anger. *She a baddy Polly.*

Mouth open wide, Polly gapes at her. 'What!'

A terrible ripple of laughter grips her, *Polly look a fish.*

'Oh my, you nasty, nasty girl! Your swear words don't bother me one tiny bit. If you don't get that shovel and fix those flowerbeds, then I'm going to get Dave Warner over here. That's right, I'll have you charged with damage to property!' Polly's eyes go small and snake mean.

'Fuck-er-doodery.'

Polly Goodman has had enough. 'One last time, get the *bloody* shovel.'

Sofie inches her way back to the door. *Polly scaredy.* She spots the shovel, picks it up and eyes it. 'Maybe Sofie Dove crack ya scone in, eh.'

Polly's large frame starts to quiver. She inches along the back wall, one arm outstretched as though the shovel will magically appear in her hand.

Sofie moves in closer. 'Ya a nasty bitch. The rose red cows! Moo, moo!'

'Now, dear …'

'Sofie know what ya do to Rilly n our house! Doze it down ya wanted to.'

'Now, look that had nothing to do with me. Put the shovel down, Sofie.'

'Huhuh, one of em fancy bitches! Like that Victoria bitchtoria!'

'I … I… somebody help me! Help me!' Polly screams.

Sofie brandishes the shovel at her. 'Poohpooh, cryin for ya mummy now, missus sookygirl!'

Somewhere a voice cries out, 'Sofie, what are you doing?' Nancy McIntyre appears at the shed door.

'Nothin.' Sofie pants.

Nancy enters the shed cautiously. 'Polly, are you right?' She touches her arm.

'Oh, goodness me, Nancy, I swear she was going to belt me one with that spade.' The Goodman woman's eyes are large with fear.

Nancy turns to Sofie. 'Come on now, luv, give Nancy the shovel.' She puts out her hand.

Eyes downcast, Sofie hands her the shovel.

Nancy moves closer, takes Sofie by the arm and guides her to the door. 'Sofie, come on and I'll take you home. Polly, I'm sure Murilla will see you about this later.'

'To Dave Warner she will. My oath!' Polly gathers the dressing gown tighter around herself.

Sofie follows Nancy out onto the street. When they reach the other side of the road, Nancy turns and with a look of pity and concern says, 'Sofie, luv, you mustn't do things like that. Missus Goodman's upset now. Why don't you go on home and stay away from Polly's, otherwise she just might get Dave Warner over. You know what he's like when he gets called out.'

'Polly sad?' Sofie asks, her heart thudding low and heavy.

'Yes luv, she's sad. But never you mind, just go on home.' Nancy then makes her way up the street.

Sofie's thoughts churn, she's got to get away, gotta run fast before Warner will come and say nasty stuff to her. She tears off down the road.

\* \* \*

All of Mundra knows about the neat-as-you-please house, sitting back from the footpath like a picture-book cottage. But it's not only Archie Corella's spruce house that amazes them.

Passers-by are struck by the sight that greets them in Archie's front yard. Sitting near the front steps are bags and bags of fertiliser, tottering stacks of pots, hoses, shovels and spades in a yard that looks like the wasteland of an abandoned mine claim, with great piles of dirt and unusually deep holes dotted across the yard. Along the fence are countless pots of withered rose plants.

One of the stickybeaks, Freddy Wenhem, curried up the nerve to question Corella about the deep ditches. Never the one for small talk, he went straight to the point, asking, why on earth would someone dig so many holes and so deep. What was this, a war zone? Didn't Corella realise they make an ugly sight, especially considering how neat the house looks? Does he have plans to bury someone out there? Freddy would later go back to his friends, a peculiar look on his face, and report, 'Corella says the roses won't grow in his yard. The dirt won't give to him; he can't grow roses at all, they always die. But he reckons the deeper he digs, the more chance he'll have of one taking root, surviving. Geez, that poor stupid bugger.'

Nancy McIntyre, shakes her head with wonder. 'Just goes to show. That Corella is dedicated.'

But there is someone who comes close to understanding his dedication. She halts, peers down into one of the ditches. 'One day, ya nasty dirt, you'll grow somethin, just for Arch.' She jumps over the ditch and goes to the door, knocks and shuffles her feet impatiently. The door opens and Archie's head appears.

'Hey, Archie.' She looks down at her hands.

Archie opens the door wider. 'Sofie, that you?'

'Sofie be in trouble. With Polly Goodman.'

Archie frowns, his amber eyes clouding over. 'Oh no, what now?' He motions her inside.

Sofie, her expression deepening, and with slow, deep breaths, responds, 'Sofie did a thing.'

Archie stops in his tracks, 'What thing?' His long, narrow face shades waxen.

'Done piss on her flowers.'

'You pissed on her flowers!' He roars with laughter, holding a hand to his heart. 'Oh Sofe, oh Sofie!' He takes control of himself, and guides her into the kitchen.

'She dob to Dave Warner. Nancy Mac ... Mac ... something her name be, tell me.'

Archie pulls out a chair. 'Here sit down.' A look of concern mars his features. 'Sofie, what ya want to be pissin on her plants for?'

Anger carves an ugly mask on Sofie's face. 'She get us bulldozed out n she won't let the old lady in the rose reds.'

Archie sits down beside her, taking in her face. 'Yeah, well, never mind. A Red Rose lady, huh. Should have known really.'

'What about Dave Warner?' She chews on her fingernail.

'Probably nothing. He'll rouse is all. Anyway, what do ya mean bulldoze the house?' Archie rubs a hand across the stubble on his jaw.

'One day when the sun that Rose Red Polly n her fancy friends they telled Rilly her's is a dirty old shack see. But Rilly fight em all. Cos the house, Rilly say, were falling to pieces. That one Tamara Dalmaine she do the bad thing, that what Rilly sayed.'

'Oh yeah, the Red Rose women. Seem to me they got their noses in everything around here. Yeah, they a funny mob, all right.'

'Pooh yeah, Nana Vida, she a smarty one, she tell Rilly

stay right away from em. Oh yeah, cos think they own the town! Can't do that, Archie? This be Sofie's, Nana's n Rilly's town too!'

'Well, whoever this Nana Vida is I reckon she might be right, they think they might own Mundra, but they don't. Never ...' Archie stops mid sentence, a film of confusion crossing his expression. 'Nuh, no one can own a town.' He finishes on an odd, cracked whisper.

'Nana live ... onetwothree ... four ... five houses that way. She one hundred years old. Older n the river.' She offers him a wide smile, 'Say, Arch, can Sofie have Milo today?'

'Milo. Yeah, Milo for Sofie.'

Sofie goes to the kitchen cupboard. Instead of grabbing the Milo, she looks out the window. A sudden jerky terror catches at her heart. 'Archie, Archie! The copper out there. *Sofiescaredsofiescared.* Archie, Archie, Archie tell him a thing.' She drops to her knees and crawls under the kitchen table, cowering with her head in her hands.

Archie peers under the table at the shivering woman–child, 'Sofie. Sofie, come on up. It's okay. Ya right.' He extends his calloused hands, trying to reassure her. But Sofie's fear is too great. 'I'm here, Dove. I'm here. No one's gonna hurt ya,' he says gently, one hand smoothing her white hair back from her tight-set face. 'Ain't no one gonna hurt ya, Sofie. Never.' He gets to his feet and answers the door.

Dave Warner stands stiff and official in his slightly grubby uniform. 'Archie Corella?'

'Yes, boss.'

'Look, I'm after that Salte girl, Sofie. Is she here?' His voice is laced with authority.

'Why, what's happened?'

'Apparently, and this is the complaint I received, she urinated all over Missus Goodman's prize flowerbed. Just tell me what you know ... I'm sick to death of these women and their bloody feuds!'

'Feuds?' Archie's voice carries a hint of bewilderment.

Warner sighs deeply, he is sick to the very stomach of having to explain himself once more. 'It's those women again.' He tightens his miserly lips. 'Been going on for years. Ah, they've got me worn to the bone. Well, anyway, I'll have to see the Salte woman, if she's here bring her out.'

When the outside conversation stops, Sofie hears the sounds of footsteps approaching.

Archie kneels into view, 'Come on out.'

'Can't, I don't wanna.'

'He knows ya here, Sofie. Now come on. There ain't a lot he can do, he'll just have a yarn to ya and that's all. Might as well get it done with.' He reaches out and encloses her hand in his. 'I'm not gonna let him take ya.'

Sofie crawls out. She holds Archie's hand tightly as they walk to the front door.

Warner offers a dim smile. 'Sofie, Missus Goodman said you peed on her flowers.'

She looks sideways at Archie, waiting for some indication as to what she should do. He nods, go ahead.

'Um ... um ... what if I say no.'

Warner shifts his weight from one foot to the other, notepad in hand as he looks at her. 'Well, someone did and she said it was you.'

'That rose red woman a bitch! She nasty!' Sofie blurts out, then claps her hand over her mouth.

'Look, you can't be doing those sorts of things to other

people's property. Missus Goodman is seriously upset. Anyway, where's Murilla?'

'At the old one's.'

'The old one's?'

'Missus Drysdale's.' Archie puts in, one eye on Sofie.

'Sofie, I'll have to have a talk to Murilla about this. Right, I don't want to hear another complaint about you again, understood?' Warner goes down the steps, looking curiously at the yard as he leaves.

Archie releases Sofie's hand, points a finger at her and says, 'This has got to stop, Sofie. It's not good to have Warner sniffing around all the time.'

Flushed with relief she says, 'He gone now, Arch. No bad words for Sofie.'

Archie steers her back into the house. 'Here sit down so I know ya can't run away.'

'Why, Archie, something funny here.'

'I know what ya did.'

'So, ain't the only one to piss on somebody's flowers, eh?'

'Sofie, I'm not talking bout the flowers.'

'Oh ...' *Gonnasay a bad thing sofie feel it.*

Archie moves closer. He begins, his voice slow, 'I saw you at the river that day. You pulled Donald Drysdale under, didn't ya?'

She jerks back in the chair and covers her eyes with her hands, peeking out between open fingers.

'Sofie, I think you know what I'm talkin about. If anyone finds out then you'll be in terrible trouble. See, Sofie, that's a bad thing and they put people away for a long time if the police find out.'

She can hear his voice coming from far away.

'I saw you there and I just don't know what the Cleaver girl saw.'

She blinks through filmy eyes. When she looks down all she can see is a vague, apparitional outline. She can hear the wind sighing, the river flowing. Calling to her.

'Sofie, now listen careful. No, don't look away, this is important. Who were the other girls? The girls Donald done things to.'

Soft voices rise, singing to her, soughing the uncertain silence. *That sweet summer we had my love, my love, then ya had to go away tears of sorrows that I have shed for ya ... my love, my love.*

'Sofie, stop this now!' The scar on Archie's face whitens.

She gets to her feet and races down the front steps, dodging the postholes and pots.

\* \* \*

Murilla glances at the tattered slip of paper, then turns her attention to the mixing bowl. 'Right, milk, one egg, Golden Syrup, self-raising flour, butter and bicarbonate soda.' She pours together the ingredients then hands the bowl to Sofie. 'Righto, make your favourite. Mmm, Golden Syrup pancakes. Good tucker, eh Dove.'

'Bake a cake Missus baker woman,' Sofie laughs, grabbing the bowl.

Murilla pulls out a chair and sits. Something like fear shadows her face. She heaves in a deep breath, then begins. 'Sofie, I gotta talk to you bout Archie.' She stops, looks at Sofie's bewildered expression, then pushes on. 'Sofie, Mundra ain't nothing to Archie. When he's sick of it here, he'll go on to some other place. Just because he's your friend that don't mean to say he's gonna be here forever. People like Corella can never rest too long in one spot.'

Sofie stares down into the mixing bowl. The sweet smell of Golden Syrup encloses her senses. 'Why, why for that, Rilly?' she chokes out.

Murilla fiddles with the oven mitt, picking at the lint. 'They like gypsies. Gotta keep going. They have it in their hearts. I've always known that bout him. Known that he'll hang round here for a while, then when his feet walks all the way cross this town, he'll be gone. Sorta expected it before now though.'

Sofie glares at her sister, 'Rilly, ya lie.'

'No lie, Dove. I'm telling ya now so that when the time comes you'll be ready for it. I know you're good mates with him but he's a loner, Dove, always has been n always will be.'

'Oh, nah, he not lone. He got a best friend now!'

'Settle down, love, now I could be wrong bout all this, right. But ya gotta know, there's a million Archie's in this old world n it's always the road that they belong to.'

Murilla's voice bleeds into the surface of Sofie's mind, her ears roar.

'It's just that I don't know a lot bout him. He just turned up out of the blue like that.' Murilla halts. She notices the tears on her sister's cheeks. 'All right, come on, love, Rilly didn't mean to make ya cry.'

Sofie bows her head. She hears her mother's voice. *My dove, my little Dove. A birdy, you see, is my Dove.*

'Dove, don't cry, I haven't seen you cry since ...'

The bruised clouds gather and besiege her mind. She goes back to the time ... when ... *when mum went down to the ground, sad Rilly n Sofie. A man, Rilly's man, he come to live with Sofie n sister.*

*First thing, he take all our money n grog it up n when the sun run away he come home yellin. Names he call Dove n sister — black bitches, sluts. A feed, he be shouting.*

*No tucker here. Ya be drinkin all the fucken money. Rilly anger.*

*He see Sofie hidin hind the wood box: Get the fuck outta there, red hot. Sofie pee scaredy. Oh, the dress, rip it do.*

*Get from her! Get ya hands off her ya bastard!*

*He laugh, dirty bitch! He chuck Sofie cross the floor. Oh, the blood run outta that girl. She cry. All too sad. Mother, she wants her mother.*

*Bastard! Get outta this house. Now! Rilly anger up.*

*Then he laugh like he do a funny thing and Rilly's face fallin in, blood, cry n snot all ova me sister. Sofie gotta run, oh that girl runned so fast. Run with the moon.*

*First place Nana's. She don't hear Sofie knockin, less she aren't home. Old people can't hear asleep.*

*That Sofie knowed nother place. The moon runned her to the old ones.*

*Last time Sofie see that bad egg he walk right outta town uncle Treacle behind him.*

Murilla is shaking her by the shoulder. 'Sofie, love, Sofie, come on, love.'

Sofie's eyes pop open.

'Ya right, Dove?'

'I good, Rilly,' she answers, turning her attention back to the bubbling mix. *Ain't a true. Rilly lie ... lie ... This Arch's town.*

Murilla exhales a deep breath as though she's finally released of a burden. She's about to grab the frying pan, when there's a knock at the door.

Murilla goes out to see who it is.

Sofie hears loud voices. *Bad news.* She gets to her feet and sidles along the hall, ears cocked to the conversation.

Archie Corella stands on the steps, hat scrunched in his hands. 'Murilla, I come here to ...'

'Archie?' Sofie moves closer towards them.

'Sofie, I've got to tell.' He looks away.

'Corella, what is it, man?'

Sofie freezes then lets out a wild scream, 'Sofie gonna hate ya! Archie Corella ya ... ya fuckerdoodery, go away!'

Murilla is caught in confusion. 'Archie?'

'I have to tell you about him ...'

'Who? Archie, who?'

'Shut up ya mouth! No more, no more ya friend!' Sofie jumps at him, arms chopping the air as she thumps his chest with powerless little hits.

'Sofie! Sofie, get offa him!'

She stops, exhausted. Archie squares his shoulders and says, 'I came about Drysdale. Donald Drysdale.'

Sofie falls back against the wall, clutching her throat. With a pitiful wail she pushes past him and down the road, hugging and singing to herself as she makes for the river.

*Now the moon gonna run away*

# nine

# lillian gee

Doris watches as Nana clutches the hen by the throat. It squawks and flaps wildly as it makes a last attempt to free itself.

She reaches for the butcher's knife, then looks across at Doris. 'You sure you can stand this?'

Doris sits down on an empty kerosene tin. 'Hmm, reckon I can.'

'This one here has got some sorta disease. When you got one bad one in with the rest of the mob, it's no good. The thing is, it infects all the rest. Bad blood, ya see.'

Nana brings the knife back and swiftly runs it deep, across the hen's throat. A stream of warm blood spurts forth. She lays the carcass on the ground and it bucks and shudders as though still alive. Its silly eyes glaze over, then it lays stiff and still.

Nana stands back and looks down at the hen. 'Cos all its chickens were infected too. Same disease. It passed it on to its littlens. Ain't no real good. Had to kill all the chicks. To think, she were one of me favourites, that poor ol girl. Suppose I can always see Treacle Simpson bout getting another one, eh.' She pulls out an empty flour tin from under the tank stand and drags it across to sit down beside Doris.

'Speaking of Treacle, how is he? Haven't seen him for a while.' Doris has an eye still on the dead hen.

'He's good. He's been working across the other side of the river. Building fences for old man Cleaver. You'd have thought Cleaver woulda fixed them fences long before now.'

'Down near the river road, eh.' Doris watches as a swarm of flies blankets the hen's carcass.

'Why, I remember when his father, Joseph, first bought that property. One time there, this was Ruby Midday's boy, Paddy, he used to walk in from the old dump way there. Back then, most us fellahs camped there in tents n humpies. Weren't allowed in town here, except to get tucker then get out again. The copper, Berne Lloyd, would be right on our backsides! Walk behind us to make sure we leave when we finished. Were like we lived in the world's largest prison, eh!' Nana laughs, but it doesn't reach her eyes.

Doris is curious. 'I thought Dave Warner's father was the cop back then?'

'See, this where people get their stories mixed. Weren't never any Warners in this town till later on in the piece. Dave Warner only came here in the seventies or thereabouts. So he's really a stranger. A lot of people forget. See, they *think* Warner a Mundra boy born n bred but the older ones know better. Most people round these parts are Mundra since generations.'

Doris watches her warily, wondering if she should bring up the subject of history again. She risks it. 'Nana, what about us mob?'

For a few moments Nana scrutinises her. Finally she

says, 'Don't count. Never counted then, don't count now. I thought a lot bout what ya said to me the other day and I believe it's true. People need to know their history, otherwise there's this terrible feeling of being lost. There's things I know that may hurt ya real bad, Doris ...' She leaves off and looks across to the riverbank. 'But the time has come.'

Doris feels a sense of dread but also elation. After all this time she's going to find out the truth.

Nana begins, 'Now, the Midday boy, Paddy, used to go fishing on the riverbank. Loved old Cleaver's place, he did. Now here's the thing: Paddy used to have this little hessian bag he carried round, kept the snake in it. Can't recall what sort it were but I know it were poisonous. Never saw anyone handle a snake the way Paddy could. Can't say any of us mob were scared of it but Ruby'd be always rousing on him that one day it'll kill him, aye. Paddy loved that snake. Well, on the day Paddy went down there, Joseph Cleaver were standing on the bank with a shotgun. Waiting for that littlen to turn up. When he got there Paddy were hunted off like a dog.

'Now, Ruby were a woman who could get mighty riled! I see her leave the camp that day, Paddy with her. Later on, Treacle Simpson's father, Gus, told me about it. Ruby had an argument with Cleaver and it seems Joseph told her that they were all *trespassing*! Claimed it were all his river n all ...'

'The river! He claimed to own the river.' Anger ripples Doris's face.

'As things go, Paddy was terrified of Cleaver. Aye, wouldn't go nowhere near that river. Then, on the anniversary that Cleaver bought the property, the thing happened. Chopping wood, he were, when a snake slithered out of the blocks and got him on the ankle. Later that day he died.'

Doris throws her an incredulous look. 'The boy taught the snake to *kill* him?'

Nana pauses, as though searching for a reasonable explanation. 'No, don't reckon even Paddy could have done that. You see, it was much later that something else happened. Yes, that old camp brought a lot a things out in fellahs. Young Paddy were one.

'Fellahs gotta have roots and at that time we didn't know what he was! Like some of us didn't even know where we came from! Such a thing ...'

A flock of crows lands on the fence, eyeing the hen's carcass. They remind Doris of sable-coated men at a funeral. It's like you feel bad about being black so you try to forget everything. Some fellahs did. Ya ask em where they came from. They say they can't remember. Like their minds were washed away. So what I want to say is fellahs looked to other things. Young Paddy with the snake, for one. It were that snake that gave him something back. Made him feel all right bout who he were.' Nana's wizened, leathery face has a far-away look.

'I don't think it's stupid, Nana. I just don't know what youse went through here.'

'Right, to get back to the story. One day Paddy went missing. We didn't realise at first that he were even gone. It were like him to go round the camp so quiet. Ruby looked for that kid high and low but she couldn't find him.

'It was Gus Simpson who found him ... What happened to Paddy I'll never really know. When Gus found his little body it were caught in the roots up the side of the bank. It seemed that when he went in to unhook his line he got his feet caught up. The more Paddy moved, the more he got stuck. Eventually, he musta tried to go under and untangle the line. All the while that snake bag were on the bank, just out of reach. What happened next is anybody's guess. The *thing* is, while Paddy was drowning, the snake got out of the bag! It were later on when Gus found the marks on his arms. The snake had bit him! I can't pretend to know anything much about it, but I know this much: *that snake killed Paddy before he drowned.*'

Nana halts for a moment and catches her breath. 'As I said, there ain't a great deal I can answer about it. I reckon it goes back to that kid having something with the snake. Aye, in times of strife there's magic in a lot a things. Like a strong hope, or a love that can't be held down. What do I reckon happened? Well, the way we were treated out there on the old dump road, anything coulda happened to anybody. Young Paddy was trying to take part of that river as his own place. It was much later, when the other thing happened with Belle Gee ...' The old woman stops, her milky eyes straining. She looks off towards the river. Memories and grief wash over her face. She hunches forward, hands between her legs as she peers off into some remote place.

From the end of the street a horse trots into view. It stops on the dusty road and raises its pretty sorrel head. Its smooth chestnut coat ripples as flies swarm its rump.

A gust blows in from the west. Leaves and paper scurry about in a dusty dance as the breeze gathers force and with a quick swoop it lunges over the carcass of the hen. The horse's nostrils quiver and it throws its head back with a sharp, bone-cracking jolt. Blood-mad from the scent of the dead hen, it rears, pawing and slicing the air. Red soil cuts through the air as it bolts down the road.

'They hate the smell of blood.' Nana goes over to the carcass and lifts the bloodied hen. 'Reckon we oughtta bury this poor creature, eh.'

The soil breaks away easily as Doris digs into the dirt. She takes the hen from Nana and lays it in the hole. 'Do you think that's deep enough?'

'Yes, my girl,' Nana answers, looking into the hole with a frown. 'It seems the dirt ain't what it used to be, either. I can't grow anything much in the yard now. That's why I have to plant the chrysanthemums in those tubs over there. Aye, the ground just won't give.

'Okay, Doris, let's have a cuppa, love. Then I'll tell ya the rest of the story.'

\* \* \*

Nana places the teacup on the ground. 'Right, where was I?'

'The thing that happened to Belle Gee.'

'Oh right. Now Doris, there are people here that still hurt very badly about what I have to tell you. Mundra is full of fellahs that like to cover things over, especially certain ones that got something to hide. I'll start by telling you a little bit more about this town because this is where it all began.' She stops, picks up the tea cup and takes a sip.

'Too much dust in this old place.' Doris winces at the dusty seats and sets her mug on the ground.

'Yep, dust morning till noon. Okay, this town ... as I said, all us mob lived on the old dump road. Were around seven families there: Gus Simpson and his mob; Treacle's parents; Mertyl and Jimmy Salte, Murilla's people; Ruby Midday and Paddy; and your parents. The thing is, we had to live there cos there weren't no other place for us to go. We didn't have a choice.'

Doris interrupts. 'No black fellahs were *allowed* in any town back then, isn't that right?'

'It is. Most black fellahs lived on the fringes of town, in shacks, tents and humpies. We used to come into town here on the odd occasion for flour n things like that.

'We had our own meat, kangaroos, rabbits, goanna n fish, that we hunted for. The humpies n tents we lived in we built ourselves. Canvas n hessian bags were used most of the time. I remember we would go across to the dump, that place stank worse than a sewer — it wasn't far from our camps — and we'd scavenge for wood and materials the white fellahs chucked away.

'The river when in flood used to back up and the water would channel out through the dump road. We were flooded many times. And it were only a matter of time before sickness set in. Edna Thursday were the first one to go: pneumonia got her. Edna n Buddy had their tent a lot closer to the dump and one night the water rose and flooded them right out. Walked around for days she did, so sick. There were no doctors for us. Although, she weren't the only one to get that sick. Were plenty others too. Aye, Doris, that was our lot and we put up with it.'

Doris grits her teeth, trying to imagine what it must have been like.

'We were all pretty mad after Edna passed on. No doctor in town wanted to see her because we weren't allowed in Mundra. But there were one person who wouldn't take to that ...' Nana stops, drops her head for a minute then looks across at Doris.

'Lillian Gee were a striking woman. Hair blacker than coal, eyes the colour of that green shirt over there on the line and a smile that would make ya melt. Had this nature about her, happy and always smiling at people.

Lilly were much loved by a lot of people. She hated the fact that we weren't allowed in town and said that Mundra wasn't our God. She went into town every Tuesday to stock up on tucker. She'd stay there for most of the day. See, not all the white fellahs here were whatcha call bad people. No, there was some that was good and Lucinda and Barry Hughes, one of the few ...'

Doris cuts in, 'Caroline Drysdale's parents?'

'That's right. Lilly became friends with them. They met when Lilly come out of Bluey Seddon's with a large sack a potatoes. Lucinda saw her trying to struggle home with it. Big sacks, they was. So Lucinda drove Lilly home that day. Fairly soon she were picking Lilly up and driving her in and outta town. Gentle, kind soul that she were, Lucinda. That's how the friendship started. Eventually, certain white people started to notice the way Lilly used to be in town most of the time.'

'She didn't do any harm, did she?' Doris bursts forth angrily.

'No, our Lilly never did. Lilly and Joe, that were her husband, had only two little ones, Belle n Raymond. That Belle, she were just as pretty as her mum. Never forget them till the day I die. Still have dreams about them, after all this time. Raymond loved his sister, worshipped the ground she walked on.

'Anyway, to get back to the town. People started to notice the way Lilly used to go in all the time. *Certain* people, that is. Back then it was Edward Drysdale who was the big honcho round these parts.'

'Edward Drysdale? Caroline's father-in-law?'

'Same man. One day I'm at the campfire cooking fish, when I hear a woman's voice from behind. I swing round and there's Lilly. She don't look too good, so I ask what's wrong and she says that she has to talk to somebody about something. She goes on to say that she's having a bit of trouble with some people.' Her words stop and start again, 'If I had a known then what I know now ...'

Doris feels a surge of guilt. Should she be asking her to remember these things? Murilla's voice echoes in her mind: *Remember, Doris, ditches are deep.*

'Nan, I been thinking ...' She pauses, watching Nana's face closely. 'Maybe you shouldn't bother telling me everything. Too much sadness.'

'No, Doris, this is me last chance to get this off my heart. I must go on.

'Lilly comes to me and says she wants to talk. I know something's wrong, cos there's no smile. She tells me there's a bunch of people who'd threatened her about going into town. I'm mad now and tell her they're all piss n wind. Fancy such talk from an old one, eh.' Nana allows herself a small laugh. 'I tell her that it's okay because she has white friends in there and there's nothing anybody can say or do. Lilly seems to feel a little better when I say that.'

'Did she say who the people were?' Doris reaches into her pocket and pulls out a crumpled pack of cigarettes.

'Here, Doris, give me one.' Nana reaches for a smoke.

'Bad for your health, Nana,' Doris laughs, handing her a cigarette.

Nana shoves the smoke in her mouth, takes a deep drag, then begins. 'Who they were ... well, let me tell you that later. But now, to Lilly. I was worried about her. Mainly cos of the men. Her being so pretty, I got to thinking a lot of things, all bad. I couldn't sleep after that, knowing how easy it would be for anyone to be dragged down that road, and no one would hear a thing.

'It was Tuesday Lilly went into town. It were one of the days Lucinda couldn't make it out to drive her. So I decided to follow, not right into town, but staying behind in the bushes and just waiting for her to come home.

'I'm there a good while when from the distance I see her coming along the dirt road, a bag of sugar in hand. I heave in a gust of air, scared she might hear me, she were that close. But then a long sedan crawls up over the hill, lurking along. Me hair stands on end, goosebumps cover me from head to toe. I know it ain't a good thing bout to happen. I keep me eyes to Lilly. She don't hear the car till it's nearly on her. I look back to the camp and at that moment Belle n Raymond come tearin down the flat. I think they must have seen their mother from up in the tree, where they played. Their small legs motor along past me in full sprint to Lilly.

'By this time, the car stops. Out steps four men I know all by sight. Ronald Artbuckle, Willy Dalmaine, Tom Cleaver, and Edward Drysdale.

'Dalmaine is the first to speak. "Keep out of town, woman!" he orders. Lilly bein Lilly just smiles n replies, "I ain't hurting anyone, am I?" Then Drysdale thunders, "No black gins allowed." His laugh come out low and fulla nastiness. His face is getting redder. Lilly having the gall to talk back to him like that! Make him angry. "People of Mundra don't want niggers roaming in *our* town!" he spits. That's when Lilly loses it. She laughs, really laughs. When she can gather herself together, she says to Drysdale, "I got good friends in there and you ain't gonna stop me from seeing them." By this time, Drysdale has enough. A black woman smart mouthing him just don't go too well. My heart smashes against me chest so loud I swear they'll hear me in the bushes.

'I was really fearing for her. Cleaver walks round to the other side of the car and steps up to Lilly. He says, "People can have accidents on this road and no one would know or care." Lilly smoothes the hem of her frock and looks down. I can feel her fear. The two children, by this stage one on each side, hold onto their mother's hand. My heart stands still. Drysdale looks from Belle to Raymond, like he was weighing em up. Finally, Lilly turns with the kids and they walk back to the camp. I don't move from them bushes. I watch them get back in the car n take off into town.'

Doris feels a shadow steal across her heart. 'Weighing them up, Nana?' she says softly. 'Anyone could see Drysdale had a plan.' Nana closes her eyes for a moment, then continues.

'After that happened I went and seen Lilly. I don't like them men following her home like that. And what they said made me think what they could do to her, to all of us. So I walk up to her tent. Lilly sees me and she comes out. I grab her by the wrist and speak hard. "Lilly, this has got to stop, please! I'm worried for ya. Those men are dangerous." Lilly just shrugs me off. "They'll get sick of me soon enough. They're all talk, Vida." And she gives me one of her smiles. I know I can't allow this situation to go on. I go n see Joe n tell him about the men. That night they have their first fight. Lilly's most a the time lovely voice screeches through the camp, "You're just like them, Joe! You can't stop me from going into town!" Suddenly the tent flap flies open, and out rushes Lilly, taking off to the river. She was hurt real bad.' Nana pauses to catch breath, a dry cough rattling her frame.

'Poor Lilly,' Doris shudders.

Nana goes on. 'Yes, poor Lilly. But I felt bad, very bad

bout going to Joe like that. I just didn't want to see her hurt.'

Doris puts out her cigarette. 'You done the right thing, Nana.'

'I suppose I did. The next day Lilly come to see me. "They can't make me stay away from there, Vida. They don't own the town." As I look at her I know she's gonna be in town come every Tuesday. Knowing that she's angry at me for going to see Joe, I say, — Now, Lilly, I ain't ya enemy here. But I frightened of them men and what they'll come at. It's true what they said, Lilly. — She knows, but she asks, "How do you know about them anyway?" And her face falls in with hurt or disappointment. "Vida, you followed me!"

'I told her I had to, feeling very snaky, like I was spying on her, which I were. She ignored me for days after. And it were about five, six weeks later when everything came to a head.' Nana leaves off, sad and tired.

As Doris watches Nana's desolate face her guilt returns. Before she can open her mouth, Nana shakes her head firmly, 'No, Doris, I'm going on. This is the story you want to hear. We'll go back to Tuesday, Lilly's day.

'I stand at the camp fire, waiting for Lilly to come out of the tent. I notice she's wearing one of her pretty frocks. I follow along behind as she makes her way to town. I try to stay out of sight best I can, especially when we get into the main street. I lower me head, trying to ghost, hoping no one will take too much notice of an old girl. Hoping I'll be invisible. I watch as Lilly walks up Mary Street, not caring for the dirty looks she's getting. Some white women actually stop and speak to her. Laughing n joking around, they are. That were Lilly's nature, to draw people to her like that. When she smiled it were like nothing bad in the world could touch ya. Some of them liked Lilly. And it so happens one of em be Tom Cleaver's wife, Jenny Anne.

'Jenny Anne were the type a woman to laugh at the wrong time or say something outta turn. She didn't have a place in town, on no committees or such. Mosta them town women tolerated Jenny only because a Tom's friendship with Drysdale. Jenny had a plain, blank face, eyes like a fish and a tiny, tight mouth n she were a short woman, no higher than that there fence post. Anyway she just looked lost all the time. Like she don't belong anywhere. She were a nice girl though. Her heart were in the right place.'

Doris follows in serious concentration. 'Oh yes, she'd be related to old Cleaver then?'

'Ex-daughter-in-law,' Nana responds. 'To get back to the story, there was this friendship between Lilly n Jenny. I'm standing by the grocers, watching as Lilly and Jenny are talking. Jenny had, a few days before, given birth. It were the most natural thing in the world to do, Jenny hands the tiny bundle to Lilly. Cooing and giggling over the baby, they are, when Tom appears. His face drops, mouth hangs open, and he halts. As though something has hit him in the gut and winded him.' Nana pauses.

She reaches across for a cigarette, lights up and watches the tip as it burns. With a slight painful movement she turns and studies the road.

Doris follows Nana's gaze, trying to see what has her attention. There's nothing there. All at once, a loud snort breaks the silence. It's the sorrel horse back again, whinnying softly as it trots up near them. Doris watches it with trepidation. She's never trusted horses, not completely.

As though knowing her thoughts the horse looks across at her, then trots off towards the riverbank.

As it disappears Doris asks, 'Who owns that?'

'No one. It's a brumby. Remember I were tellin you about the Corellas, the mob that used to live here years ago? And how the young fella, Archie, got kicked in the head?'

It comes back to Doris. 'Oh yes, yes I do.'

'Anyhow, after the accident they let the horse loose. No one in the camp would have it because of what happened to Archie. Some of em were scared of it. Somewhere along the line it musta bred with the Hetherington horses, and now there be a whole mob a them running free in the bush. I'd guess that sorrel belongs to the mob. Funny though, for that one to come close to people like that. I've seen it many times, but always at the riverbank. They can be real dangerous creatures, horses.'

'Yeah, that's why I keep my distance.'

Nana gets to her feet, stretches her arms, then sits down again. 'To the story. Now, where was I? Yeah, Tom Cleaver. So there I was in town, standing near the grocery store, watching Lilly with the baby.

'Tom runs, runs all the way down the street to the women. He screams at Jenny Anne, 'Stupid bloody woman! Letting them touch my son!' But it's for Lilly he saves his nastiness. She hands the bundle back to Jenny. Soon as Lilly does that, Tom shoves her hard in the chest, so hard she stumbles back and falls onto the footpath. Some people stop, others just walk by nodding their heads, as if ta say, that's right teach that woman a lesson. As I look at Jenny I see her face collapse n turn bright red. She screams, "That's all you're good for, Cleaver, hitting women!" I feel my gut sink, poor Jenny Anne. I never see her again, neither does Lilly. For the resta the day I follow Lilly, always watching every move she makes, all the while close to dying from fear.'

Doris gasps. 'What do you mean, never saw her again?'

'No one saw Jenny Anne again. I reckon Cleaver kept her locked up in that stinking little house by the top paddock, the one old man Cleaver's in now. Always felt bit sorry for that girl, didn't fit in anywhere.'

'Yeah, Nana, a bit like us, eh.' Doris grins tightly. It seems to her there's more to the history of Mundra than she ever imagined. Nana's voice cuts through her thoughts.

'Yeah, Doris, ya can say that. Righto, here's what happened next with Lilly.

'Missus Hardacre, one a them women who did bother to talk to Lilly, were driving down the street and she musta have seen the commotion with Cleaver, Lilly and Jenny. Then she musta gone over to Lucinda and Barry's house, telling them about the incident. Lucinda and Barry turn up on the street. But Cleaver was long gone. What happens next is the end of everything. Bad blood starts. Lilly, Lucinda and Barry are all heading for a gutser. Lilly musta told Barry and Lucinda about the men threatening her that day on the road. Anyway, it's Lucinda who sees Edward Drysdale come wobbling outta the pub, he's had a few drinks ...'

Doris interrupts. 'It's hard to believe that Lucinda was Caroline Drysdale's mother, eh. Then again, Caroline Drysdale's got steel running through her veins, I swear! Don't know how Murilla puts up with her.'

Nana smiles to herself. 'Murilla Salte, well, she's a Salte n there ain't too much in this world'll rattle her, I reckon.'

Nana takes up the story again. 'Drysdale wobbles outta

the pub. Lucinda spots him and makes a beeline straight at him. At first he looks down at her, like she's a piece a garbage. "Get out of my way, Hughes," he barks. Lucinda stands her ground. "Mister Drysdale, you have no right threatening Lilly like that. She's done no harm to anyone here." Barry is standing back watching, holding Lilly's arm.

'Then Drysdale says to Barry, "Getting a bit of black velvet, Hughes?" Barry's ruffled. "You dirty bastard! Step up to me, Drysdale," he's shouting.

'Drysdale laughs, "Throw the leg over, do you, Hughes? Little white wifey no good in the sack." That's done it now. Barry shapes up to Drysdale. He hits Drysdale square on the chin and Drysdale lands on the footpath like a sack a watermelons. When Drysdale gets up, blood pissin from his wounds, he gives each a them a look that'd curdle milk. Hate is written all ova him.

'I'm real stunned when I see Drysdale just walk away. Common sense tells me that's not the end of it. Lucinda and Barry and Lilly think it is. Two days later … someone dies.' Nana drops her head in her hands and starts rocking back and forwards.

Doris goes to her and puts an arm around her shoulders. 'It's okay, Nana, ya can stop now. I can hear this another day.' Doris is again overcome with shame. She shouldn't put Nana through this grief.

Nana brings her head up. 'I must go on with the story, Doris. It's comin to me, clear.'

'Nana, ya really don't have to.'

Nana seems not to hear, she slips back into memory. 'It's Sunday, a hot day, so hot the ground burns the soles of ya feet. I'm hanging out the washing and happen to look over at the river. I think I see someone on the other side. Where the Cleaver's property is. I make out a shadow movin through the bushes, movin very fast. It just don't *look right* ...'

'Nana?' Doris quizzes.

'Before I go much farther, go switch the wash-room light on, Doris. It'll be dark soon and I don't like the darkness. Pull that drum over closer to me, Doris,' Nana motions. 'Alright, here goes. The shape's movin fast. I turn to see if anyone else is about, but most of em are down on the riverbank swimming n fishing. I spot Mertyl Salte close by, stirrin the billy tea. "Mertyl, over here, look," I yell. She joins me at the line and looks over at where I point.

"I'd say, Vida, that's Tom Cleaver over there." Thinkin she was right, I don't worry about it too much; after all, Cleaver spying ain't nothin new. I walk back to me tent when I notice some of the fellahs have come back from fishing. Joe and Lilly have caught some cod and are gutting them on the ground. A few minutes later Mertyl comes back ta join me as I stand countin how many fish be caught. Suddenly there's a loud bang! First I think it were a car backfiring up the dirt road. But a terrible feeling tells me that it were a gun. No one panics; after all, people shoot pigs and roos down near the river. Then Mertyl says, "Don't feel right. I don't like this, Vida. Where's everybody?' Someone pipes up, 'We're all here, except for Lilly's littlens.' Everybody freezes. All eyes turn ta Joe and Lilly. Lilly's mouth drops wide and she places a hand over her heart. "No," she whispers ...'

Doris feels her whole body break into a tremble. 'No, Nana, no!' Her mouth tastes coppery, she tastes her own fear.

'Do you want me to go on, love?'

Doris sucks in a large breath. 'Yeah, Nana, go on.'

'Mertyl Salte is the first to break from the group. She gallops down the riverbank, me tearin after her. We reach the lower part of the bank. And there she were, laying against the trunk of a ghostgum. She looks like a red n white flower. She has on this pretty white frock, Lilly sewed it by hand. A red spot, like an ink stain, spreads all over the front a her dress.'

Doris shuts her eyes tight. *Smack bang in the heart.* The vivid image plays in her mind. She wrings her hands into a fierce painful knot. But still she listens as Nana goes on.

Nana's voice is now low and whispery. 'And there's Raymond, alive, holdin his sister's hands, wailin. He's only a twelve-year-old child. But Belle's still alive, barely. As she lay dying, her last words be: 'Raymond, help me ...'

Doris feels the shift in the now shivery night air. Her eyes fix on Nana.

A small wail escapes the old woman's mouth. She stands uneasily to her feet, shaking a frail fist up into the darkness. She stumbles against the tank-stand. Doris shoots forward, grabbing her by the arm before she falls. She gathers Nana into her arms. 'I'm sorry, Nana. I'm sorry,' she murmurs, hot tears burning the back of her eyes.

'Nana, I'm staying the night.' She leads Nana up the steps and makes for the bedroom. She pulls back the blanket, arranges the pillows and helps her into bed.

Nana crumples amidst the pillows. 'There's more, my girl. That's half the story. You got the power to change things, Doris,' she finishes.

Doris nods. She can't answer. She has lost all power of speech. She turns from the room, goes into the kitchen and looks from the window out into the night. From the end of the road she can see something in the half-light. The horse stands by the undergrowth, seeming to look straight at her. Doris turns away. Suddenly the night feels very lonely.

When she sleeps she dreams of many things.

# ten

# those voices

Archie waits for her anger. He hopes his face doesn't betray the fear skirting his mind. His head goes damp. Then the pain starts. It begins in his arm and shoots up to his shoulders. A dull pang throbs under the thick, puckered ridge of his skin. The scar takes on a life of its own. The agonising brush of pain spreads across his face. Archie draws in a sharp, jagged breath, his throat catching on the air, his lips numb. He fights the mad desire to cry out, to just drop to the dirt and surrender to it.

Archie should have known that this is what it'd amount to. Coming here to Murilla's house might well be a terrible mistake. The pain tells him that. He tries to convince himself that he's doing the right thing, doing what he has to. He knows he's done all he can for Sofie. Now it's up to Murilla.

He catches hold of the door as Sofie jumps out at him and pommels his chest, useless little hits, then with a shrill scream tears off down the dirt road, white hair flying behind her like a flag. He looks at Murilla. Her face tells him that she's not gonna take it easily. Her shadow falls upon his unsteady form.

'Spit it out, man! Haven't got all bloody day to be muckin round with you!'

'Drysdale. I come about Donald Drysdale.' Archie watches the way her face changes into a slate of dread.

'Righto, Corella, what about him?' Murilla's voice drops to a low threat.

'He's done that to Sofie.' He takes a step back, preparing for her fury.

For a brief moment Murilla just stares at him, her hard eyes clouding over. A peculiar silence fills the air. *The eye of the storm.*

Her mouth opens then closes, like she has no words to speak, and he knows that just can't be so. Finally, she makes a small move: one arm crosses over the other.

'He done what to Sofie?'

'What he did to other girls, ya already knowed he did, Murilla. I ... I ... Now, dontcha be looking at a man like that!' He struggles to go on. 'I comed here on good will. I thought ya needed to know what he doned to her ... I ...' Archie stops, thoughts eddy in his mind, words come to his tongue then leave. He wants to tell her everything, wants to tell her that Drysdale didn't *really* drown and that it was Sofie held the man's head under the water. Archie's heart races and his body feels distant.

'He interfered with me sister, is that right, Corella? Is that what I hear ya say?' Murilla looms over him. Sweat glistens on her face.

He hears himself, almost whisper, 'Yeah, that's right. I just can't stand it anymore, Murilla. I have to tell ya. Can't ya see I'm tryin to do the right thing.' Archie stumbles back from her fierce gaze.

'I believe ya gotta lot of talking to do, Corella.' She motions him to step inside. 'Here, sit down there and

I'll brew us a coffee.' She turns, her large shoulders humped forward.

He doesn't like it; she's way too quiet. He pulls out a chair and falls into it. When she's not looking he sneaks quick glances around the room. Sitting in the far corner is a cane basket full of dried flowers with a frayed, pink ribbon tied around the base. Dangling from the kitchen window is a delicate wind chime, the tiny gold pipes tinkling against each other as a breeze snakes past. A wooden counter runs from the stove to the sink and sitting at each end is a vase full of freshly-picked magenta geraniums.

Archie feels a ripple of something like confusion. This room isn't her. This room couldn't belong to her. It's too ... well, he doesn't really know what it is.

'Here ya go. Might be too hot, eh?' Murilla's hands tremble slightly as she passes him the cup.

'It'll do.'

She sits quietly then she asks, 'How'd you find out?' Her eyes keep moving away from his.

Archie clears his throat. He's gone way too far to turn back now. 'It wasn't long after I started work for them. One night, the first night there at the Drysdale house, I saw Sofie standing near Drysdale's work shed ... um, she were holding a fish. It scared me. I knew then something was wrong.'

Murilla runs a finger around the rim of her coffee cup.

Archie doesn't feel right. He gives an uneasy cough, then goes on. 'It was later on, that was when I threw in the towel. 'I ... I didn't know what to do! Dontcha, now dontcha look at me like that!' He rubs the side of his face. It's starting to feel hot. 'What was I to do? Murilla, I was scared, scared ...'

'Why, why didn't ya tell me!' She bangs a fist on the table. The coffee cup totters for a second then: Crash! It smashes on the floor. Archie flinches.

'Oh God, why?' She drops her head into her hands, a low growl rising from the back of her throat. She collapses back in the chair and weeps, shoulders heaving as she succumbs to the despair Archie reads on her face. Then he knows. All along he's been wrong about her, thought she was something else. Now, as he watches the broken woman before him, he realises that Murilla Salte is another person. *That* Murilla Salte never existed.

Archie feels the loneliness, and the old blood starts to roar. Nothing has prepared him for this. He starts to reach for her hand but pulls back swiftly. He wants to tell her that Drysdale got it in the end.

Murilla, emptied of hot anger, raises her head. 'You were scared to tell me?' she asks, her voice frail.

'Reckon I were.'

'Anything else I should know?'

He begins, 'Well ... uh ...' The pain returns as brutal as ever. He doesn't see the darkness yet, but it'll come for him like always.

'Tell me now, Archie, do it in one hit. I need to know how badly done me sister is.' She wrings her hands, tears start up again.

By now Archie is bending forward in the chair, one hand holding the side of his head. Any moment now the dark will come.

'He ... he ... ddiiddnn'ttt ...' The fire has started. *They're coming for him.*

'Drysdale didn't ...? Corella, is this one a ya turns, man? Archie, are ya right?' She shoots around the table, grabs his face and looks into it.

He stutters, 'ii ... tttt ... lll ... eee ...' trying to let it loose before the darkness claims him.

'Here, man, don't move. Stay right there.' Murilla grabs a dirty tea towel, runs it under the tap and races back to place it on Archie's face.

He's sinking into the pit now. 'Sssooffi ... sofiie ... She ... kill ... himm.' There. He gets it out. The darkness unfurls from the tunnel, Archie falls into it. For a moment he hears the voice: *help me hellppp meee.*

\* \* \*

Archie opens his eyes and looks around the room. For a few minutes he struggles to recall what has happened and where he is. In the distance he hears the sounds of the TV, plates rattling against each other and the tinkling of wind chimes. He's at Murilla's house. He blinks, adjusting his eyes to the gloomy room.

He lays back against the pillows. Should he get up and go home? Should he see if Sofie is back yet? Hang on, he can hear someone coming down the hall.

'Arch. Arch.'

'Sofie, that you?'

'Is Dove, Archie Corella.' Her soft footsteps move into the room.

'Sofie, please understand ...' He tries to find the words to make her understand.

'Sofie right as the rain. Dontcha be cryin now crybaby, crybaby. Archie, ya reckon things comin atcha?' She sits down on the edge of the bed.

'I dunno, Sofie. Whatcha talking about?' He rests his throbbing head on one elbow and cocks his ear in the direction of her voice.

'Like the sun jump outta the sky, no more sun. It gone.'

'Yeah, that's the way things are, Dove. Dark everywhere round us.'

'Sofie can tell ya a thing, Arch.' She attempts a whisper, reaching out to find his hand. 'Sofie got big heart for ya. Can ya know bout that?'

'Yeah, reckon I can,' he answers, knowing she is all that counts. Nothing else matters anymore, he's finished running now.

'Arch be a carin, like a good hoss. Can ya see what Sofie be tellin ya?' She finds his hand and cradles it in hers.

'Suppose that I can. You're not mad at me?' Archie swallows.

She giggles.

'Did Murilla have a yarn to you?' Her cold hands play with his fingers.

'Yeah, Sofie say, Murilla, don't be funny on things that do wrong. No way, fuckerdoodery!'

He can't help himself, Archie laughs loudly. That's her, seeing things the way other people don't.

'Where's Murilla now?' He throws one rickety leg over the side of the bed.

'Gone to the old one. Tooked off real fast.'

'Gone to Missus Drysdale's!' He stumbles about until he finds the wall switch.

'Yippee, that where she go all right.' Sofie smiles at him through crooked teeth.

'Jesus Christ! No, no, she can't. Sofie, when, think when!' Archie stands motionless, taking a deep breath.

'Ah … bout when the sun went for a walk.' She looks at him with confusion.

'About an hour or two ago? I knew I shouldn't have … That's bad, there's gonna be trouble.'

'Ain't nothin ya can do. Whatcha say, Archie?'

'I gotta go over there. I gotta get to her before ...'

'Before the sun get her?'

'No, no, there's ... the old woman.' He holds up his hand to her. 'Stay here. I gotta see the old one.'

'Nope, nope.' She jumps to her feet.

'Ya can't come! No, Sofie, no. I have to see them.' Archie makes for the door.

When Archie arrives at the Drysdale's padlocked gate, he stops and looks across at the house. Everything is in darkness, except for the weak orange glow from the kitchen window. He wonders if he's too late.

As he unlocks the gate he hears a slight noise in the bushes. He swings around, wild fear knocking his heart. 'Who's there?'

The branches part, out steps Sofie.

'Bloody hell! Thought I told ya to stay home!' Archie rages, closing the gate.

She ignores him, turning to face the house. 'Ya reckon Rilly's up there?'

'I hope not. Look, maybe you should go and knock, eh?'

'Sofie knock, Yippee.'

As she takes off towards the light, Archie steps back into the bushes. He watches as she knocks on the door. For a while nobody answers, and he wonders if he's too late. Then the door opens and in a sliver of light from the open doorway he sees Murilla's big frame. He heaves a low sigh of relief and steps out of the shadows to make his way home. Murilla's loud voice cuts through the air, stopping him in his tracks.

'No ya don't,' she yells across at him. 'Come on over.'

Archie makes his way reluctantly across the gravel driveway, wondering with a sick feeling what she's done to Caroline Drysdale. When he gets to the door, she smiles and lets him through.

'Go in there,' she says pointing towards the kitchen. 'And, hey, what are the both of ya doing here?' She looks at him, then Sofie.

'Arh, well, see arh, um ...' Archie doesn't know how to explain himself. *She doesn't look as though she's actually done anything yet.*

'Arch wanna see Rilly do somethin on the old one,' Sofie says, eyes roaming the room.

'What?' Murilla scowls in confusion. 'Now, why would I wanna hurt Caroline?'

'Because of him.' Archie's voice comes out small.

'Because of Donald!' She cocks an eyebrow.

'Something like that ... Revenge.' He stops suddenly when Caroline Drysdale walks into the room. She peers at him with intense concentration.

'Well ... I never ... Archie Corella, isn't it? By George, after all this time! Well, don't just stand there, come into the kitchen everyone. We'll have tea and cake.'

'Hello, Missus Drysdale,' Archie mutters, noting how very old she seems. The past hasn't been good to her; if anything, she's aged years in the short space of time since he's seen her.

She offers him an ambiguous grin. 'Yes, I'm dying,' she states, as though reading his thoughts.

'When?' Sofie goes up and looks into her eyes. 'Yippee, can't see the eyes are dead yet.'

'Sofie! Stop that now!' Murilla chides. 'Sit down n behave. And, Caroline, don't talk bloody nonsense. She's not dying, Archie.'

'Oh,' is all he can answer.

'And to what do I owe the pleasure of this visit?' Caroline directs the question at him.

'Oh, well ...' Archie throws Murilla a glance.

Murilla puts the teapot on the table. 'He's watching Sofie for me and he's just brought her over because she hates the dark. Ain't that right, Archie?'

Archie nods in agreement.

'We're going to the fete next week, Sofie and I. Maybe you'd like to join us, Mister Corella?' Caroline offers.

As Archie watches Caroline Drysdale, he's reminded of that terrible night when all the birds were poisoned. The tangle of bright quivering feathers and twisted claws was something he would never forget.

'Mister Corella, remember the night you found all my birds? When you found My Heart's Desire, the cockatoo?' She looks at him with a faint trace of sadness.

'Oh yeah, I remember.' Archie offers her a lopsided grin. Seems she knows everything he's thinking.

'He poisoned them, you know. It was Murilla that went to war about it. An old woman doesn't have much in life ...' She stops, casts Murilla a glance and says no more.

'Here, drink this.' Murilla hands Archie the tea and a saucer of biscuits.

'They were always like that, you know. All the Drysdale men had a mean streak. Yes, goes back generations. People don't think I know anything about this town, but I do. And I even know what those Red Rose women are!' Caroline bursts out.

'Maybe you should stop right there.' Murilla walks around the table and pulls out a chair to sit beside her.

'Why should I? See, Mister Corella, I was never good enough for them. I was a Hughes to begin with and my parents were considered nothing here. I was a Hughes, yes, always was, and, am proud to say, always will be.

'They tried to get Murilla and Sofie out of town, oh yes, didn't you know about that!'

'Archie doesn't want to hear this,' Murilla puts in, casting an annoyed look at Caroline.

'Tamara Dalmaine, Polly Goodman, all those women on that committee. They went to the Council and told George Featherfew that the house had to be bulldozed because it was an eyesore to the community. The audacity of those women! They always thought they owned this town, ran it like a bunch of skirt-wearing Hitlers!' She laughs, knocking her legs together with glee. 'So, when I heard about what they had planned, well, I went to George and had a quiet word to him. I might be only a Hughes but at that time I *was* a Drysdale.' She stops and takes a small sip of tea.

'All the story, old one. Gorn then.' Sofie giggles behind her hands.

'Now, George wasn't the type of man to do certain things without first consulting his wife. Mary Featherfew happened to be good friends with ...' She comes to a halt throwing Murilla an inviting look.

Murilla gets to her feet and walks around to Archie, bending to whisper, '*Polly Goodman.*'

'Righto, I see,' he says, thinking: *what a strange pair these two are.* But, he's learnt something else tonight. Knows that they don't hate each other. In the glow of the kitchen light, seated among them he wonders to himself if it all has to do with the way Drysdale treated these women. He knows why Donald hated Murilla — she was a thorn in his side, for sure — but your own mother.

'Naturally, she told him, George's wife, that is,' Caroline

plays to the room, 'she told him that she agreed with the ladies from the Red Rose Committee. A report or some such thing was drawn up and handed to Murilla. They told her that if she didn't fix the house, then they'd bulldoze it to the ground! Those ... those ... cows!'

Murilla stands. 'Okay, that's enough for one night.'

Caroline ignores her. 'They didn't beat me, Archie. I got them on that one, Murilla, didn't I?'

'No they didn't beat you. Come along, Caroline, and I'll tuck you in for the night.' Carefully, Murilla lifts her by the arm.

'Archie, Sofie'll be all right here with me. You go on home n have a camp, man. Look like death warmed up.' She shoots him a funny look: *our secret*, her eyes say.

Caroline turns. 'I say, Archie, do be careful. There are people here that will hurt you. They'll take you apart like skinning rind off an orange. Walk with purpose and know your enemies.' She says her piece then leaves the room with Murilla and Sofie by her side.

Sofie shouts, 'Night, Archie Corella.'

'Night all.' Archie gets to his feet and has a last look around. He'll never be back in this house anymore. When he left last time he swore he'd never cross this threshold again, but here he is. A sense of shame overcomes him. Murilla would never hurt Caroline. He wonders if Murilla has told Caroline about Sofie. He thinks not.

But one thing Archie does know is that what happened today somehow brings him closer to understanding the mysterious events of his own life.

\* \* \*

Archie makes his way towards the gate. He passes that little square, white building, his first home in Mundra. His skin crawls as he recalls the nearby shed. Thinking about Donald Drysdale, Archie wonders who else that sorry bastard might've messed with. The town could be full of abused women and children — all at the hands of Drysdale — and none of em would say a word. That's small town life; the shame and guilt would keep his secrets forever buried.

Archie unlatches the gate and peers down the dirt road. For the first time ever, he looks in the other direction. The scrub-lined road appears bright and silvery. The full moon casts an even light across the landscape. Trees jut from the undergrowth, their shadowy heads bowed down as though in mourning. Shrubs hunker in the darkness, their ragged shapes moving gently as a small breeze sneaks through the undergrowth, rustling leaves and rattling branches.

Still feeling anxious and unsettled, Archie decides to take a walk. He heads off in the other direction, the direction he never looks. As he moves along, the distant sound of flowing water increases to a steady murmuring.

Somewhere to the left he picks up the noise of a dog howling. He reaches the end of the road and looks around. To the right he notices a track. Funny, he never heard of any other tracks along this way. He wonders if he should go along it, or if it's part of someone's property. He'd hate to get a bucket of lead thrown at him — it'd happened once before. Yeah, the old bastard took several pot shots at him with a .303.

He decides to chance it; it's more than likely part of Caroline Drysdale's place. With that thought, he makes his way down the track. He gets halfway through the bush and stops for a breather, sitting down on a dead tree branch. His thoughts go back to the women. The best part of him is relieved that all is said and done with em, especially Murilla. But for some reason, a tiny slug of doubt invades his mind. It all goes back to them: Sofie, Missus Drysdale and Murilla. A thought tells him that something is shying away in the shadows, crouching and biding its time. There's nothing that should go wrong from here on in, he *knows* that, but like everything else in his life, sometimes the flow changes, just like the Stewart rushing downstream. It has the strength to pull away the banks at any time. Go against the flow and you're on ya own.

He sighs and gets to his feet in the silvery moonlight. Time to go home, call it a night. Archie walks towards the river, deciding to go along the bank. The sound of the rushing Stewart River fills the night, closing out the shrill of insects. Up in the treetop an owl hoots, wings flutter and branches rustle.

He slows his gait and curses himself for being scared. Something ahead of him is moving on the edge of the darkness. Archie stops, waits for a second and stares hard from side to side; probably only a feral cat or possum, he assures himself, then continues. Suddenly his face flares bright with pain. He puts a hand on the scar, holding the pressure to his face.

It hits him hard.

*Murilla, sofie, caroline drysdale, get em up there, boys, pen em pen em, the steer has broken loose it's out over by the bottom paddock, shear that bastard, clip im, me sister, me sister's eye, me sister, archie, the red rose ladies wanted to bulldoze her out. I luv ya arch, man ya broke her down, man ya broked murilla salte down to nuthin! The baby, sofie I told you that woman's cryin for her baby, kenny austin, kenny austin, he gone missing drowned in the stewart never had a chance, sofie stoled that baby it all amount to kidnapping, gotta lie, mister drysdale he done that to em little ones, messin with they bodies, bad, bad business, ain't normal, ain't normal to treat ya mother like that archie, help me, archie help me, raymond, raymond gee, help me, ya me eye, were lillian gee brought em out this way, lillian n her fancy ways arch, raymond, archie, raymond gee!*

Archie's howl shatters the night air. 'Nnnnnoooooooo-ooo!'

He drops to his knees, head cradled in his sweaty hands, trying to drown out the chanting voices. 'My name's Archie Corella, my name's Archie Corella.' He stops.

There.

There.

They're going.

Fading.

Fading out to nothing.

The voices are weakening off.

Go, that's good, go away.

Archie brings his head up and with small, cautious movements looks around. Images float past his foggy vision. What? What is this? He sees ... a woman? A woman screaming with rage, pelting down towards the water. Archie blinks and opens his eyes to see a man, standing below him on the bank, the woman kneeling before him, her ghost fingers holding something — a fish. *A fish can't be landed.* She tosses her head back, wet hair shining, and laughs, a deep sound that skims across the water. The man throws out his arm and hits her across the mouth. Tears fill Archie's eyes. The woman, no, the fish, she's a fish now, flicks her glistening head and knocks the man into the river. Before he goes under, before he disappears beneath the furious pull of the river, his sickening eyes look across at Archie and his mouth moves: *Not allowed in my work shed, it's my own space.*

As though from some high space above, Archie sees something else. A road. He sees himself walking along it, a hessian swag draped over one shoulder and a billy in hand. Then the road comes to a stop. There's nothing at the end of it except a pitch black curtain of space. He hesitates, one foot nudging the edge of the dirt track. Should he enter the darkness? A raw urge propels him forward. That's when he hears it, a familiar voice: *I love you. I have always loved you.* He reels back, clutching his chest as the old blood roars, rolling like the Devil.

*Whhooowhooowhoo.* Archie opens his eyes at the owl's call. Where is he? A cold dampness spreads down the middle of his chest. He puts his hand under his shirt and touches a wetness. Soaking wet, he's soaking wet! How ...?

Feeling light-headed and sick, he struggles to his feet. He had a dream? No, a nightmare? His mind was playing tricks again, only this time worse than ever before.

Somewhere in the back of his mind the roots of fear entangle him. The voices and images could well be a part of something larger, something decayed within his mind — madness even. What is all this strangeness that belts into him?

As he walks limply towards home, an invisible weight crouches on his tired shoulders. When he reaches his house he doesn't enter, but pulls out a chair from the corner of the verandah and crumples into it.

Archie thinks about the river, about those phantom people. Somehow it makes sense to him. It all feels the way it should feel, yet that in itself makes no sense at all. As his mind churns out all the possibilities, a name comes to him, leaping forth like chalk on a blackboard: *Raymond Gee.*

He knows that name, can feel it in the bottom of his

aching heart, yet can't put a face to it. He lets it pass, puts it away to that other place that keeps all the confusion and pain, that part that shies away. Heaving himself up, he places the chair against the wall, and has one last look at the street.

He tells himself that if he walks down three houses, turns left to Purcell Street, then looks across to the river, he'd find what he's been looking for. He's never walked in that direction in all the time he's been in town, yet he knows without a doubt the final answer is down the dirt road.

He must go there.

## eleven

# the devil in caroline's kitchen

'I can't see what this is gonna prove.' Murilla's voice is loud, her back turned to Caroline as she runs the iron over a frock.

'Probably nothing, but, then again, maybe I'll run into some old friends.' Caroline selects a tube of lipstick and carefully shades her lips.

Murilla turns. 'Who? Now, tell me who. What old friends, Caroline?'

'Oh, people I know.' Caroline turns away and bothers with her hair.

'I don't like it. You're wasting your time, you know that don't ya?'

'*Am I?*' She cocks her eyebrows, purses her tinted lips and shrugs. 'You would know, would you?'

'Don't start, now don't you start this up! Yeah, I do know!'

'Oh what a sour puss! How the hell would you know who my friends are?' A dark scowl crosses Caroline's face.

'Oh no, I wouldn't know anything, would I? I oughta

take this frock and put it back where it came from. That's right, put it back to stop you from doing something that I know is gonna cause a lot of trouble. It'll all end up like the way it always did. I'm sick, sick to death of tryin to tell ya!'

'Salte, you're a pain at times. The one time I want to go into town, and you have to ruin it for me. You're just like them!' Caroline's face flushes a pale shade of pink against the plastic red of her lips.

'I know it ain't fair.' Murilla tries to placate her. 'Come on, I didn't mean it that way. Ya know what they're like. Maybe ya have something else in mind, do ya?' Murilla drapes the frock over a chair then walks over to her.

'No, I don't. But maybe we could bake some lamingtons, pies and scones to take in, eh?' Caroline gives a guilty smile.

'Cakes! Lamingtons! Caroline, for who and what?' *This again.* 'You'll never give up, just won't accept it at all, will ya?'

'For the fete. Maybe I could enter them in the contest. You know, the Red Rose Committee's cooking competition.' Caroline turns her attention to the window.

'It won't work, not now and not then. They ain't gonna let you in, that's that. For Chrissake, *I'd* have a better chance of getting on their shitty little committee than you, Caroline Drysdale.'

'Oh nonsense. No, this is how things are, they'll see how helpful I can be. I might even start a fund-raising charity in the Drysdale name. That's sure to impress them, too.'

'They won't see anything. Nope, they wouldn't give a piss to the wind for anything you do, Caroline. Listen, for the last time, let this go. You're driving me mad!'

Murilla returns to the ironing board, spits on the iron and grabs at another dress. She feels the sour taste of disappointment in her mouth.

Turning back from her view onto the garden, Caroline declares, 'Now, when you go to town bring back some icing sugar, flour and eggs — not the ones from Bluey's, go over and get some fresh ones from Vida Derrick's. Hmm, let's see then, get a small carton of fresh cream. Ah, yes, that'll do for today.' She gazes up at the ceiling, unable to meet Murilla's eyes.

'Waste of time. Total waste of time!' Murilla glares at her.

'Right you are then. Get the money out of my purse. Now, no tricks, Murilla. I want those ingredients and that's that. If you don't return with them then I don't care. I'll pick them up when I go in this afternoon.' Caroline grins: *There, you see how clever an old woman can be.*

'No more. This is the last time I'm ever gonna do this! The very last time, I mean it, Caroline!'

'Okay, okay, no need to get excited, Murilla.'

'All right then. But hear me good: last bloody time, Caroline Drysdale!' Murilla unplugs the iron. 'Now, you'll be right until I get back?'

'Do hurry, Murilla. I don't have a lot of time to bake all those things.' Caroline turns back to the window.

\* \* \*

Murilla walks out the front door, thinking of Sofie, Drysdale, Caroline, the Red Rose women and Archie Corella. Her thoughts veer to Sofie.

*Drysdale was a huge man, strong and dangerous. Sofie just don't have the strength, don't add up. How can I live with the possibility that Sofie done something to Donald Drysdale?*

Murilla's mind races. She wouldn't put anything past

Caroline, either. Seems there's a lot going on and Murilla Salte's always the last to find out. Well, she muses, as long as it stays with Corella, there ain't a lot anyone can do. Except that don't solve the problem of Sofie. An unhappy realisation dawns on her. *She needs help with Sofie, and soon.*

As she walks along the road she glances across at the river. *He's in there, down in the mud. Someone, somewhere would have eventually brought Donald Drysdale down.*

She walks up to the embankment and looks down at the eddying, coffee-coloured water. It doesn't look so frightening in the daylight. She goes down the slope, her feet sliding as she descends. When she reaches the bottom she turns and looks around. Where was it? Where did he go in? She searches the ground, looking for anything that might belong to Sofie. Tears begin without warning and a deep sadness crowds her heart, her body folds down slowly on the damp bank. Where did I go wrong? Maybe it was mother's death that set it in motion — drove Sofie over the edge. A flush of guilt courses through her. She wonders, could it have something to do with Andrew Murray and the time he bashed her and Sofie? The night Sofie raced to Caroline and told her what happened? That same night Treacle Simpson turned up and drove Andrew off.

She knows it was Caroline Drysdale who sent Treacle over. Thinking of her makes Murilla despair. Caroline ain't ever gonna win the Red Rose ladies over.

\* \* \*

Murilla remembers the summer of 1982, the year after Polly Goodman had turned up at the Drysdale house for a dinner party and been caught with Reginald going at it in the hallway.

That year was the worst in the entire time she'd been

working there. Caroline had a crazy idea that if she baked enough cakes and made new friends, the Red Rose ladies would finally invite her onto the committee.

That summer was a stinker with temperatures soaring to the high forty degrees. All throughout town people tried to keep cool. Some swam in the Council pool and others just sat in the shade under garden hoses. And if that wasn't bad enough, the red dust would fly in from the flats, covering houses, washing and town people alike. The windstorms got so fierce people even swore the wind burnt their faces. If you happened to go outside barefoot and stepped on the cement or bitumen, the soles of your feet would burn as though they'd been torched with a flame.

Young and old hid in the shade of trees. Some people even refused to move from their houses for fear of heatstroke.

It was Mundra weather — cold as ice in winter, hot as hell in summer. But over in the Drysdale house the Devil had parked in Caroline Drysdale's kitchen.

Every day from morning to noon Murilla lit up the wood stove and piled blocks of wood in the burning furnace, keeping it as hot as possible. The kitchen was an inferno. Sometimes Murilla could see heatwaves dancing up from the table and the floor. Even the fridge felt hot to the touch. Murilla would have lost a stone or two just by sweating. And this happened every day.

Caroline would bake, fry, cut, julienne, stew — anything and everything. Her mission was to create something no one else had thought of. This was her idea for getting onto the Red Rose Committee. Fresh eggs were ordered from Nana Vida, fruit was brought in from Bluey's straight off the truck and the milk was directly from old man Cleaver's milker. There were new recipe books: French,

Asian, Chinese and just about every other cuisine that had books devoted to it. For hours, days, weeks she'd slave over them, occasionally asking Murilla's opinion: 'Do you think they'd like this one? Do you think that eggs would be too heavy for this cake, this scone? Do you have a recipe?'

Murilla observed all this with a creeping sense of dread. But it was never enough for Caroline. It was as though she was searching for that one 'special' recipe — one that didn't exist for her already.

Finally, wearied by Caroline's frenzied emotion and obsessive searching, Murilla decided to give her a recipe, one she knew Caroline would never have come across before. At first it was more of a joke than anything else. Murilla wrote it down and handed the folded piece of paper to Caroline.

Caroline glanced up from the Asian cookbook. 'What's this?'

'Um, well, since you're so mad on trying to find something that no one else can have, or cook, I thought this might help.' A small smile played at Murilla's mouth. She really didn't think that Caroline would bother.

Caroline, looking puzzled, opened the paper.

*Kangaroo Fillet with Orange Sauce*
1 x $1/4$ pound kangaroo fillet
$1/2$ cup port
$1/2$ jar raspberry jam
$1/2$ cup orange juice
$1/3$ cup red wine vinegar
2 chillies sliced
1 cup beef stock
*Cook the Roo Fillets (in an open pan) to medium rare with a small amount of butter and oil and allow to rest. Place the Port, Jam,*

*Orange Juice and Vinegar in a saucepan and simmer slowly until consistency is that of a syrup. Now add the stock to the syrup and simmer until reduced to sauce, then add the Chillies and re-boil prior to serving with the Roo Fillets.*

Caroline drew her brows together with a look of absorption. 'Okay, so what does kangaroo taste like?' she queried, looking down at the crumpled paper.

'Let's see ... um ... It's a tender, red meat, much like rabbit, but sweeter. Good tucker, for sure.' Murilla smiled.

'I doubt any of these Red Rose women would have come across anything like this. It's original and has a certain appeal. And it tastes like rabbit, huh? As crazy as all this sounds, perhaps you're onto something here, Murilla. Being as desperate as I am, I'm willing to try anything once. Okay, when do we start?' She folded the paper into a neat square then shoved it into her apron pocket.

'Well, if ya really want to ... I mean, it was sort of a joke, you know,' Murilla shrugged. She didn't expect Caroline to take it seriously.

'Well, it's backfired on you. Now, if you can get those ingredients together, then we can begin. Oh, this is the one, I can just feel it in my bones!' Caroline laughed wildly, delight written across her face.

After seeing Treacle Simpson, who in little time found a kangaroo, Murilla trotted in through the back door with her 'special' ingredient. Caroline jumped up eagerly from the chair, rushed at Murilla and grabbed the newspaper-wrapped parcel from her.

Caroline looked at Murilla with big, expectant eyes. 'This is it?'

'That's it. All ready for the pan. Now, sit those fillets down here and we'll begin.'

Caroline opened the parcel and plonked the fillets on the table, eyeing the meat warily. For a moment her features screwed into a look of repulsion. 'It looks like steak but …'

Murilla laughed. 'Mightn't look too flash but good to eat!' She reached across the table for the chillies. 'Here, slice these.'

The women worked quickly side by side. Finally, Murilla stood back and declared: 'That's good, now we'll put it into the pan.'

After cleaning the kitchen, the women sat down and had a cup of tea and a biscuit. Caroline had a serious expression on her face, one of her I've-got-a-good-plan looks. 'Murilla, I might have a dinner party tonight, what do you think?' She smoothed down the hem of her dress.

'Yeah …?'

'Thinking I might just invite the Red Rose ladies over for a bite to eat. Why, yes! Yes, I will. Hmm, now when they ask me what they are eating, what do I say?'

Murilla shook her head. 'Oh no, Caroline … um … is that the right thing to do? I mean, what if they ever find out?'

'They won't, trust me. Now, think what I'll tell them.'

'Tell em that it's, um, it's um …' Murilla shrugged. 'I dunno.'

'Imported! Yes, that's it, imported meat! I'm sure they wouldn't know any better. Our little joke, Salte.' Caroline put a finger to her nose.

That night, the Red Rose ladies turned up on the doorstep, dressed to kill and ready to take Caroline Drysdale apart with their sharp tongues. Murilla met them at the door. Polly Goodman and Tamara Dalmaine were the first to arrive. Polly threw her long nose into the air and sniffed. 'Smells lovely, Caroline,' she said, as Murilla led her to the dining room.

'Smells like ... like steak.' Tamara wrinkled her perfectly made-up face.

'We'll have to wait and see, Tamara. It's a big surprise.' Caroline winked mischievously at Murilla.

Five minutes later, Gwen Artbuckle and Libby Purcell arrived and swept through the door in a cloud of perfume, leaving a trail of mud on the carpet.

'Bloody bitches,' Murilla muttered under her breath.

When everyone took their seats, Murilla poured each one a glass of red wine and passed the peppercorn pâté around. When she finished arranging everything, decorating the fillets, buttering the paper thin slices of damper, she walked out to the dining room, a wild laugh bubbling in the back of her throat. She wondered if they would know any different.

'Here we go, Missus Drysdale.' Murilla uncovered the carefully arranged slices of kangaroo fillet and stepped back with a wide smile.

The women all bent forward in their chairs, eyeing off the food and casting each other tiny glances. Finally, a wavy *whhhoooo* went around the table. They were impressed.

Murilla's lips twitched as she watched Tamara nudge Polly in the ribs, her mouth moving slightly. Murilla strained to hear what they said, but was distracted when Libby Purcell asked for another glass of wine.

'So, who else has applied for a position on the committee?' Caroline regarded each of them.

'Oh, no one in particular. But you're the first one on our agenda this week.' Tamara tittered, as she slyly glanced at Libby.

Polly took a delicate sip of wine, then enquired, 'How's Reginald holding up?'

Murilla knew what Polly was doing. She recalled the night of the last disastrous party, when Reginald had deliberately bumped into her so that she fell and the soup landed on Caroline. That was another thing she hadn't told Caroline: her husband was having an affair with Polly Goodman. Caroline had worked that one out for herself.

'As good as can be, I guess.' Caroline's eyes narrowed.

'Fine man, lovely man. You're so lucky, Caroline. Yes, you've done well.'

'Speaking of Reg, is he away?'

'Business trip or some such thing. Here we go, please help yourselves.' As the women piled the food onto their plates, a silence fell on the room. It was as though they all were weighing everything up: the shape of the plates, the cut of the meat.

Murilla waited patiently with her heart in her mouth. Libby took the first bite of meat, chewed slowly then exclaimed, 'I say, Caroline, that's the best cut of meat I've had in years!' By the tone of her voice Murilla knew she was sincere. Carefully drawn eyebrows were raised in disbelief.

After the meal was finished, Murilla brought in a tray with port and coffee. She smiled at each of them: you just ate kangaroo! She'd have loved to voice her thoughts and seen the looks on their snooty faces. She looked over at Caroline, who was looking at the women with cunning eyes.

Tamara began, 'We should discuss Caroline's application.' She gripped the port glass tightly in her elegant, manicured fingers.

'Um ... I don't believe we can be so hasty, Tamara. I

mean, we have all the other women to consider, too.' Libby looked annoyed as she fiddled with her pearl necklace.

'I say, Caroline, where on earth did you get that brilliant cut of meat!' Polly offered a smile — foxy and fake.

'Oh that! Well, now, that's my little secret. I'll tell you this much: you'll never be able to get meat like that in a butcher's shop. Oh no, it's imported. I have a woman in the city that arranges everything for me. It's very, very expensive and few people actually know of it.' Caroline smiled, her fingers drumming on the table.

'That was an extraordinary meal, Caroline, you have really outdone yourself this time!' Gwen exclaimed. 'Now ladies, we really should discuss Caroline's application.'

As Murilla watched them she knew what they were going to say — the same thing they've said for years — but it didn't lessen the hurt. It was the way those women went about it that sickened Murilla. Dressing Caroline up just to cut her down again. And as cunning and mean as Caroline could be, she never really tried it with them. Murilla stepped back against the doorway. She waited with a sour taste in her mouth. *It was all happening again.*

Tamara hesitated for a moment, and with apparent disappointment said, 'Unfortunately, Caroline, I really don't think you can join this year. Don't lose hope, there's always next year.'

'But you have come along, and that's the important thing, isn't it Libby?' Gwen wriggled on her seat, her face showing a faint tinge of pink.

'Oh yes, I agree whole-heartedly! You're showing promise, Caroline, and that's part of the *importance* of being a Red Rose lady.' Polly's voice dripped with false promise.

To see Caroline then was like looking at a photograph

that's been left out in the rain. Everything washed away slowly, her face fell back in, her eyes watered and her lips trembled. For a moment the whole room wrapped itself around Caroline. Not a word was spoken, nobody moved. The Red Rose women threw sneaky looks at each other and Polly's face was a picture of triumph and gloating. They had torn Caroline Drysdale down like a piece of stained linen hanging on the clothes line.

Caroline Hughes wasn't fit to be in their company. Caroline Hughes had married a Drysdale. And for this every single one of them punished her.

As they got up to leave, smoothing down their dresses and smiling vaguely at Caroline, a thought crossed Murilla's mind. She led them towards the door, the gravy pitcher still in her hand.

'Keep a good watch on her, Murilla. She's not ...' Polly pointed to the side of her head, '... all there, if you know what I mean.' She grinned: see what a good person I am to tell you this!

'Oh, really!' Murilla's hand flew across her chest, pure shock registering on her face.

'You didn't know!' Libby whispered in a fierce, disbelieving tone.

Tamara gasped. 'All the Hughes had that in them. Madness. Yes, Murilla, they all had a problem or two. Her parents were crazy as old man Cleaver!'

'Goes back it does, right from Lucinda and Barry Hughes, that's why they never really fit in the town. At least you *know* your place, Murilla.' Gwen gushed, her spite-green eyes opening wide with apparent goodwill.

Murilla's stomach curdled. 'Yeah,' she muttered, disgusted.

'Right then we are. Here, Murilla, help me into my coat.' Polly turned around.

Murilla grabbed the coat from the wall hook and then tripped herself forward, right into Polly's back. Hot sauce drenched her and Polly dropped to her knees, squealing and pawing the air with pain and shock. Tamara swung on Murilla, 'You stupid bitch!' she shouted, her face a mottled scarlet as she moved towards Murilla.

Gwen raged, 'God damn hopeless cow!'

'Useless, useless. Bloody stupid woman!' Libby hissed, mouth twisted, eyes gleaming wildly.

Murilla turned. 'Who the hell are you! You all make me sick! Coming here like a bunch of high bitin bitches! I got news for you and that's ya can all go to fucken hell n back!' Murilla made a move at Tamara, her body quivering all over.

A second later Caroline came out into the hall. 'What in God's name!' She looked from Murilla to the women. Realisation etched itself slowly into her features.

Caroline put out a hand. 'Murilla, are you okay?'

'Yeah,' Murilla uttered, nodding at Polly's crumpled form.

'Oh dear, a nasty little accident. Well, hop to your feet, Polly, I'm sure that you'll survive.' Caroline smiled at the group then walked away, a soft laugh trailing her.

'I'll never forget this, Murilla,' Polly spat, as the women gathered around and led her sauce-splattered, indignant figure through the door.

'Neither will I!' Murilla screamed.

There was never to be another dinner party in the Drysdale house.

Later on that night, after Murilla cleaned everything up and was ready to leave for home she heard Caroline's bitter sobbing coming from the bedroom. Murilla left her to it. She'd had enough of all of them, even Caroline.

Three weeks later the Council threatened to bulldoze Murilla's house down. All the Red Rose ladies gathered force against her. That was supposed to be her lesson. They never succeeded, of course. But then, there seemed to be a lot of people doing a lot of things at that time, all aimed at revenge. It was in the Drysdale house when everything finally came to an explosive end. As Murilla knew it would.

It was about a month after the dinner party, Reginald had smashed Caroline's photo frame of Josephine Rose, that he finally got his dues paid in full. At that time, Murilla knew he was on all sorts of tablets, just as Caroline was.

Reginald was a thorough man. Nothing happened by mistake, ever. He was obsessive about anything and everything. Even the floor rugs had to be positioned just right and the bed linen starched until stiff.

All the while Murilla worked he watched her with close, crafty eyes. Looking out of the window on wash days, hanging around the lounge room when she tidied up, appearing behind her in the kitchen unexpectedly.

But it was the day he came back from town that Caroline and Murilla felt the full force of his rage.

They had just finished putting the edges on one of Caroline's crocheted rugs and were sitting down to a cup of tea, when he charged into the living room, his face blood-stained. He panted and puffed for a second or two then looked at each of them with murderous eyes.

'You, woman, are a bloody disgrace!' he bellowed at Caroline, moving at her, hands curled into tight fists.

'What? Reg, what?' She cowered into her chair, her face pale with expectant dread.

'You hire this ... this ... this here! And what does she do! Pours gravy all over Polly Goodman!'

Murilla shrank back from his deadly rage.

'I ... I ... Reg, what are you talking about?' Caroline's lower lip quivered.

Reginald's jaw tightened with fury. He grabbed Caroline by the shoulders and shook her violently. 'You know damn well what I'm talking about!'

Murilla got up from her chair, legs feeble from fear. She faced him. 'Um ... um ... Mister ... Drysdale ... it was ... It was an accident.' She could barely string words together.

'No. I know what it is. It's called low breeding. Yes, that's right, Caroline Hughes, low breeding.' Then he turned on Murilla. 'As for you! Well, you can't help your stupidity, it's inbred! Your employment here is finished, you bloody incompetent!' he yelled with such vehemence that Murilla stumbled back.

Then he stormed out of the room, hurling the freshly finished rug at Murilla's feet. Murilla turned to Caroline, eyes downcast. 'That's it, eh. Maybe it was a stupid thing to do. Sorry, Caroline, seems I got ya in all sorts of strife now.'

'No, Murilla, don't apologise, please.' Caroline's voice regained strength.

'What you did was the right thing to do given the circumstances. How many times have I wanted to do the same thing? Reginald is just Reginald. I've put up with his spiteful, cruel behaviour for years. Oh, I don't know, Salte, but his image to others is more important than me, you or anyone else.

'They've always been that way, the Drysdales. They are the lords of Mundra. They control everything, including their staff and wives. I've made my bed, Murilla, now I must lie on it.'

'Ya don't have to ... Leave, you *can* leave ya know. You don't have to put up with that all the time! Caroline, he might hurt you bad and I won't be here for ya.'

'I can't leave. That's the thing, I can't go anywhere. Where would someone like me go? Nowhere.' She stooped and collected the rug.

'Now what am I gonna do? He's sacked me!'

'Never mind, Murilla. Some situations have a way of working out. As for you being sacked, well, I wouldn't pay no mind to that. You didn't come here to work for him.' She smiled mysteriously as she folded the rug. 'Things happen, Murilla, happen every day to old people that forget.'

Murilla took Caroline's word and stayed on. Later in the afternoon, after Murilla had just brought the washing in from the line, she noticed Caroline hanging around Reginald's bedroom door.

She saw an ugly, purplish-blue bruise covering Caroline's forehead. Murilla didn't say anything because she knew what had happened. Caroline had been punished for something that she did. Murilla, not wanting Caroline to know that she was watching, stepped back behind the linen closet and peered curiously as Caroline glanced from one end of the hallway to the other. She just didn't seem *right*.

Then, with a wily swiftness Murilla never knew Caroline possessed, she stepped into the room. Minutes later, Caroline crept back out, clutching a brown bottle in her hands.

By this time, Murilla was very concerned. She wondered if Caroline had stolen Reginald's medication to take herself. How many times had Caroline threatened to kill herself? Maybe this time she actually meant to do it.

Placing the basket of washing on the floor, Murilla made to go after Caroline when suddenly Reginald's bedroom door swung wide open.

Her first thoughts were that he was so angry he was going after Caroline. Wrong. Reginald staggered forward and fell against the wall. His hands clutched his chest and his face swelled into a red mask.

A shivery realisation hit Murilla: he was having a heart attack. She barged forward dropping to her knees, trying to sit him against the wall. It made no difference. Panic-stricken, she tore down the hallway and into Caroline's room. Panting with urgency she stood before Caroline. 'Jeesus! Get up! Get up! He's having a heart attack in the bloody hallway!' she shouted, heart pounding like a jackhammer.

Then, to Murilla's horrified disbelief, Caroline cocked an eyebrow and just said: 'Oh, well, suppose you should get an ambulance over.'

Murilla walked closer. *What? Did I hear right?* She wondered if it was all some sick joke, if Caroline had gone crazy in those seconds before she came to the bedroom. It took a few moments for her to realise Caroline was dead serious and wasn't going to help. She just didn't care. And all the while Reginald lay dying out in the hallway.

Finally, when Murilla could move, she sped back to his side. But by the time she got there he had stopped breathing and his face was ashen-grey.

He'd died in the few seconds she'd been gone. When

Murilla looked down at him and studied his face, suspicion rose through the confusion and panic. *Did he take the wrong medication? Did Caroline swap bottles? Mix his tablets?*

It was later on, when the ambulance came and took his body away, that Murilla confronted Caroline.

She was in her usual spot, reading, smoking and eating chocolates, when Murilla barged into her room. In all the time Murilla had worked for Caroline, there was one thing she knew: Caroline never smoked. As Murilla watched her, she knew without a doubt that Caroline had something to do with the awful turn of events.

Fury raced through her. 'Caroline, what have you done?'

'Huh, what on earth are you talking about?' Caroline offered a cool smile.

The sweat rolled down Murilla's burning face. 'You swapped his tablets, didn't ya?'

'Tablets, whose tablets? Salte, are you okay? Must say, woman, you don't look too good.' Then Caroline laughed, laughed so hard that tears rolled down her bruised cheeks.

In all the time Murilla had known Caroline Drysdale, not once did she suspect that something was wrong. But that day, Murilla began to doubt. At that moment, as she watched Caroline, she knew she was looking at a seriously desperate woman. It chilled her blood.

Murilla's breathing slowed. 'Do you care that he's dead?' She sat on the edge of the bed and watched closely.

'He's dead?' Caroline shrugged, putting a hand to her pale, bruised face.

'Dead. Dead as he'll ever be. I know what you've done. I saw you, didn't I! Yeah, that's right, Caroline, I watched you go into his room. I saw you come back out with a bottle!'

'So you're upset now, are you?' Caroline tipped her head in a gesture of indifference.

'You ... you ... but why? Why do this?' Murilla felt a deep weariness in her bones.

As she gazed silently at Caroline she realised that of all the things she had witnessed in the Drysdale house, there were plenty more things she didn't ever see.

'Murilla, you believe what you will. Just remember, things can happen to people all the time. Things happen to good people. I've washed my hands of it all. Reg was so stupid to take the wrong tablets — that's his undoing. I was in his room to drop off the full bottle that Doctor Sheffield left him. That's it, nothing more!' She opened her book and began to read.

Murilla never knew the whole truth, but she always suspected that Caroline did swap the bottles.

After all, both Reginald and Donald had tormented her and Caroline for years and they had lived with their hate as best they could. In the back of Murilla's mind, she still thinks: *Reginald deserved everything he got.*

\* \* \*

As Murilla walks along the dirt road, she lets the memories fade out, and sits down on a fallen log. She's in no hurry to get the ingredients for Caroline's bloody cake.

She catches her breath while casting a glance across to the other side of the Stewart River. For a minute the sun blinds her eyes. She shades one hand across them and tries to make out the shadowy thing moving in the bushes. She stands for a better view.

Lurching and stumbling along, a branch in one hand and his hat in the other, is Archie Corella. Murilla wonders if he's drunk or having one of his turns. She knows that if he goes any closer to the water he might fall in and drown. She walks nearer to the edge of the bank.

'Archie, Archie, over here, man!' She waves her hands. He swings around wildly, and for a horrifying second she sees the look on his face. Stark terror. He throws himself back into the undergrowth with a shrill scream.

Panic grips her. *Can I swim across? The man's in trouble. He's ... He's? Something ain't right.* she looks down into the water. She's frozen to the spot — she can't do it. There's a dead man in there.

'Wait! Wait! I'm coming!' she hollers, tearing off into the bushes towards the other end of the road.

She hears noises coming up from the far side of the bank, distant like the echoing of voices crying out into emptiness. She ignores them and keeps going, running as fast as she can.

Towards the old dirt road.

# twelve

# sofie do that thing

Sofie crouches back in the bushes, eyes narrow, as she looks over at the neat, cream-and-tan-trimmed house perched by the footpath — Polly Goodman's. She screws her face into a tight grimace and looks across at the flower beds.

She squats lower when she spots Ron Goodman at the window. Her mind races, *gotta creep along like a spider to that ol car shed. Uh oh! Car comin up the driveway! Move, move, move!*

She puts a finger into her mouth and chews on the already bitten-to-the-quick fingernail until she feels a sharp stab of pain. Her bottom lip quivers. She knows the hateful car coming up the drive belongs to Tamara Dalmaine. Her mind churns. *It were Tamara that wanted to doze Murilla n Sofie outta they house — they mother's house, that one she loved, that one she gave up to Rilly n Sofie before the big man he called her up.*

Sofie sits back on her haunches, heart heavy as she begins to softly chant, her voice breaking as she strains to remember the words of a tune from long ago.

*That summer we had mylovemylove*
*Then you had to go away*
*Tears of sorrow that I have shed for ya mylovemylovemylove*

Then the voice comes, the loud, nasty voice.
*Sofie whatcha reckon bout that high bitchin piece*
*She a bad one*
*Taking things away from Rilly n Sofie, the house, mother's house*
*Things don't happen lest ya make em ya got a kettle to boil boil it*

The hot rage creeps up on her. 'Arh shuddup! Can't fuckerdoodery when fellahs at home! Sofie gotta stop that Polly one bein mad at her,' she hisses at the bushes.

*Just gut it along already gone whatcha scaredy bubby or something crybubbycrybubby got her knickers in a twist eehh*

Sofie starts crawling slowly towards the car shed. When she reaches the shed, she stands up, tries the door and slips in. Against the far wall is a lawnmower and a tin of petrol. She goes to the tin, looks down at it and frowns. Ideas tell her many things. She picks up the tin, unscrews the cap and splashes the fuel on the mower engine. *Sofie mow the yard, Polly mad be gorn. Come on giddyap ... How to ...? Ah yeah, gotta put some fire in the mower ... gotta get it movin.* Sofie looks around the room, *There! Box a matches.* Whoosshh! Whoosshh! The room explodes, the crimson-yellow blaze leaps forth, licking the walls, snatching at the curtains. The shed is alive with heat and smoke.

Sofie falls back. *The fire gonna eat Sofie! Oh nnoo ... Run, you run, rabbit.*

She tears out of the shed, a shrill scream rising in her throat as she beats desperately at the creeping flames on her clothes. She rips open the top half of her shirt, the flaming fabric coming apart in her hands. Panting hard, not yet feeling the pain, Sofie crawls back into the bushes and watches the flame-engulfed shed. *Sofie scaredy. Ouch ... ooww Sofie's skin burnin.*

Suddenly a yell comes from the driveway. The fire brigade truck pulls to a screeching halt and men jump out, shouting orders as they run to the blazing shed.

Sofie shivers and bites down hard on her tongue. She feels the bad dreams coming. *What ya done there dove? Bad bad dove.* She cradles her head in her hands and smells the burnt flesh of her fingers.

She clenches her charred fists tightly, feeling a familiar shuddery emotion. Her heart thuds a terrible rhythm of terror as a warm trickle runs down her legs. Then other voices reach her.

'Started in the shed, didn't it?'

'Yeah, then it must have caught onto one of the curtains, then burnt up the wall.'

'There you go, can never be too careful with fire. Nope, as I said to Dave the other day, this weather is perfect for fires. Everything being so bloody dry and all.'

'That's Mundra for you, worst weather in the country!'

'This is a terrible thing to poor Polly. What is she going to do?'

'For a start they'll have to think about building another house. I believe that one is well past saving. Oohh, step back, Bertha, those flames are getting close!'

'Here comes Warner. Wonder what he'll make of it all?'

'Nothing. It must have, well ... It could have been one of Ron's lawn mower tins that exploded. Happens all the time, especially with this heat.'

'Why, it was only three days ago that Minnie Purcell

had one of her stove's electrical wires short out. Almost started a fire in the kitchen!'

'Tamara! Tamara, over here, luv!'

'Oh hello, Davidson, Betty, Doreen. Dreadful situation, isn't it? What are we to do?'

'Come on, Tamara, there's nothing you can possibly do now. You're too good-hearted, that's your problem. Always worried about other people. Now, here, sit down on the grass and I'll pop inside and get you a chair.'

'Thanks, Davidson.'

'Well, looks like we'll have to have a charity drive next for poor Ron and Polly. They've lost everything. Betty, Doreen, you'll have to come over next week so that we can all arrange something for them. If we can get enough money together, enough to set them up anyway, just for a while, until they can get back on their feet.'

'Look, Tamara, I've got that house over on Mary Street. They're more than welcome to stay there for as long as they please.'

'I'm sure they'll appreciate that, Davidson. The best thing we can do as a community is to rally behind them, let them know they have our support.'

'Look, there's Polly! Polly, over this way!'

'She doesn't look too well, does she, Betty?'

'You wouldn't either if your house burnt down.'

'I say, did anyone happen to see that funny girl from Purcell Street here about an hour ago?'

'What girl, Doreen?'

'That strange Salte girl. What's her name, Betty?'

'Murilla, I think.'

'No, no that's not her. Murilla's the big one. The other one with that bloody crazy white hair. The slow one.'

'That'd be ... um ... oh what's her name! Sofie, that's it! Sofie Salte.'

'Bit slow in the head isn't she, Davidson?'

'Mental age of a kid. Gives me the creeps that woman — well, both of them do actually.'

'Doesn't the big one work for the old Drysdale woman, Tamara?'

'Caroline Drysdale. Yes, Murilla works for her, has done for years. She's a right pain in the you-know-what, too. See that shack those Salte women live in? It's an eyesore isn't it? We tried to have it demolished, my oath we did!'

'How come the council didn't do anything about it? Disgrace is what it is.'

'Well ... Davidson, that Drysdale woman stuck her nose in, as usual. No, as I said to the other ladies, it's not fair on the decent people around here to have to go past that disgraceful sight and be reminded of that sort of filth. Pity it wasn't *that* thing that burnt down! As I was saying, did anyone happen to see that Salte girl here?'

'Come to think of it, I did see someone in Polly's shed, but thought it might have been Ron.'

'Didn't Polly catch her peeing on the flowerbed the other day?'

'Oh yes! Polly said that when she told her to dig all the ruined flowers out, she almost hit Polly over the head with the shovel!'

'Betty, did you actually see her in the shed?'

'Well, Tamara, I was at the kitchen window, looking out, peeling spuds for supper, when I happen to notice that girl loping along the road here. Talking to herself, she was, talking and laughing.'

'Oh, come on, Tamara, surely you don't think she would have deliberately lit that fire, do you?'

'They're strange people, Davidson, and I wouldn't put anything past them. Especially that girl and after what she did to Polly's garden. Polly was getting it ready for the hospital fete, was going to enter it into the garden competition. She was so distressed about it all. Bawled like a baby.'

'Polly should have gone over to the sister and made her replace those plants! Who do they think they are?'

\* \* \*

Sofie huddles silently, body blistering with pain. She looks down at her mottled chest. A pink trail of burnt skin has spread across her stomach and breasts. Her ears ache.

'They bad talk bout Sofie n sister. What Sofie do?'

*Sit there n shut ya gob is the thing to do*

*Might be a good idea to get under that bush cos they smell ya shit n piss then whatcha gonna do then shame people seein Sofie with shit all ova it proper shame*

'Sofie can't help that thing Ya shud up!'

*Only bubbys shit emselves*

*Owwwhh crybubbycrybubbycrybubby missus sooky cucky pants gonna cry cos she pissed n shit herself oh now what sorta thing is that*

Sofie hits out at the bushes. 'Shut ya fuckerdoodery! Mixin me head like a cake ... pplleeaaassee shuddup!'

*Eyes gotta be peeld on ya at all times*

'Fucken shitty shit talk! talkin bout eyes! What ya know bout that!'

*That's where ya wrong DOVE I know eyes like the back a me hand n rilly ya eye ya be sorry ass hoss when she get hold a ya told ya not to mess bout that she did no sooky girl cant get it in her headbusted head!*

'Lookat ya make Sofie doin! Stop that. Stop that!'

*Boohoo n all that jazz gone then cry it all outcha system ya is lettin peekaboo puttin his hands on ya wee wee what sorta Sofie is ya a dirty Sofie that what lettin em hand fiddle n can't say ya didn't like that old pink snake gone then put it in ya mouth*

*kill murilla kill ya friend kill ya if ya talk*

*Shhhhhhhhhssssss our secret*

*Ya can't have a bubby*

'I wanna bubby'

*No bubby*

'Hey there, stop that now! Em women are lookin ova this here way!'

Sofie too scaredy. Back, back in the bush, now! Listen close to em.

\* \* \*

'Maybe, you should go over and tell Warner what you saw, Betty.'

'You think so, Tamara?'

'Oh yes, if this is that girl's doing then it amounts to arson. Go on, go and see him.'

'Yes, but I didn't actually see her with matches or anything.'

'Go and see him, Betty, otherwise I'll call him over and tell him.'

'Tamara, I just don't want to get involved!'

'Betty, the whole town's involved when someone deliberately sets fire to someone's home. How do you think Polly and Ron are feeling at this moment? Get moving, the town depends upon you.'

'I say, Davidson, do you think you should go over and take a look around at Purcell Street? To see if that Salte girl is there. The eldest one will be at Drysdale's, that's for sure. But the other one, well, walks the bloody streets like a lost dog. Never did trust those women. Of course, my parents knew all about them. Said they been troublemakers in this town since dot.'

'Tamara, I just don't know. I mean ... we can't really point the finger at this stage, can we? What if it wasn't her and Dave Warner turns up with the handcuffs?'

'Nonsense you people go on with! You don't think the Red Rose ladies just sit around all day, do you? It's our organisation that works for this town, that knows who's who and what's what. There's only three — wait ... make that *four* undesirables in Mundra: Caroline Drysdale, the Salte women and that halfwit gardener with his minefield yard. The sooner we get rid of them, the better! Now get along, Davidson.'

'I say, Tamara, do you think that's wise, sending Davidson over there like that?'

'Doreen, don't you start in on me. Those people are all the same. They all have a connection to each other. I'm not that stupid! And that connection is Caroline Drysdale! No, I take that back — Caroline Hughes.'

'That's all fine and well, but Caroline Drysdale hasn't set foot out of that house in years! Why, I can barely remember what she looks like. Tamara, what are you getting at?'

'Caroline Drysdale hates us, all of the Red Rose women. She's been trying to get on our committee for years, but we won't have her. It was Reginald that told us the real story. Few screws missing up here,' she jabs. 'I wouldn't put it past her to try and get some sort of revenge against us.'

'Sorry, Tamara, I just don't see how.'

'Well, Doreen, she's thick as thieves with those Salte women. All she'd have to do is play on the silly one's sympathy. See, people like that aren't like us. No, and it shouldn't come as any surprise to you. They're outsiders. That's what happens when black ...'

'Hang on, just hang on a minute. You mean black people, Tamara? But ... um surely being black has nothing to do with this fire. I mean you can't accuse a person simply on the colour of skin. I have to say, I've always liked the Salte girls and never had any trouble with them.'

'Yes, I did mean black. Oh, come on now, Doreen, don't burn my ears with your Christian goodwill. That won't help you a damn if anyone happens to burn you out! If we were to leave the goings on of Mundra to people like you, we'd be in serious trouble!'

'There's no need to take that attitude with me, Tamara Dalmaine!'

'Come to your senses, Doreen. Anyone would think they were family, the way you go on. Good, here comes Davidson. Was she there?'

'I knocked on the door but no one answered. Tamara, I don't think we should point the finger just yet.'

'Oh, look at that! Polly's trying to get the cat out! Good grief, why don't they stop her?'

'Christ Almighty! She'll go up in flames! You there, why don't you get Missus Goodman away from the door! Man, pull her back!'

'Mate, just shut up and let us do our job! Now get back away from the road, all of you! This isn't a bloody show! You, with that chair, get back!'

'Dave Warner, over this way. Dave, Polly has just gone through the side door!'

'She's trying to get the cat! Where the hell is Ron?'

'Holy shit! Her dress has caught fire!'

'For God's sake, hurry, someone hose Polly down! She's burning up! Ron, Ron!'

'Tamara, I don't think he can hear you. They've got Polly bundled up. What ... Oh yes, they're putting her into the ambulance.'

'Here comes Ron. Ron, are you all right?'

'Yeah. But Davidson, did you see where they took Polly?'

'Well ... um ... didn't you see her at the side of the house trying to get the cat out?'

'No, I was being held back by Barry. I tried to get into the back door and save some of Polly's photo albums. Why, what's happened?'

'Um ... they've taken her to the hospital. She ... er ... she tried to get the cat out. The flames caught her dress. I don't think it was too bad. Why don't you ask Warner.'

'*Davidson, you idiot!* You shouldn't have said anything! Ron's not a well man. Leave it up to the professionals to do their duty.'

'Look there, Tamara, did you see that bush move? Something's in the bushes!'

'Might be the cat! Hurry, Davidson! If we can save the cat, that's something at least.'

The sound of footsteps approach, then someone starts pulling at the bushes. Sofie drops her head and stares at the ground. A sour taste fills her mouth, like blood. Looming above her, the shadow speaks.

'Well, well, well. And what do we have here?'

Sofie brings her head up slow, knowing ya gotta be careful with the eyes, always the eyes that give ya ova.

'Tamara, I say, Tamara, I believe we have that Salte girl over here.'

*That high bitin bitch come across n look down at Sofie.*

'What the hell! Davidson, race across and get Dave Warner. Now, now, just you stay right there, madam. Did you do this to Polly's house, eh? And where on earth is your shirt?'

'Ain't done nothin!'

'Oh see, I think you did. What's wrong with your hands? Oh my God! You caught alight! You set fire to Polly's house, didn't you? Speak up, girl.'

'No! No! Sofie doned nothin!'

'You lying little heathen! That's right heathen! And do you know what God does to heathens? He hates them, sends them to hell to burn. That's right, burn for all eternity! You'll burn forever, Sofie Salte! Perhaps that old woman sent you over to do this, did she?'

*Sofie don't wanna burn in hell. Don't want God to burn her. Oh no! That girl a heether …!*

'Polly Goodman is very sick because of what you have done. Now, get to your feet! And for God's sake put your top back on!'

*that sweet summer we had mylovemylove*
*then you had to go away*
*tears that I have shed for ya n everyone mylovemylovemylovemylove*

'Ya shudd up! Ya shudd up! Ya … ya … ya … ya f-u-c-k-e-r-d-o-o-d-e-r-y!'

'Stay back, don't you dare come near me! Davidson, Davidson, hurry! Dave Warner get over here now!'

Sofie swings wildly, confusion and panic pummel her senses. *Run rabbit, run, down that road, fast as ya can.*

She throws her arms skyward and belts down the street, past houses, towards the river. *Where to? That road, that street? No! Not that way. Scat cat!*

Gasping and sobbing she tears up the driveway, screaming gutturally, eyes wild with fear. She comes to a sudden shuddery stop, looks behind, then ahead at the house at the end of the driveway. Quivering, she takes flight again, and pelts forward to the gate and scrambles over it. When she reaches the front door, she pounds on it, burnt hands throbbing painfully. 'Open! They comin for Dove!'

The door opens and Caroline Drysdale peers out. 'Sofie! My God! What's happened? Where's your shirt? Sweet Jesus, look at your chest! Are you okay? In pain? Here, here sit down.'

Sofie garbles, 'They comin for Sofie! Sofie doned a bad thing n now she a heether! Goin down to the fires of hell!'

Suddenly Sofie drops heavily to her knees and crawls in through the doorway, past Caroline Drysdale. 'Dave Warner, Tamara Dalmaine n Polly Goodman they want Sofie in hell,' she whispers, one hand across her chest, eyes roaming the room frantically.

'What ... why, Sofie? Have those women done something to you?'

'Done set fire to Polly Waffle's house! Sofie was gonna fix Polly's yard, mow it n all.'

'Okay, so you set Polly Goodman's house on fire, is that it?'

Sofie backs against the wall. 'Reckon so. The mower wouldn't go. Boom, boom the room went.'

'The mower ...?'

'Sofie put fire to it to go, see. But ... but ... now Sofie goin to heethers! That what Tamara said that ... nasty ... heart!'

'Calm down, Sofie. Don't listen to anything that woman has to say! Now, look, was Warner behind you when you came down here? Think, Sofie.'

'Right behind her. Ohgeeeee ... God gonna get her n burn Sofie. Ohgee, old one ... gee.'

'Shh, shh, settle down. Take a breath and settle down. Let me think. Sweet Jesus, oh Sofie. Oh dear, what am I to do? Where's Murilla?'

'Sofie never seened her sister's eye. Could be anywhere. Polly Goodman go up in flames! In flames she go! Oh ... oh ... bad Sofie.'

'In flames? She caught alight!'

'Reckon so. Burnin she were.'

'Oh God ...'

A loud, impatient thump begins on the door. Sofie crawls farther down the hall.

*Run, run away girl. Fly away, birdy.*

'No, stay there, Sofie.' Caroline says in a low, urgent voice. 'Stay there while I talk to him. I can smooth things over.'

Sofie whimpers covering her face as she cowers against the wall. The door swings open and a loud voice breaks the air. 'Missus Drysdale, I'm after that Salte girl, is she here?'

'No, she's not. And what are you doing on my property, Warner!'

'Caroline, bring the girl out. I need to question her. There's been some serious trouble and Sofie may be involved. As the law here I order you to send her out!'

'Don't you dare speak to me in such a tone of voice! I'm not one of your flunkey Red Rose women! That's right, Warner, I know what you've been doing all these years. Running this town on the orders of those women! I'm no fool!'

'Step aside, Missus Drysdale, I'm coming in! Being a Drysdale doesn't carry any weight with me, out of the way!'

Sofie crawls along, making for the kitchen door. *Dave*

*Warner wanna get Sofie n send her to heethers. That girl she'll burn.*

'Stop right there! Warner, don't you dare come into my house! You're just like the rest of them!'

'Step aside, Caroline.' She swings the door open and stands in the centre of the threshold, her jaw set hard and determined. 'Sofie Salte, I know you're here. Come on out. I just want to ask you a few questions. It's me Dave Warner, your mate, Sofie. I won't hurt you. There's no need to be frightened.'

'Don't listen to him, Sofie. He's lying, just like that Goodman woman and all the rest of those Red Rose women. Lies.'

Sofie reaches for the back door knob. Heavy footsteps tread down the hall. *Dave Warner footsteps! Ya gotta fly, birdy, away, away.* She opens the door and rushes headlong into the backyard, making for the river.

*The fires of hell will getcha.*

*God hate heethers*

*Burn you'll burn in eternal*

*Come on down the waters fine ya got mates in the house here keepin a spot for ya*

*Dove where ya been bubbylooo lightin fire*

Sofie stands on the dank edge of the swollen river, trying to catch her breath, her skin biting with pain. A small sound comes from the bushes. She swings around in wild panic. It's Archie Corella!

'Arch! Archie, over this way, it's Sofie here!' She waves at the staggering figure.

He looks up, then screams, one hand holding the side of his face as he lurches out of the bushes. Sofie hears shouting and turns to the weir. Murilla, Dave Warner and

Caroline Drysdale motion wildly with their hands, yelling incoherently as they rush towards her.

'Sofie! Sofie! Stay there. Stay there!'

'Come on, Sofie. No! No, don't go into the river,' Dave Warner hollers, above the roar.

'Get away from the water!'

'Sofie, listen to Murilla!'

*That sweet summer we had my love my love*
*Sweett suummeerr wwee haadd*
*My love, my love*
*Then you had to*
*Go away*

## thirteen

# all those words went to another place

As Archie stumbles along, he can hear someone calling. Murilla Salte comes towards him, mouth moving rapidly as she points to the river. When he looks up, he sees another woman, an old woman standing at the top of the embankment, yelling at a man wearing a uniform.

The side of Archie's face throbs angrily and the pain spreads to the back of his neck. Already he knows where it's going. He crashes back into the undergrowth, howling like a cornered animal. For a brief second the sun goes behind the clouds and everything falls into darkness. Then, as in the last glimpse of a dream, Archie hears a bird calling. This time he knows what it's saying, what it means.

Like a light switch being thrown, the sun shows its face for a bright moment. Within that time he feels the tingling shoot all the way up to his shoulders, exploding in the top of his head.

*It's comin.* The fire is moving. He waits, mouth dry, heart thumping. *Go. Go. Go!* he garbles, spit sliding down his jaw.

He wonders if this time he can fight it, keep it away long enough to get back home.

'Archie! Archie!' The voices are sounding from the bushes, but he can't move.

He prepares himself as best he can. Head cradled in his hands, he bends slowly and lays down in the dirt. The dark is nearly upon him now.

He waits for the void that will claim him, and somewhere in the far reaches of his mind he tries to hold it back, tries to keep it down like always.

It's closer now, he can feel the fingers of pain crawling along his scalp.

He wets his lips and his scalp tightens and prickles.

A soft moan escapes. 'Pleaase,' he croaks.

A red film crosses his vision.

It's almost here now.

Archie writhes on the ground, burrs and twigs digging into his flesh.

His head falls to the side and that is when he sees it. A snake. It slithers by him, dead eyes mocking his torment. And that makes him cry out with unstoppable terror.

Above him somewhere Archie hears noises. *They've come for him.*

'Leave me alone! Leave me alone!' he screams as the dark rivers of pain wash over him.

*help me*

*raymondddraaymmonnddhheeelllppppmmmeeeee*

*she always went in on tuesday that were her day aye loved bubbies always did our lilly raymond gee get outta there hey hey lookatthis a cowboy n indian thingamajig hey belle bee belle bee where ya goin boy huh I ain't going nowhere ya stay away from that river now ya hear me archie corella ya keep way from that horse kick ya in the head one day it will funny creatures horses can't really trust em their nature can't be broken down ever they free will raymond ya keep an eye on belle there ya sponsible for ya sister now raymond come down the river we'll go fishing go fishing we will*

*nnnnoooooonnnnoooo!*

He holds onto the ground, no voices, no voices. They fill his head, accusing, shouting, screaming. His body is out of control. His arms flex and one leg shoots into the air. His hands slowly unclench.

There.

Fading off.

Going.

Almost gone.

Archie blinks until his vision clears and looks around at the bush. It doesn't look right, nothing seems right. The trees look faded, the ground looks like its been washed by a fierce storm. He stands up slowly and takes an unsteady step forward, in the direction of the children's voices.

Parting the bushes, he looks through. There, hunched back against the scrub like metal monsters, are shacks scattered across the clearing, pieces of rusty tin held up by rotting posts and branches. At the end of the clearing is a huge hole. Inside it are up-ended washing machines, papers and bottles. A sour smell of decay and damp reaches his nose.

Near the first shack he sees a campfire, the dim flames flickering weakly as a breeze lifts over it. Sitting above the fire is a smoke-blackened billy can with steam rising from the top. A lifeless yellowbelly lays in the dirt, ants march across its dull scales.

He turns his head and sees them.

Kids. A mob of children laughing and playing around

the campfire. But it's the girl he watches with an aching heart. A girl: long, black hair tied into a ponytail, her legs pumping as she moves around singing and clapping. She's wearing a white dress.

> *ring around the rosie*
> *a pocketful of posie*
> *atichoooatichooo*
> *we all fall down*
> *ring around the posie*
> *a pocketful of rosie*
> *atichoooatichooo*
> *we all fall down*

A small boy walks into the clearing. Trotting along behind him is a pretty sorrel horse, its hooves beating a steady rhythm on the dirt. It brings its head up and looks straight across at Archie, nostrils flaring as it paws the earth. A breeze kicks up, blowing across the carcass of the fish.

The horse snorts wildly, flesh trembling as it throws itself back with a hard jolt. The boy swings around, fear crossing his soft face as he spots the creature's wild eyes. The boy pulls on the lead, stepping back to keep the horse from bolting.

With one swift bone-breaking pull, the horse rears, its hooves slicing the air.

The boy, so small, stumbles and the lead whips through the air. A desperate cry is heard, 'No!'

Eyes white with terror, the horse crashes back to earth. Crack! The boy's face collapses. He topples to the ground.

An old woman bursts through the group of children. She drops to her knees and a deep wail makes its way out of her mouth. '*Archiiiiiiieeeeeeeeee!*' She lifts the boy in her arms. And Archie knows that the child's eyes are unseeing.

Then, everything starts to fade out.

The children, holding hands, their faces no longer smiling, blend into the scrub. All the shacks bow back, dwindling into the odd light.

Archie finds himself at another place. He can sense his mind is not his own anymore. He looks around him and realises he's on the riverbank.

The day's heat holds him down and he watches as small lizards scurry over scorching rocks, burying themselves under the cool stones which jut out from the earth. Hopping steadily along the embankment, a kangaroo stops and lowers its head to the water. It takes a drink then bounces towards the thick scrub.

The day takes on a tricky light: everything moves, hazes and melds together. Archie hears and sees it all clearly, smells the fishy stink of river-water and mud and senses the river churning against the banks.

The loud, brassy laugh of the kookaburra heehaws and echoes into the silence. He takes a step, his breath catching when he realises that he's no longer Archie Corella. He's another person, from another place. Images flash into his consciousness and his mouth fills with the taste of mud and something else.

Another taste he can't name.

*He hears the gun first, then a low thwump! Like something his friend has told him about: cowboys and indians. The cowboys always get the indians. When he grows up he's gonna own a gun n be a cowboy.*

*He looks out across the clearing to where the blast has come from.*

*He spots the stick-thin frame of Edward Drysdale crouching among the bushes, holding a gun. A slow smile spreads itself across his face. Huntin roos or feral pigs, that's what he'd be doin.*

*He turns to his sister Belle to tell her that maybe Drysdale will let them watch him hunt. But she's not there, standing beside him, she's on the ground. He's looking down at her, his mind tellin him that she's kiddin bout. Just playin up with him the way she always do.*

*'Belle?' He kneels down. There's a red patch on her chest. Mother will be angry bout her getting that new dress all dirty like that the one she sewed by hand. The patch is unfurling. He brings his face down closer, to its centre, and pulls away. An odd smell races up his nose, a coppery smell. Blood. It's blood!*

*'Belle! Belle! Ya gotta wake up now! Come on, Belle, ya kiddin, I know ya is!' He shakes her shoulders as the red stain spreads.*

*Her words come out hushed: 'Raymond, help me ...'*

*'No! No! No!' he screams. The riverbank echoes back, the birds fly off, the river stops running, small lizards scurry across the earth to hide away.*

*He knows now what's happened: Drysdale has shot his sister, has mistaken her for one of em indians. He gets up and swings about, searching for help.*

*Like an illusion, his mother and father fly down the embankment. Their faces are already shattered.*

*He is crying. He can't look at them but he can't turn away either. They don't see him; all they look at is Belle.*

*'Belle! Belle! My little Belle!' his mother screams into the awful stillness. His father kneels down and lifts the doll-like form of the child into his arms. She's gone, she's dead, she won't be back.*

*Minutes, maybe hours, pass. People come down from the camp. There is crying, screaming, shouting. Some throw themselves into the river, the water washing away their tears.*

*And as he stands back from the mob, he knows they've forgotten him. He drops to his stomach and crawls into the undergrowth, towards the other end of the bank, the lower end. When he reaches the other side, he parts the bushes and sees the crouching form of Edward Drysdale. With a terrible scream he flies through the air and lands on him. He fights with everything he has, struggling to free the gun from Drysdale's hand.*

*'Let go, you little black bastard!' Drysdale hisses as he tries to shake himself free.*

*The boy knows plenty about rolling and wrestling, did it every day with his best mate Archie Corella when they played together. He charges, feints from side to side, and finally grabs hold of the butt of the rifle. With one swift pull he has it in his hands.*

*With a yelp of surprise the man falls backward, the gun exploding into the air.*

*He hauls himself to his feet, pointing the gun at Drysdale and from deep in his gut a howl rises; he's about to kill a man for the first time in his life.*

*He cocks the trigger, 'This be for me sister Belle,' and pulls, the awful kick of the rifle sending him reeling back.*

*Nothing moves. The air explodes with sound, the smell of gunpowder fills his nose and the weight of the gun hangs solid in his hands. When he opens his eyes it's too late. He's missed his target.*

*Drysdale springs at him. Then that's all there is. He falls into a darkness, with the feel of warm liquid trickling down the side of his face.*

\* \* \*

It was Vida Derrick who found him later on that night, curled up in the dirt with the side of his face smashed in. Drysdale had flogged him with the butt of the rifle.

When Vida got him home, she sat him down on an empty petrol tin and studied him with tear-filled eyes.

'Raymond, son, are you right?' She put her head in her hands.

He couldn't answer, words had all gone to another place.

'Son, they all gone. They tooked ya father and mother away. The police came out n there were all sorts of trouble. Don't look like they comin back this way again. I can take you into town and find out if I can send ya to wherever they went. When you took off we all looked for hours, but no one could find ya, son.'

He stayed on for a little while, then on his twelfth birthday he made a swag out of a hessian bag, borrowed a billy can off Teddy Simpson and walked out of the camp. Walked the roads for the best part of his life until he started to forget things. Over the years his mind closed off those images.

At some point he became Archie Corella, and Raymond Gee became someone he didn't know, Raymond Gee didn't exist. At times his mind would try to tell him, try to explain certain things. Dreams tried to make him relive the incident on the riverbank but he couldn't see those things.

He would walk for years until he'd walked full circle. Came back home without even realising.

Sometimes, late at night, Archie would lay wherever he could get a bed, and a deep sorrow would come over him. He'd be racked with depression for days. Guessing that it was something to do with his nature, the way he were birthed, born a Sad Sack.

It was much later on that he started to get the headaches, those crazy thoughts, the pain on the side of his face. Like everything else, he thought it was part of who he was, part of his nature to have such pain. Often he'd look in the mirror and stare at the disfigured face looking back at him and wonder what made those ugly marks. His ugliness made him shy away from people.

\* \* \*

The big woman is almost upon him now. She scrambles up the embankment, dress hitched around her knees.

Murilla stands before him, reaching out to him. 'Archie, are you all right? You don't look good.' She runs her hand across his aching face.

'Lillian it were. Always with her fancy ways.'

'What? Archie, what are you talking about?'

'Lillian and Joe Gee.'

'Yeeaaah ... and what about them?' Murilla straightens up.

'Were Lillian they hated, not Belle or Raymond. Lillian it were.'

'Who, Archie, who?'

'Drysdale's men.'

'Archie, what are you talking about! Now look, I've come for your help. Sofie's in trouble. Come on, please.' She pulls him forward.

'Edward Drysdale, Ronald Artbuckle, Willy Dalmaine n Tom Cleaver.'

Murilla's voice is urgent, edged with hysteria, 'That's enough, now come on!'

'They warned her to stay away from town. They told her to keep out. Not Lillian, no. She had to go in every Tuesday to see her fancy mates.' He points to the old river road.

'I see.' She takes a small step back, eyes fixed on the side of his face, on the scar.

'They told her, warned her: no niggers in town! She wouldn't listen! Ya see, she just wouldn't get it through that head a hers!' His voice is wild.

Murilla pats his arm. 'Okay, now just you settle there,' and points to a fallen tree branch. 'Sit down here for a bit.'

He sits, legs cramped and weary.

'They spied on us there.'

Hands on hips, she gazes in the direction of his finger. 'The old camp? The old dirt road?'

'Reckon that's about it. Guess they thought we was gonna take their town from em, eh.' He looks up at her through squinting eyes.

Suspicion fills her face. 'What's this got to do with anything? Anyway, Corella, how do you know about it? How do you know about the camp?'

'I was there. I was there.' He drops his head and stares down at the muddy riverbank. A fierce pain knocks at his heart.

'I'm expected to believe that? Look, Archie, I think ya need to see a doctor. Taking turns like that ain't normal, mucks up your head. Right, now Sofie needs you, so let's move along then.' She tries to haul him to his feet.

He clamps himself to the log and looks up at her with terror in his eyes. 'I'm not Archie Corella. My name is Raymond Gee.'

She stares hard at him. 'What ... What are ya talkin about?'

'I'm Joe and Lillian's boy, Raymond. I saw what Edward Drysdale did to my sister. It was me, Raymond. I was there when it happened.' There, he'd said it. Now he's ready for what must follow.

'That shooting of the Gee girl ... That was years ago. You can't be her brother, he's dead!'

'I come back. All this time walkin around this town n not knowin that I come full circle. Back to the place I were to start with.'

Murilla folds her arms against her chest. 'Someone told you this story. They must have, otherwise how could ya know?' Her face drains, eyes wide as she takes him in.

'Edward Drysdale was hiding in the bushes, gun aiming right at us. He took Belle down.'

She points at him. 'You need help, Archie.'

'I'm Raymond Gee.' He closes his eyes. His body feels so tired, his bones ache. 'Left when I was twelve. Roamed bout for years ...'

'Listen, Archie, don't try that bunkum on me. I dunno what you're trying to pull, but it ain't gonna work!' She waves an open palm at him.

He mutters, 'Why do they all have these groups? Drysdale's men, the Red Rose ladies?'

Her voice is piercing, 'Because that's the way they are! Now, enough of this. Come on!'

He gets to his feet and follows behind her, whispering to himself, 'It's all done now. What's done can't be undone.'

Murilla falls back to join him. 'I don't know what you're getting at but I'll tell you this much, that sort of talk won't do in this town. Lot of people hurt real bad about them little kids. Things never the same again. I can't say I knew em as such, but my mother told me a story, all about that old road, the camp n Lillian Gee.' Murilla nudges him hard in the ribs, 'Hurry up, for Christ's sake!'

Archie doesn't hear her, though he's done what he has to. He throws his head back and looks up into the ever-darkening sky. The low sound of thunder reaches him. His knees catch and the side of his face burns.

'Just like her. Of course, she got her own problems too. Caroline Drysdale's just a thorn in they sides ...'

She goes on and on, chattering away to herself. When they reach the bottom of the slope, Murilla turns to him. 'Corella, please help me now. Sofie's in trouble.' She points. The river is the colour of the sky and sliding furiously past.

He looks down, but can only see sullen sky.

*He hears the low thwump, then sees the men trying to catch her.*

*She is screaming, her white dress spotted with blood. Blood. Blood. A dead smell.*

*She's trying to fight them. This time he can't let them do it. He knows there's a man across the river with a gun, pointing at him n Belle.*

With a roar, he jumps and lands in the middle of the group. His head explodes with the voices. *They've come back, they've come back to get them all! They want him to pay the price for what his mother done.*

Murilla is screaming above the noise of the pounding river, 'Archie! Archie! Let her go!'

'No, don't go near the water!'

'Come away! Please, come away from the river!'

'You'll drown her!'

'Me sister! Me sister!'

'Archie, let Sofie go!'

'Arrcchhiiee ... you can't take her with you! My sister, Corella!'

Archie Corella? Sofie's call echoes above the roar.

He feels himself going down, the river washing over him. He lets go, feels the scar on his face cooling in the river's embrace.

White hair fanning out, Sofie waves an arm above the cold metallic surface of the water then vanishes. *Me sister!*

# fourteen

# ghost rider

Doris treads the old road, still troubled by her visit to Nana's. She shades her eyes with a hand and looks across at the coursing river. Something cruel grips her throat until she's barely able to breathe. She makes her way towards the embankment and looks down into the coursing water. Her attention turns to the riverbank, where she spots something white on a fallen tree branch, jutting out of the water. She makes her way carefully down the slope, grabbing hold of a sapling to steady herself. When she reaches the branch, she can see it is a piece of scorched white material. The remnants of a shirt.

A dreadful realisation hits her. And as she watches the rip and flow of the water, she knows what she must do. She makes her way further down the bank, stepping with caution. She reaches the fallen branch and crawls out along its slimy surface, over the roaring water.

In one quick motion, she tumbles into the rushing flow. Quickly she grabs a branch, straining to keep her head above the water, but the powerful rush pulls her back. Panic-stricken, she screams, 'Help! Someone help me!'

Somewhere above, the harsh sound of crows answers, *kaaarkk, kaaarrkk.*

She manages to get her leg above the water and throw it over the branch.

Easing back on the branch, closer to her quarry, she extends an arm as far as it will reach, trying to grab the fabric. In an instant it is torn free and flutters down into the water. Disappointment rushes through her. She edges backward, cold and shaken on the log, making her way to the safety of the bank. When she reaches ground, she stands on wobbly legs. Once back on the embankment, she looks down into the raging flow. The white material sails downstream, untouchable, untouched as it floats out of sight. Shivering and weak, she drops to the ground.

When she can finally gather herself together, she sets out for Nana's house.

\* \* \*

Shaken and wet, Doris stands on the side of the dirt road and looks across at the house. Everything is still and quiet. She decides to make her way home when the voice reaches her.

'I've been waiting for you.' Nana Vida stands on the verandah, motioning her forward.

'Come on inside, girl, I believe the time has come.' Nana opens the door wider.

They reach the kitchen and the smell of boiled potatoes and roast lamb fills the air. Placed neatly on the battered wooden table is an old teapot, two tin mugs and a place set for two.

'Have a seat, me girl.' Nana points to a chair.

'I'll begin with Belle Gee's murder,' she says, watching Doris closely. 'The time has come for you to know it all,

Doris. I have my reasons now, but more to that later. You've been there, Doris, you've been down there.' Nana points to Doris's damp clothes.

'Yes ... it nearly had me ... I ... Sofie ...' She can't go on.

Nana nods, understanding. 'That's where it all begins, down there by the river.

'It started with Belle Gee.' Nana pauses for a second, looks at Doris, then pushes on. 'The day Belle was murdered there were a witness. Her brother, Raymond Gee, or Archie Corella, as he calls himself. When Raymond left the camp he must have changed his name to that of his best mate, Archie Corella. Life has a funny way of comin back at you at times. But there's another story yet untold.'

Doris peers at Nana. 'Another story? Nan, you knew it was Raymond all along, didn't you?'

'Yes, love, I knew. Not all along, but I saw him up the street one day. I near lost my heart when I realised who he was. When I could move again I went up to him and said hello. We spoke like strangers. Finally, I asked him where he were from. "Don't know, missus," he told me. As I went to leave I said, "Goodbye, Raymond Gee." His face went grey, then he pelted, yeah *pelted* down the street like a madman, holding the side of his face.'

Doris swallows a hard lump in her throat. 'Nan, do you think he came back for revenge?'

'No. He didn't even know who he was. I could see it in his sad, lost eyes. I don't even think he knew he'd come back home.' The old woman drops her head for a minute, staring down at the table.

'That makes no sense. You'd have to remember the place where your sister got murdered!'

'The thing is, when Edward Drysdale bashed the boy with the rifle, maybe he done some damage to his head. The scar on Raymond's face were caused by Drysdale. Raymond Gee didn't know who he really was! Somewhere along the line he must have put those bad memories away. When you're numb from pain and can't take it anymore, your mind tells ya many things. That poor, poor boy put it away so far that he lost himself, lost all or part of his memory. A lotta people survive by forgetting the sorrow in their lives.'

Doris passes Nana a steaming mug of tea, her eyes fixed on the old woman in the fading light. 'And so, Nana, Drysdale's men, what's their story?'

Nana takes a small sip of tea and places the mug on the table. 'That's the question ... What were Drysdale's men? Hard to say really. But from my reckoning they were a group of men dedicated to keeping black fellahs out of town. They formed their group sometime after winter, around the time they re-named Kangaroo Creek Track to Purcell Street. It were then things started to happen.'

Doris's feels uneasy. 'But Nan, you weren't even in town, or anywhere near them. Why, why would they bother youse?'

'For a lotta reasons, love. To them, we was something of a problem. The only time we did spend some time in town were the night of the carnival. The hospital held a fete every year. One night we decided to bring the kids into town, something for those little ones to see. This is the story, Doris. I'll go back, back to that time.'

\* \* \*

It's late evening and Mertyl Salte and I make our way into town, walking along the dirt road. The others are already ahead of us. We reach Mary Street. Balloons are tied to streetposts, coloured paper trails from street signs and white kids march up and down, banging on cymbals and drums, their parents throwing pride-filled glances as they move past.

As we're walking I see a merry-go-round. Deciding to be a kid again I jump on and go for a ride. While I'm in the air I look down at the bar, a makeshift bar, and see Edward Drysdale glaring at Mertyl. Goosebumps prickle my scalp. I get off the ride, telling Mertyl that I'm going to get a soft drink, then I walk over to a stack of hay bales near the bar behind them. I cock my ear in the direction of Drysdale's voice. 'What are we gonna do about this problem?' he's asking Purcell as he takes a swig of beer.

'Have to do something and soon. Why, just look at that gin across there. Like she has a right to be here!' Purcell points at Mertyl.

I watch the way Drysdale's mean eyes follow the little ones, our kids. This is a year or so after he killed Belle and my heart is still paining. I realise they're gonna do something. I shrink, shrink back into the hay, barely able to breathe.

Purcell goes on, 'We ought to teach them a lesson. Teach them they can't just come in here like this. We have to act now.' He stops then and watches as cousin Treacle's mother goes by. He stares at her with such a hate-filled glare that my guts crawl like a thousand snakes moving about in me.

I listen to the men knowing they're working under the cover of decency, chatting politely to others, yet plotting hatred all the while. Time wears on. My legs cramp, and my mouth is so dry I think I'll drop from thirst! Finally,

I hear Drysdale say to Purcell: 'We'll go out there tonight. Do some work.'

I ask myself: work, what does he mean? Common sense kicks in. I realise they're planning to do something out on the old dirt road. For a wild second I think of going to the cop, but then realise he's probably in on it too. I try to think a step ahead of their plan, and guess they're gonna do something when the show starts, when the big band from the city comes down. Sick with the idea, I reason that what with the noise from the band and all the townspeople in one place, well, Drysdale's men can do what they please out there to us.

Even though Drysdale's got plenty of people in his pocket, there's still a lot of white people very angry and upset bout what happened with Belle. But there'll be no witnesses, that's what he's counting on.

I leave the bales and go looking for Mertyl to tell her their plan. I tell her about the conversation. We stand staring at each other scared and not sure what to do. After much thinking we go to Treacle's dad, Burra Simpson, and tell him everything. Burra tells us that he has a plan, something we'll see later. So the day falls into night, and we all head back to the camp.

Burra gathers everyone round, telling them what's about to happen. A big argument breaks out — some want to move away from the camp, fearing for their kids — but in the end, Burra wins out.

We huddle back in the scrub, waiting for what we know is gonna come. I stand with the women at the front. Mertyl beside me. We have a good view of everything. The moonlight is strong. Then we hear the sound of a car comin down the dirt road, the tyres crunching along. Like a torch being shone in your face, the car headlights sweep over the camp, past us. I swing round slow to see where the men are, but Burra has posted them in the bush as lookouts. The car stops and out step the men. It's Edward Drysdale's tall, thin frame I'm drawn to. He steps in front of the car lights. In his hand is a gun, looks like a pistol. He motions to the others, meaning they are to search around.

Then I see in our rush to hide we had all forgotten about Teddy Simpson's little dog, Buddy, tied to a tree.

Drysdale calls out, 'Look here, boys.' The sound of the gun hangs in the night air.

Mertyl's beside me, crying and whispering, 'They killed Buddy, Vida, Buddy.'

It's then Mertyl breaks, when in the fire's glow the men lift the dog's body up and toss it in the campfire. She howls, howls with such a noise that we others push back further into the bush, terrified, knowing she's just given away our location. Before anyone can know, Mertyl crashes out from the bushes and goes straight for Drysdale. She moves so fast, so unnatural, I'm seein it but not believing. The men swing round, fear written cross their faces. She tears towards Drysdale. He's out of his place here, on our patch now. He's walked into something no one can get away from, *walked right into the anger and power of Mertyl Salte.* Straight into the storm that's her.

Burra and the men, our men, are making their way to Drysdale, but Mertyl gets there first. She lands on Drysdale, the gun gets knocked from his hand and ends up near the fire. Mertyl has her hands wrapped tight round Drysdale's throat, screaming, screaming, 'He loved Buddy! Loved him!' I see Drysdale's life is running out of him n I know what's gonna happen next.

I tear from the bushes, rush at Mertyl and try to pull

her away. Out of the corner of me eye I spot Burra near the fire holding down Ronald Artbuckle. Suddenly shots go off! Bang! Bang! Bang! I swing round, releasing Mertyl. Like a nightmare vision I see Drysdale's face weeping blood. He's been shot.

Lurching forward, Artbuckle points the gun in Mertyl's direction. The aim is for Mertyl but by the look on those two faces — you can read it — he'd misjudged and hit Drysdale instead.

Moments pass, someone checks a pulse then one of em signals and they hurry back to the car, leaving their dead friend on the ground.

Later on, Beazely Blackman, the cop, comes out to the camp and questions all us. Turns out that Artbuckle and his mates told Blackman that it was Burra who shot Drysdale. There's not much hope for us — no one will believe a black fellah's word. Days later, they charge Burra with murder.

Nelly, Burra's wife, walks along the dirt road every single day, waiting for her husband to come back home. She doesn't understand that she'll never see him again. As the time passes, Nelly realises. She packs up her things, walks into town and stands in front of the Drysdale shop, cursing the Drysdale name forever. Nelly's never heard of since. She vanished, ghosted to some other place. That's the story. I let it go now.

Doris sits straighter in her chair. 'I'm sorry, Nan, sorry to make you go through this again.'

'No, love, you had to know.' Nana puts a hand to her forehead, wiping away the sweat. She resumes, 'As time's moved on, some things changed for us, not many but some. And I see, Doris, those women are still holding to their group just like the men before them.'

'The Red Rose women, Nan?'

'Yes, those women.'

'Polly Goodman's the only one left. When she goes that'll be the end of them.'

'Yeah, let's hope so.' Nana sighs deeply, looking past Doris's shoulder, her eyes faded and distant. She gets to her feet. 'What I told you, pass on, girl. Keep this alive, tell em all. Funny thing, is history. If you remember what others went through to get ya here then all is not lost. Some died for you, others fought for you. Always remember where you're from. There's hope. Always hope.' Nana pats Doris gently on the shoulder. 'Must go, my girl. Terrible pain in my body. I'll have to rest.'

Doris gets to her feet and leads the old lady down the darkened hallway. She shuts the bedroom door, steps outside into the evening light and walks to the other end of the road. Out of the stillness comes the steady beat of hooves and she turns to see the horse coming into view. In the near dark Doris makes out a rider on its bare back. It's a boy; he rides as though the creature is part of him. The horse and rider blend into the night, vanishing as quickly as they appeared.

In the distance Doris hears voices rise on the night air:

*ring around the rosie*
*a pocketful of posie*
*atichoooatichooo*
*we all fall down*

# fifteen
# corella's roses

On the horizon bruised clouds gather and out of the dusky sky a flock of cockatoos swoop down and perch on the clothesline, their brilliant white wings fluttering like butterflies as they settle on the wire.

Murilla stands over by the washhouse, taking in the yard. Pigweed and thistle grow at the edges of the shed, paint peeling away from the walls. It squats back into the long shadows of the jacarandas, huddling as though in fear.

Caroline joins Murilla in the direction of her gaze. 'It's being bulldozed away tomorrow. Always hated that damned ugly thing. Was never much use to me anyway.'

'No, it never was,' Murilla replies. *Funny thing about time, it pulls things apart, strips them naked.*

Caroline bursts out excitedly, 'I'm thinking of putting in another garden bed, what do you say, Murilla?' She shades her eyes with one hand and scrutinises the yard.

Murilla studies her closely. 'What do ya think you'll plant?'

'Well, you know I've always had a fondness for fresh roses. They're not hard to grow, are they?'

'I guess not but rot can kill em.'

'Yes, yes it can. But that's neglect. Roses need attention.'

The two women stand quiet, both looking at the garden bed. Murilla drops to her knees, grabs a handful of soil and stares hard at it. Then gets to her feet, the soil enclosed tightly in her hand.

'Queer things can happen to the dirt, Caroline. It might be bad to start with. Plants won't grow if there's no life in the ground.' She opens her hand and looks at the dry, crumbling soil.

'I believe you're right there, Murilla. But only people can give it life.' Caroline turns around, shuffling in her oversized slippers, looking towards the front gate.

'The soil were always bad here, Caroline. You live at the dead end of the line.'

Caroline looks squarely at her. 'Yes, that's true. But nothing ends, Murilla, don't you see? The ground, the soil improves. Quite simply, it must give again.'

Murilla tightens her grip around the handful of soil. 'Yeah. Yeah, ya right.' She turns in Caroline's direction when she hears the sound of a vehicle coming up the driveway.

Treacle Simpson's battered ute pulls up near the clothesline. He jumps out and looks over at the women.

'Here they all are, Missus Drysdale, just as ya asked. Can't say some of em are too good.' He quickly unloads the pots of rose bushes. As he slams the tailgate closed, he turns to them and says, 'Well, I'm glad someone offered to take em. I reckon Corella would've been happy for somebody to have a go at growin em.'

Caroline faces Murilla. 'Well, what do you think? Do they have a chance here?'

Murilla studies the soil in her hands. 'Yes, yes, I think they do.'

'Looks like a storm coming in from the east.' Treacle watches the darkening horizon. 'Good time to be plantin.'

Caroline bends to her knees and peers at the soil. 'Here, I think some roses here. What do you think, Murilla, Treacle?'

'Good a place as any,' Treacle answers.

Murilla looks up at the sullen sky. 'Yeah. Yeah, good spot.'

Caroline stands. 'Righto then, let's get those bushes in and let's hurry.'

Treacle goes to the shed and returns with a shovel.

'No. No, thank you, we can manage.' Caroline smiles at Murilla.

Murilla takes the shovel and begins digging into the earth, the soil breaking away easily with the rhythm of the shovel.

Treacle leaves them and drives slowly out the gate, looking in the rearview mirror as the two women work side by side.

When the last rose is planted, Caroline and Murilla step back to study the garden bed. The bushes are lined side by side, as neatly as stitches in a frock, each hole carefully dug to the same depth and each bush clipped and scrutinised for aphids and disease.

'Murilla, I think they might just grow here afterall. Don't you?'

'They just might but we have to keep an eye on things.'


The garden soil scrubbed from their fingernails, waiting for the kettle to boil, the two women sit before the window and watch as lightning dances across the sky. The wind picks up and tears across the paddocks, scattering leaves and rattling the window pane. With a deafening clap of thunder the sky opens and the landscape blurs into a silvery sheet of water.